High Jack de Conqueror

Also by Whit Frazier:

Harlem Mosaics

Robert Johnson's Freewheeling Jazz Funeral

High Jack de Conqueror

Whit Frazier

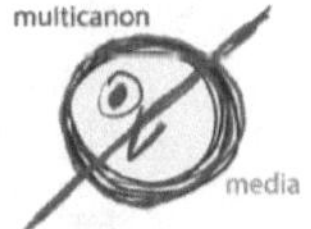

The Multicanon Media Company, LLC
New York

www.multicanon.com

Paperback ISBN: 978-1-7372149-4-6
ebook ISBN: 978-1-7372149-5-3

The Multicanon Media Company, LLC
45 Rockefeller Plaza, Suite 2000, New York, N.Y. 10111

For My Mother

High Jack de Conqueror:

Original (ca. 2222) Edition

By Whit Frazier

CONTENTS

-Three days after the shooting, the president died
Then came back again, great
Glory to God!

-- Cudgo Loo, "3"

Two days after the shooting, on the sixteenth of February, 2046, at 7:17 in the evening, President Lena Powers, the hope of our nation, succumbed to her wounds; this documentary uncannily captures the deep malaise of those dark days. (loc. 84)

-- From Janice Bloodtree's review of *The Mystic* (2048).

From *Collective Unrealities* (2041)

by Tyrone Grant

Movement III: Movement

I

I've only been awake for a few minutes when the calls start to come in. The first one is from Lena. I reject it, but she follows up with a text:

What the hell happened to you yesterday? You need to call me back NOW.

The second is from an unknown number. I reject that one too.

A third call. I flip to the news, and there it is, the demonstration, front and center on the *Washington Post*. I'm not ready to deal with this yet. First things first. I need coffee. There's none left, so I throw on some clothes, put on sunglasses (I'm not feeling so hot) and head out of my Adams Morgan apartment.

Yesterday's rain has passed and left in its wake a perfectly lucid autumn morning. Red and yellow leaves scatter Kalorama in patterns like an African tapestry. A crowd has gathered on the street. There are reporters and police and curious bystanders. I'm working my way towards the coffee shop when I realize they're there for me. Like metal shavings to a magnet, the crowd moves as I move, and before everything clicks in my head, I cross the street and a reporter is talking to me, a square-faced twenty-something white guy, and he's looking at me like I'm something to eat, like I might be his first big story.

"Care to make a comment?"

"Um."

Before I have the chance to say anything, there's a police officer on the other side of me.

"Do you realize you just jaywalked?" he's explaining, a dour looking middle-aged Black cop. He scowls in an oddly friendly ironic way. "I'm going to need to see some ID."

"I don't have any."

That friendly scowl turns unfriendly quick. "Well see, that's a problem. Because then I have to take you downtown."

"Take me downtown?"

"Either you show me some ID or you come downtown."

I look around, up and down Kalorama Road, across the way to the park. At least there's a crowd here: cameras, reporters, innocent bystanders. He can't just shoot me or something, can he? But I'm not awake enough to think of what's clever to say. I turn to the reporter. "I'd like to officially protest this as an unlawful arrest."

The reporter scribbles something in a notebook. "Noted."

I frown right back at the police officer. My scowl doesn't feel as effective as his. "I don't have to wear handcuffs do I?"

"Actually, sir. Yes you do."

II

This arrest isn't going to help things with Lena. Or maybe it will; it's hard to say. It's like the day I met her: I'm researching an obscure Harlem Renaissance artist named Richard Bruce Nugent for my thesis on catachresis one afternoon, and when I walk into Howard's Research Center, there she is, sitting at the front desk in a puff of purple sunlit hair, reading Franklin Frazier's *Black Bourgeoisie*.

The first thing she asks is to see my ID.

Normally I'd offer to go back for my Howard ID, but I feel like flirting: "I actually don't have any."

"How do you not have any ID?"

"I dunno. I don't drive. Never bothered to go get myself registered with the State."

That makes her smile. "Did you at least register with Howard?"

"That I did. But do I really have to go all the way back to my room and get my ID for you?"

Lena wrinkles her forehead, like she's thinking about something, but then her face lights up, expands into a wide round bright blinking dimple smile, "I guess it's alright this time. But if you need to come back I'm going to need to see some ID."

"Well, don't you sound just like Five-O?"

"It's regulation," says Lena. "And besides, the way things are right now, I don't know that it's such a good idea for a brown person to be walking around without identification, just in general I mean. Speaking of Five-O." She smiles a smile as sly as an invention. "You're bound to get disappeared."

That makes me laugh, and then I decide I kind of like her style. "Well, maybe I can take you out for a coffee sometime, and we can get to know each other better. Then you won't need to ask me for my ID every time I come through."

"Really? That's the best line you got?"

Okay, so maybe the line was a little cornball, but it worked. Ever since then, well, up 'til yesterday at least, we've been aspects of each other.

III

For example, soon after we graduate we go to Rosemary Thyme for dinner. It's time for a serious talk, one of those. It's been hanging around the air for weeks like an uninvited guest. We walk to the restaurant through a summer evening so even and cool it feels like folklore.

After we're seated, Lena says, "So what are we doing with the rest of our lives?" Her face is like a laugh or an apology.

"Well we're both staying in DC"

"For now at least." Lena hesitates. "Who knows where my work might take me eventually."

"Well, I've always been a wandering type."

"I just don't want you to end up resenting me."

"Resenting you, how?"

"Like I got in your way or something."

She can't really get in my way, but there's something else she's not saying, and I guess I don't know how to bring it up either.

"Not even my whole straight edge thing."

I take another sip of my beer. "Why would that bother me? Half the people I know are straight edge."

"Yeah. But."

Don't drink don't smoke don't fuck, at least I can fucking think. I guess it's that third part where things get complicated.

"Well, Lena. We've talked about this before, and I told you, it doesn't bother me." I frown when I try to smile.

Lena frowns too. "I know it does, but it's cool of you to say it doesn't."

I open my mouth, close it. Take another sip of beer.

"Anyway, I've been thinking; and I think we need a project."

"A project?"

"Well you're always talking about your poetry, and I'm always talking about my politics, and now that we're out of school, well. We need some sort of common thing, don't you think?"

"I guess. What do you have in mind?" I can tell by the look on her face, something like a wink and a kiss, I've been lured into a separate conversation.

"A demonstration. Actually bigger than a demonstration. We should start an activist group."

"Right. Become a Movement."

"Oh I'm serious. I've been thinking about it. And we can launch ourselves with a demonstration. We just need to get people together first."

This is what I mean, though. Just as I'm about to protest the demonstration, she hits me with this, and maybe it's just me, but I'm sold:

"And I think it should involve you reading one of your poems. I've been thinking the poem should get you arrested, and then we demonstrate to get you out."

IV

Well, I'm sold on everything but that me getting arrested part. Someone should definitely get arrested, but that someone shouldn't necessarily be me. We laugh for a while about it, and then the night really settles in around the patio of that restaurant, and the moon comes up thick and gold between midnight blue wisps, and Adams Morgan lights up around us with music and food and street theater, and we're suddenly closer than we've ever been. Aspects of each other.

V

The demonstration idles with us a while. We talk about it but we never make any plans. Expand our social media networks, but never make any plans. It's something to talk about, it keeps us close, maybe it's like expecting a child, as long as it doesn't happen, it's full of opportunity and wonder and partnership.

In retrospect, we were probably afraid to lose that.

Eventually we start a Meetup group at Rosemary Thyme. We meet every Wednesday evening. It helps. We start out as a group of seven and after a while swell to thirty. One night this real punk rock Parliament Funkadelic brother shows up. I don't know who invited him. Maybe no one. It's another one of those perfectly mythical mystical nights, just like two years ago, and we've gathered a crowd. He comes in dressed in a long purple and yellow robe, and beneath that he's just sporting jeans and a "tHIS iS NOT a FUGAZI tSIIIRT" t-shirt. You might expect an Afro or braids or dreads, but he's close cut.

"You two must be Lena and Tyrone, the leaders of this movement."

"Leaders?"

"Movement?"

"Do I have it wrong?"

7

"Well, for one thing, we're not a movement."

"And we're more or less against the idea of movements with leaders anyway."

"So, yeah."

"My bad. Listen, my name's Cudgo. Cudgo Loo. I've just heard a little bit about you cats, but what I've heard sounds interesting."

"Who do you know here?"

Cudgo laughs. "Listen, I'm an actor, man. I don't know nobody and don't nobody know me."

Lena squints, pauses. "Okay. Well, you're welcome here Cudgo. It's like Tyrone was saying. We're not a movement. And *us*? We're certainly not leaders."

"That's cool. Listen, what are you cats drinking? Let me spot you one."

"I don't drink."

"A coffee then."

"I wouldn't mind a beer."

Cudgo flags the waiter.

"What kind of theater do you do?" I ask.

"I've done it all, from Othello to off-off-off the block. It's a kind of foolhardy question, you know, because -,"

"Well, damn. Foolhardy."

"Well, foolhardy only in that a real actor realizes he's always playing a role, and so there is no kind of theater that I do, everything is theater. But I can hit you with a fly cliché if you like: you can just say I play the theater of life."

Lena groans. I smile.

The waiter comes and Cudgo orders drinks: a double bourbon, a beer, and a coffee.

"Say what you will. This Meetup here is a little theater of its own, that's what I'd say."

"Someone here is certainly playing a role."

"Do you mean me or you?"

The drinks come, and for a moment no one says anything.

"Because, you know. What are you two really up to with these Meetups? It's more than just a coffee klatch." Cudgo squints, shakes his head slightly, "Oh no, I can see it, my brother and my sister. There is certainly something else afoot here."

"Well, we have talked about staging a demonstration."

Lena nudges me. I glance at her quick, a look like a shrug.

"A demonstration? Well, God damn brother. You are forming a movement!"

"Well, if you have to know," says Lena. "It's not so much a movement, as an awareness program. Inspired by Occupy and Black Lives Matter. But meant to be even broader in focus than those two programs."

"An honest to God, movement. Well, I'm impressed." Cudgo gauges us. "Well, I'm not much for joining movements, but if I like some of the ideas, I'm always happy to help out on the periphery. Like the two you mentioned, Occupy and BLM. Both worthy endeavors."

"Well, we've just talked about things so far, so there really is no movement," I say, almost apologetically.

"Brother, it's like you say, you just need the demonstration. I bet you have the people already, and don't even know it. People who'd be willing to demonstrate, I mean. I mean, what you demonstrating against anyway?"

Lena and I exchange a look.

"Well, that's the thing," I say. "It's like. Well, I'd have to read a poem and get arrested for it. And we'd demonstrate against. Well, that. I guess."

Cudgo winks. "And who you say don't know nothing about how life is theater and theater is life? Oh no, see now I like this idea of yours now. You a poet, or something?"

"Or something."

"So why not go on and do it. Can't you write something pissed off enough to get you arrested? A young-black-movement-leader-poet like you?"

"I'm no young black movement leader, and of course I can write the poem. But for what – just so I can get arrested?"

"And stage the demonstration, man. That's the whole point, right? What? You afraid to get arrested or something?" Cudgo shakes his head. "I guess you ain't much of a young-black-movement-leader-poet after all."

"Are you always this antagonistic?" asks Lena.

"It's part of my charm."

"Well, why don't *you* go on and get arrested then?" I suggest with a little acid.

"What? You mean *I* read your poem, and then *I* get arrested?" Cudgo takes a moment; sips his bourbon, like a consultation. "Well, all right. I guess I'll do it. But people got to think that poem's mine. Don't worry, just for now, I mean. You can still publish it in your *Collected Works* later."

That actually makes me laugh. "Yeah, sure why not. I'll do it like a playwright. I'll write it as a dramatic monologue, just for you."

VI

I look out the window of the police car. Dupont Circle is disappearing into Downtown DC. The funky shops and colonial old row houses replaced by arid Greco-Roman architecture. In the distance I see the Monument, not far from where we staged the demonstration. It brings back all the memories suddenly. Just a day later, and so much of it submerged. In its wake, just a feeling. Made even stronger now seeing the outline of the city.

VII

Here's an excerpt from the *Washington Post* describing our little project:

DEMONSTRATION ENDS IN APPARENT VICTORY

August 26, 2019

By Scott Brittle

On Sunday morning some 300 demonstrators gathered on the Washington Mall to protest the arrest of Kujo Lou, an African-American poet who had been arrested on disturbing the peace charges after reading his inflammatory poem, *Ozymandias*, on the steps of the Lincoln Memorial Saturday night. The demonstrators gathered, recited the poem as a group, and then staged a sit-in, which lasted through the day, into the evening, throughout the night and only ended Monday morning, when Mr. Lou was released. The demonstrators have announced themselves as belonging to the ADO (Africanist Diaspora Organization) cooperative, and claim they are the beginning of a new civil rights movement that focuses on 'identifying and annihilating institutional racism throughout America at its source'.

"It was just awful," said Martha Huntington, from Columbus, Ohio, regarding Mr. Lou's poem. "It all came out of nowhere. I was there with my kids! We're here in Washington to honor our country's history, and then to have to hear something like that! We certainly don't allow our children to be exposed to that kind of language at home."

Mr. Lou's own relationship with the ADO remains unclear.

Attempts to contact lead members of the ADO have so far been unsuccessful.

VIII

There's a small dirty commode in the back of the cell and all around the sides of the room, benches. There's probably about twenty of us in here total. All of us Black except for one white guy who's huddled up on the floor in a fetal position.

"Man, fuck these cops. Who's got a match?"

"I got you, but I ain't gonna smoke in here."

"Man, I got you too. Any of these motherfuckers tries to step to you, you know it, I'll fucking smack 'em down."

"Shit, it ain't gonna come to all that."

"Hey, you. What you in for, J. Cole?"

It takes a moment before I realize this last question is directed at me. I frown. "Being Black in America."

"Amen, brother. That's what we're all in for, ain't it?" A bald young man next to me.

"Man, you're in for shoplifting and hustling. What you going on about?"

"You're talking about the surface. This brother's getting at something deeper."

Everyone laughs.

"No really, what you in for? Lawyer telling you not to talk or what?" says a man with short dreads, a black t-shirt, and black slacks.

"I honestly don't know. I guess because I didn't have my ID on me."

"Guess you looked suspicious."

A titter around the room.

"Dangerous. I'd say he looks dangerous."

"Hell yeah, dangerous."

I laugh, taking it all in stride.

"They just gonna take your prints and let you go," says the bald brother. "Unless you wanted for something else."

"Maybe so. They took them now, just before they put me in here."

"Well, there you go. You'll be the fastest brother out of jail in history."

"And how about you? What you in for?"

"It's like the man said. Shoplifting. Rite Aid. Hustle gear."

"Word."

"Yeah, but I'm done with all that now."

"Right on," says Dreads. "I don't hustle at all man. I don't steal, none of that. The shit comes back to you. God sees what you're doing."

"Yeah, but sometimes bad shit keeps happening to good people. I don't see nothing wrong with stealing from a big company. Fuck them, man. They already stealing from me. You know what I mean? I got busted stealing from a Rite Aid, man. Fuck Rite Aid."

"Those shits are getting hit hardcore. Motherfuckers are killing Rite Aid out there," says the kid.

"Okay," says Dreads. "I feel you there. These companies are stealing from us. But does that mean you stoop down to their level? Like I said, God sees what you're doing. You get your reward in the end. One time, I seen these jeans I wanted to buy up in Georgetown. Them shits was like sixty dollars. I was like, damn. Mad as a motherfucker, stomping around, making the earth shake and shit. Nah mean? Walked down the block and found a hundred twenty bucks right there. Paid me back for them jeans and gave me sixty to boot. I'd thought about snatching them shits, but I didn't. You feel me?"

"Sure, man. But you know that doesn't always happen. Some people struggle their whole lives, good people, and die broke."

"That's what I'm talking about. Life is a struggle. Look at all us sorry motherfuckers. Can't one person in here say this life is easy. It's like coming through the womb. You push and struggle, push and struggle for nine long months. But at the end of that struggle, there's life."

"Being broke ain't living. No one's happy dead broke."

"See that's what's fucking you up. Being happy isn't having money, man. Motherfuckers rich as shit, miserable as hell. You keep that mentality up, you gonna keep coming back to the same dead end."

"Yeah, well. Nothing sucks like not being able to make ends meet. Besides, I mean, I respect all that morality shit, man. But I gotta call you out on it. After all, what you in for, then? Other than being Black in America?"

Laughter.

"I was just sitting in the park, drinking my beer, and reading the wise words of Brother Iceberg Slim."

"So they got you on open container."

"Probably public drunkenness," says the kid.

The bald guy snickers. "That's what's up. Besides, who'd you say you were reading? Iceberg Slim? So, what is you a pimp?"

"You goddamn right."

"And you think preying on women is okay?"

"If they consent to whatever, man, they consent to whatever."

"Taking they money and making them sleep around and calling them hoes and all that."

"So long as you don't force shit. And I'm not into that pimp shit where niggas be hitting women and shit."

"So, say it's your sister. And I'm pimping her. And she's giving me her money. And she's giving up that ass. All that shit. All by her choice. That's okay?"

"All I could say to her is," and here Dreads throws a condom down on the floor. "Be careful out there."

"Well, if that's really how you feel, I guess that's you. But that's not how I get down, and I don't suffer for nobody."

IX

The police officer returns. He scowls at me. All the irony of morning is gone. He just looks mean-spirited now.

"Do you have any medical conditions that would prevent you from spending the night here?"

"Spending the night?"

"That's what I said."

"No – I mean? Why? Why would I spend the night here?"

No one else in the cell says a word. I can hear the curious gazes in their silence.

"Machine's broken. You'll have to wait until we're able to process the prints."

"But."

"That's just how it is. Someone will let you know when the results are in."

"When will-?"

But he's already on his way back down the hall.

"Damn brother."

"Somebody don't like you out there."

"For real, man. What you do?"

"Looks like the brother has plenty of time to tell us now."

X

"It might have something to do with yesterday," I say to no one in particular.

"Why? What'd you do yesterday?"

"I was part of a demonstration."

"What, the one downtown?" says Dreads.

"Yeah. You heard about it?"

"Yeah, I heard about it. Over that poet whatshisname. You knock out a cop, or what?"

"No. I should have, though."

Laughter.

"Actually, I just gave a speech."

"What'd you say?"

"The brother said *Fuck Trump*. What else?"

"Basically, yeah. I mean I didn't say much. Just who we were."

"Who you were? Well who are you, brother?"

"You lead the thing?"

"There it is."

"I just helped organize it."

"Wait, wait. What's this demonstration you talking about?" says the kid. "I ain't heard about it. They shoot some poet or what?"

15

"Locked him up," says Dreads. "He got let go, but looks like they just traded in one brother for another."

"His name's Cudgo Loo. All he did was read his poem on the steps of the Lincoln Memorial Saturday night."

"Shit was dope, too."

"Yeah?" says the kid. "How's it go?"

<h1 style="text-align:center">XI</h1>

And it goes a little something like this:

Ozymandias

A Brick through your window, Mister
Charley, Uncle Sam, The Man vs. Ozymandias,
America, land that I hate
Full of sound and fury,
Signifying Monkey

Back up on your block,
Climbing up your tree,
Dropping drones like shitting
Down on thee.

Let's get lit,
And light into these crackers real quick:
If you looking for a fresh image in this shit
You can fucking forget it.
Nothing for you to parse
For your academies to understand,
Just the lay-it-down-low
Of another Black man
Talking, and?
Mocking your democracy, it's hypocrisy, it's worse,
It's a fascist plutocracy, and I'm shouting it out, verse,

I'm probably somewhere you don't want me to be
Like next to Lincoln, in front of your reflecting pool,
Hollering at your monument,
Feeding off your economy,
Built by me.

Dem bones, dem bones, I see dem bones
What built this town, don't think I don't,
They crawl the pool, they crawl the grounds,
Assemble up, look bleak around,
And stretched and bare they standing there,
They see the city I see right here,
From Eric Garner to the Trail of Tears,
I trail my gaze, I plough the years,
Dem bones, dem bones, I see dem bones,
I see dem bones, don't think I don't,
I hear them poems, don't think they won't
Tear down this town, they
Live as ghosts.

XII

"I don't remember most of it, but it's basically about Fuck Trump, fuck MAGA, fuck America's racist history, and shitting on the Government. That kind of thing."

"Well, that's cool with me," says the kid.

"So what the hell did *you* say, that they got you in here now?" asks Dreads.

"Just who we are. It's like I say. I really didn't do anything wrong. It probably just pissed someone off that they had to let him go, and now they're taking it out on me."

XIII

Yeah, maybe, but then why do I feel so guilty?

It's a long night. I have a lot of time to think about things.

Lena and I only have that one real difference of temperament - other than her being political and me artistic — she's real old school Washington DC Straight-Edge, and me, well not so much. Not that I'm some out-of-control Hunter Thompson basehead druggie lunatic lush, but I do take the occasional puff now and then, and I'm certainly known to enjoy a good strong beer when one is offered. So, I come down off that stage Sunday, and when someone passes me a celebratory joint, man I puff that shit right away.

It hits me hard right away too, and then I'm walking off through the crowd, feeling pretty good about myself, folks congratulating me left and right, pats on the back, attaboys and all that shit, and every moment this weed funk is getting funkier and funkier, and then the sky goes dark, and the clouds pull in and the reflecting pool in the distance seems to be singing in a faraway old kind of way, and then Lena's standing right there in front of me, and she's frowning hard, because it must be obvious as hell that I'm working my way through the clouds, and I already left Earth's atmosphere long ago.

She says something like, "You really laid it on thick just now," and for a moment I don't know what she's referring to. I just stand there blinking at her. She looks super cute standing there with her wide angry brown eyes, hair pulled back in a bun, stern reprimanding frown playing the blues down her plump piano key lips. Black Bad Brains t-shirt. It's too much. I suddenly feel foolish and dim, and my ego comes rolling on down the steps of the Lincoln Memorial after me.

"How do you mean?"

"You made it sound like we're some sort of movement, and you're some sort of spokesperson, or worse yet, leader."

"I didn't say anything like that."

"It was all in the tone. And all that rhetoric."

"I just said who we are. I thought that was the idea. Just say who we are."

Lena looks at me fiercely. "Are you high?"

"One of the demonstrators…" I try to explain.

"How dare you treat this demonstration like a frat party!"

"Frat party? I just…"

"Are you really committed to this, Tyrone?"

"Sure, I'm committed, but aren't you taking it all too seriously?"

"Did you think it was supposed to be a joke?"

"Don't you think you're being a little unfair?"

Lena sighs. "I knew this would happen."

"What would happen?"

"I knew you'd start resenting me. Resenting what I want from us."

I open my mouth. Close it. I don't know what to say, so I don't say anything. I just shake my head, and walk back up the hill, away from the reflecting pool, off toward the circle. I walk off the circle at the Arlington Memorial Bridge, past the bronze equestrian statues of Valor and Sacrifice, and gaze out on the Potomac. I look back at Washington, the Lincoln Memorial, the Monument off in the distance, and then down and over the waters of the Potomac, beneath a sky becoming increasingly gray and unstable. The clouds begin to reach across the water like Roman columns, and the first few drops start as I stare dizzy onto that scene of Washington filled with protestors, a painting I produced myself. I'm replaying the scene with Lena in my head over and over, and I'm glowing with anger, tempered by an awkward ineffectuality I feel from the weed.

I think about Lena, and her demonstration – after all, it really is just her demonstration, and if it has a leader, it's her – and I think about the sleep we've lost, the effort we've put into it, the effort I've put into Lena, and wonder if the cause is my cause, because I'm a poet after all, more like Cudgo than Lena, and if I care sometimes to wax political, sometimes I don't care to at all. After all, after all, after all. Black Lives Matter, and Black Literature Matters too; the two aren't divorced from each other, they're two sides of the same, but if I spend all my time devising demonstrations, where will I be when it comes time to paint them and bear witness?

There's a shift in the light on the water. I look up, and there's our demonstration in the distance, which is its own thing, and then there's the image of the demonstration, which looks like a poem I wrote, and the two seem like two sides of a penny, where each is an aspect of the other. An unwritten poem that's just beyond my reach seems to expose these dualities, and as I try to catch it in the light, I think about the sky and the river, and how the two are connected, reflections of the other, and I think about Lena, how she's just an extension of myself, and Cudgo is just an extension of myself, and the change in the light is a change to an Egyptian blue, and a sense of spirituality I've long forgotten resurfaces, like one morning when I'm in the National Cathedral, and I look up and around at all the stained glass windows, and the light from the windows blends together, and for the briefest moment I feel the presence of God, and God seems to me the presence of poetry in the light.

XIV

I spend the night in that cell replaying the day over and over in my head like a dream, or a trauma, my last substantive memory of outside life.

After a while there's nothing romantic or heroic about spending the night in a box. Infernally isolated and alone, a second-class citizen, a problem to be squelched and buried. The cell gets more and more familiar over the evening, the way death gets more familiar the older you get. There's nothing I can say to these bars to dispel the isolation and humiliation of being locked up like an animal.

Dreads says life is a struggle, like coming out of the womb, and Dostoevsky says something like: Life begins on the other side of suffering: and maybe all that's true, but I don't know. The problem is how do you go about the business of living if you're still haunted by the long shadow of the other side?

XV

I wake up to a new cop calling my name.

"Tyrone Grant?" A lady cop, real stern, looks like my high school English teacher.

"Yes?"

"You're clear. Free to go."

I step out into a vivid blue morning. It's brisk, like an autumn day ought to be, but the sun is warm, and the air thrives electric. Brown and scarlet leaves scatter the steps in front of the Central Cell Block in patterns like an African tapestry. A crowd has gathered on the street. There are reporters and police and curious bystanders.

I could use a cup of coffee, but I'm not really trying to be woke up anyway. There's something about me that's still asleep back there, in that cell, trapped in an image of standing on the Arlington Memorial Bridge.

Before everything clicks in my head, a reporter is talking to me, a lean hawked-eyed brother with a half-smile, and sharp facial features that make him look half-Asian.

"Are you Tyrone Grant?"

"That's right." I'm half expecting him to ask for some ID.

"And are you the head of the ADO?"

"There is no head." I say this quietly, sleepily.

"Can you give us a statement, Mr. Grant?"

I look out at the crowd in front of me. It's almost like a demonstration of its own. People are there with *Free Tyrone* posters and everything. But where is Lena? I think about Cudgo. I even think about Dreads. I think about the night in that cell, and then I can't think of anything, only that I should say something.

I look back at the reporter. He's waiting.

"All I have to say is that my arrest was awful and unlawful." It

21

comes out a little louder than I expected, and now there's a silence coming over the crowd, like they're awaiting a speech.

"And that this is exactly the type of systemic racism the ADO is devoted to rooting out and eradicating."

Cheers.

"In every level of our society, and in every institution."

More cheers.

I squint at the crowd. Somewhere beyond the morning sun slanting through the Greco-Roman architecture of Judiciary Square, I see myself watching all this from Arlington Memorial. But the image is also captured directly behind me, below me, surrounded by a cell.

"Tell it, brother."

Beyond the crowd, lone and level, Washington spreads into the rising dawn.

From *The Mystic* (2048)

ACT II

SCENE 1

Official headquarters of the ADO. Tyrone is sitting at his desk. He is talking with Ralph, a young man early to mid twenties.

RALPH

Have you given any more thought to it?

TYRONE

I'm still where I was last time. Look, I know what you're saying, Ralph. I've seen your data. I know you're a political wizard, and honestly, I think with you on my team, we'd win the
damn thing. But I'm not really ready for that step – to be a
professional politician.

RALPH

Those are just definitions in this day and age, and you ought
to know it, Ty. You already are a professional politician. You
think you can just be an activist and leave it at that? That
hasn't been the case since Jesse Jackson ran back in '84 and
re-Negroized niggas. Obama was a community organizer for
God's sake. An activist is a politician, and that's just how it
is. The question is whether you can do more good within the
system, or outside of it.

TYRONE

Well, your namesake, Ellison, said it first, and Obama proved it: a Black president is beholden to the duties of the office more than the duties of his constituents, and I'd rather not give up that freedom.

RALPH

That's just an excuse. You'd be a different kind of president than Obama was and you know it. And as for Ellison, he was making a political point in service of an aesthetic one. I wouldn't take him for an especially canny political strategist.

TYRONE
(*folding his hands*)
Can I tell you a story, Ralph?

RALPH

You want to tell me a story?

TYRONE

It's about that day twenty some years ago. The day Cudgo Loo read his poem at the Lincoln Memorial and the ADO officially announced itself.

RALPH

Well any story about that day that I don't already know I'm more than happy to hear.

TYRONE

I haven't told anyone this, you know.

RALPH

Well, now I'm really intrigued.

TYRONE

It's about Cudgo's poem.

RALPH

Okay.

TYRONE

I was the one who actually wrote it.

RALPH

You wrote that?

TYRONE

Surprised?

RALPH

Well, yeah. I guess. It doesn't really seem like you.

TYRONE

Well, I wrote it for Cudgo; but it was me all right.

RALPH

(*shrugging*)

Who'd a thunk it? But I don't see what that changes. It was an effective poem, and that's what it had to be. Regardless of who wrote it.

TYRONE

What it changes – or rather what I'm getting at here – is that I've never really even felt like an activist. That was always Lena. I mean, I was committed too, but up until that day, I was always a poet. I mean, even that day I was still a poet.

27

RALPH

Listen, can I shoot you with your own gun here? I mean, I have to admit something to you. I already knew you had a literary background. I read your thesis before I joined the ADO. Catachresis as an African American literary trope, right? So now you say you're a poet. And not a politician. And I say, as you argue in your thesis, that all language is metaphor, and all metaphor destroys itself at the level of catachresis. Which is just to say that all language is unstable, and that's why Black folk have had this trope of Signifyin' – where there's a repetition of the word, and a revision of the meaning, which is after all what all use of language is; all use of language is just a repetition and revision of the language. So if you're a poet, okay. I respect that. But who told you a poet can't be president?

TYRONE

Yo mama.

SCENE 2

A few months later. A press conference. Tyrone is standing at the podium with Lena, Ralph, and a few other advisors beside and behind him.

TYRONE

For the many of you who have followed the ADO from our inception, some twenty years ago, I'd like to express my extreme gratitude. Doing the grassroots activism work that needs to be done has fueled my entire life's work. I simply can't see myself doing anything else. I would have been doing this kind of work no matter what, whether it was just as a neighborhood organizer or as a political poet. But I've been blessed with being granted a larger platform from which to express my ideas, and I'm just happy that we've been able to reach as many people as we have. As I have always insisted, the ADO is dedicated to several key issues in the still ongoing struggle for equality in this country. While organizations such as Black Lives Matter put issues like police brutality to the forefront, the ADO has focused more on structural racism within the system itself and has dedicated itself to eradicating these racist power structures one by one. That is why, after all these years of grassroots work, I feel the next step in my own personal work is to try to change the system from the inside. And the best way to do that is to do it from the highest position possible within the government. So today, I'd like to announce my candidacy for president of the United States.

General applause.

REPORTER 1
What does this mean for the ADO as an organization?

TYRONE
As event organizers from the beginning, Lena and I have been adamant about the idea that the ADO remain a leaderless organization. There are ADO chapters all throughout the country, and they will continue to operate as usual. Our Washington chapter will still manage administrative and organizational tasks through Lena, who will be perhaps the first First Lady who is actively part of the same political grassroots organization as the president himself.

REPORTER 1
Couldn't you say that might cause a conflict of interests? Or that it at least limits your objectivity as a world leader?

TYRONE
I've always been clear about where my political loyalties lie.

If you don't like what I stand for, don't vote for me, because
I won't change.

REPORTER 2

Do you think the country's ready for a militant Black president?

TYRONE

I think it's now or never.

VOICE

This brother ain't militant. This is just more of the same.

TYRONE

Excuse me?

CUDGO
(standing up)

You heard me brother. You ain't militant. You ain't a revolutionary. You're another phony-ass Black politician. We've
heard all your talk before.

TYRONE

Don't I know you from somewhere?

CUDGO

From somewhere? Oh, I would think so, my brother. You
keep going on about your roots. How soon a brother forgets.
It's me. Cudgo. Cudgo Loo.

TYRONE

Cudgo! Cudgo Loo! Come on up here, my man. Why are
you always antagonizing me when we're on the same side?
You always were a trickster type. Come on up here.

CUDGO

I ain't antagonizing you, brother. I'm signifyin' on you. And I don't know if you want me to come up there.

Tyrone scans the crowd.

TYRONE

I think so. Come on up. I'm not averse to a little friendly debate.

RALPH
(aside, to Tyrone)
You sure this is a good idea?

TYRONE

I know him. He's okay.

RALPH

I know you *knew* him, you know? But now, you know…

LENA

I agree with Ralph. We really don't know Cudgo at all.

TYRONE

Too late, in any case.

Cudgo joins them at the podium.

CUDGO

These white reporters wouldn't know a tough question if they chewed it over for a week.

TYRONE

Well, Cudgo. I'm glad to see you again. How long has it

been? Twenty years? Where you been? What you been doing?

CUDGO

I'm a poet, so I've been reading and writing poetry. But when
I heard you were… wait, how'd they put it? "Expected to
announce your official candidacy for the president of the
United States of America" – well, I had to come and see *this*
performance for myself. It's the best performance of your career. No doubt about that, brother.

TYRONE

I don't know what you mean by performance. But as you
know, it has always been my mission to work for the people
of this country.

CUDGO

I heard tell you were once a poet, too. And now you just
speak in platitudes like every other politician.

REPORTER 3

Do you consider yourself a poet, Tyrone?

TYRONE

I dabbled in poetry in college, yes. But my poetry was always
activist in nature.

CUDGO

Oh, no doubt about that. At least at its best, it was. But listen,
let me ask you some real questions here. Like, first off. What
do you mean the ADO has no leader? I mean, first off, how
could an organization organize without an organizer? You
know what I mean? And an organizer is a leader.

See, that's where we differ. I say an organizer is just an organizer. It can be me today; Lena next week; Ralph the week after that; someone else the week after that. There is no leader.

CUDGO

Well, look at you having it both ways, because every white boy in this room thinks of you and Lena as the leaders of the ADO, and you know it and I know it and Lena knows it and Ralph knows it and that someone else from next week knows it too.

TYRONE

Now we're just arguing semantics.

CUDGO

See, that's what I thought all arguments were to begin with. But that's all by-the-bye. The real problem here is your quixotic mission to shut down structural racism in the United States. I mean, here we have a country built not once, not twice — but thrice, on structural racism, first with the Indian genocide, then with slavery, then with Reconstruction. And you think you can eliminate structural racism in the United States, and keep the United States? You might as well ask for a Jew-friendly Nazi Germany. The shit don't work. America is built on white supremacy, and either you accept that, or you don't. And if you don't, you don't accept America.

TYRONE

Well, I think you forget the wisdom of the forefathers. "All Men Are Created Equal." The Declaration of Independence.

CUDGO

The forefathers were all fucked up. "All Men" according to them was all white men. And just men. Like no women. And certainly no Black men. And most certainly no Black women. And then comes the Constitution. The US Constitution goes on to make sure all men are not equal under the government. In fact, it lays the very ground for the racist plutocracy we're living through right now, where only wealthy landowners can join the senate. It was designed to keep poor whites, and all Black folks, out from Jump Street. And ain't a damn thing changed since.

TYRONE

Oh, things have changed. Certainly the Reconstruction Amendments changed our Constitution substantially. And after all, my brother, I don't come from money, Cudgo. I'm Black. And I'm going to be the next president of the United States.

Cheering.

CUDGO

You don't need to come from money. The money people will come find you. And you can't do nothing about that. Either you come from money, and you do things your way, or they come to you, and you do things their way. But if I may borrow and mix metaphors on a couple of your clumsy clichés, you just need to follow the money to see which way the wind blows.

TYRONE

I haven't been and won't be bought by anyone.

CUDGO

Then you won't win shit. And you know it. It's like I said.
This country is tore up from the floor up. And all your grassroots weeds won't change that.

TYRONE

So what do you suggest? Move back to Africa?

CUDGO

Is Africa a country, my brother? No, I want revolution.

TYRONE

I propose a political revolution as well.

CUDGO

Which is to say, you propose the status quo. I propose motherfucking revolution, brother. A real revolution. But it's like
the Last Poets said: "Niggas are scared of revolution." And I
think they were talking about you.

SCENE 3

Later that week. Cudgo giving his own press conference

CUDGO

This is just a brief statement. Twenty years ago, as many of
you remember, I helped Tyrone develop ADO. Since that
time, I haven't been able to support the ADO in their conservative efforts. I've always been more a poet than politician,
and I want to see change in a real and radical way. Tyrone
has always been more of a politician than a poet, and he sees
change as something that has to come from within the system. I have no interest in a crooked system. And I'm not
alone. There are a collective of us, the Poets of the

Apocalypse, and we intend to inspire our brothers and sisters to revolution with our words.

REPORTER 1

Is there any bad blood between you and Tyrone?

CUDGO

Honestly, I haven't even seen the brother for twenty years. I got nothing against him personally. Just what he and his organization stand for.

REPORTER 2

How do you plan to get your message out to a wider audience? You and your poet collective?

CUDGO

We're already doing just that. Aren't we now? Plus, we've got a self-published collection that will be coming out next month. And many of you might not know this, but as I hinted at before, once upon a time, Tyrone considered himself a poet too. Well I challenge him to a poetry battle any time, any where. But he won't rise to the challenge. The brother's straight up shook, and any man who lacks courage sure as hell ain't no leader.

SCENE 4

The next week. Tyrone's office. Tyrone and Cudgo are sitting at Tyrone's desk.

TYRONE

So, why, exactly are you doing this Cudgo?

CUDGO

This is theater, brother. It's what I've always done. The question is why are you doing what you're doing?

TYRONE

Because I grew up. That's why. And there are real issues out there, and someone needs to address them. And I happen to be in a position where I'm able to do that.

CUDGO

No, no, see. I think this is just more theater. I think we're both actors. But you always pretended to be a poet. Now you're playing politician, and it's out of your league.

TYRONE

I still write poetry.

CUDGO

You do? Could have fooled me, and the rest of the city, too, for that matter. I'm the one that's known as a poet.

TYRONE

Yeah, but you're no poet, Cudgo. You've only published one poem, and I'm the one who actually wrote it.

CUDGO

Well, you gonna take me up on my battle?

37

TYRONE

That's just childish, Cudgo. And you know it. For you it's just a publicity stunt, but for me, it can only hurt my campaign.

CUDGO

Listen to you go on about your campaign. And I thought you were a poet. Now we see where your real concerns lie.

TYRONE

Fine. You want it, you got it. You're just gonna make yourself look foolish. I'm gonna kill you up there.

CUDGO

You name the time and place.

SCENE 5

Busboys and Poets restaurant in Washington, DC. Night of the poetry battle. Tyrone and Cudgo onstage with an announcer.

ANNOUNCER

Ladies and gentlemen, we have a special treat for you folks tonight. Tonight we have a poetry battle between presidential hopeful Tyrone Grant and radical Black militant, Poet of the Apocalypse, Cudgo Loo.

General applause.

ANNOUNCER

The rules are as follows. The challenger, Cudgo Loo, will begin with a poem of his own composition. This will be followed by a response by Tyrone. At this point the judges will make a quiet assessment of each, and score from one to ten. This score will only be announced at the end of the match.

The audience can vote as well, through applause after each poem, and this applause will be kept in mind during the final tally. After the first round, there will be a second. Once again, Cudgo will lead things, and Tyrone will follow with a response. After the second round, the judges will give their verdicts. Audience participation, once again, is encouraged. Are we ready to proceed?

General applause.

CUDGO

I was born ready.

TYRONE

I'm ready as well.

ANNOUNCER
Well then, without further ado, I give you Cudgo Lee.

Applause.

CUDGO

Here I go:

SCENE 6

Press conference across town. Same time as the poetry battle. Ralph and Lena standing at a podium.

LENA
This will come as a surprise to those of our supporters who have followed our long, storied history, especially to those who have been with us since our inception. Let me begin by saying that I did not come to this decision lightly. It was only after much thought and soul-searching that I was able to

39

come to the point where I could say what I have to say today. In short, Ralph and I will no longer be associated with the Grant campaign. Instead, we will be redirecting the efforts of the Washington ADO branch into my own presidential campaign.

General chatter.

REPORTER 1

Is Tyrone aware of this development?

LENA

Tyrone is not yet aware of it.

REPORTER 2

Has Tyrone done something we don't know about yet? Should we be expecting some kind of scandal? Can you comment?

LENA

We will be not be taking additional questions at this time.

REPORTER 3

What does this mean for the relationship between you and Tyrone?

REPORTER 4

Is there anything going on between you and Ralph?

LENA

As I said, we will not be taking questions at this time.

REPORTER 5

Is there a reason you scheduled this press conference at the same time Tyrone and Cudgo are having their poetry battle across town? Especially since you aren't staying around to take questions?

REPORTER 6

And what does this mean for the future of the ADO?

LENA

As I said, we are not taking questions at this time.

From *Separate Powers: An Autobiography of a Movement* (2041)

by Lena Powers

IF YOU'RE NOT PISSED OFF YOU'RE NOT PAYING ATTENTION

That's what the sticker on my dorm room door said. To everyone, even the casual passerby. Personally, I didn't have much to be
pissed off about. Middle class Black chick who could only conceive
of the real brutalities of racism in the abstract. But I could make my
abstract explicit and make that explicit specific in the person of
Lena Powers, activist. But that's how we all begin though – in extremes. We begin in extremes because we have to find the edges of
identity before we can complicate identity with its eventual compli-
cations and complexities. So I was pissed off and I was paying attention, but I wasn't sure what I should actually *do*, or where to start,
or even what that meant.

I was a poli-sci major, and there were organizations at the University, so I had found some kind of footing, but those college years
are restless years where you think the years are getting the best of
you (I know – don't get me started), and so you compare your
achievements to those of your heroines when they were your age,
and your possible life trajectory in the coming years and you look
at theirs and you look at yours, and yours always comes up wanting,
so there I was, wanting.

I met Tyrone Grant in the last year of my M.A. studies, when I
was really freaking out about graduating and getting older and
missed opportunities, and what was I going to do with my degree?
Was I going to go on and get my doctorate, and become an armchair activist – an academic, in other words – or was I going to do
something for real, in the real world? But that's terrifying, right?

Hanging out with Tyrone helped. He was funny, he was cute,

most importantly he was an artist, and I needed that artistic temperament around me mostly cuz it helped me to chill. And he also just helped me forget about things, or not really forget about things, but not to take things, or myself, you know this Lena Powers person I had Frankensteined up, too seriously.

The question that inevitably comes up in interviews when we get to talking about Tyrone is why I wasn't there with all the other demonstrators that time he got arrested outside his apartment in Adams Morgan; after all, we had organized the rally that got Cudgo arrested together. We had planned that. I don't know how many people know this, but Cudgo's arrest was planned. The poem had been written by Tyrone, and Cudgo's job was to get arrested reading it, and then we started our movement based on that staged arrest. Like I said, I was looking for something. I guess we were all looking for something. But I looked around at all these other young people in Occupy and #BlackLives and #MeToo and I wanted to get involved myself, but in my own way, so you can say that the ego, Ms. Lena Powers herself, took over. And she got mighty jealous and confused and upset when Tyrone spoke at that rally and received such a warm reception. Was it because he was a man? Was it because he was a better speaker? Was it because he was more authentic? Was I really authentic at all? These were the issues I was dealing with, but at the time I couldn't have laid it all out for you like that, I was just under their spell, and reacting to this witchcraft of emotions brewing in my body. And then his arrest, well that was just the double double toil and trouble to top it all off. That damn near turned him into a living martyr. I mean talk about automatic identity, and me in the middle of my identity crisis.

It was my lowest point, but it was a necessary shock. Religions have these conversion moments, you know, like Paul on the road to Damascus, and I don't read those so much as revelations from an external God, but as a sort of revelation about yourself, a stepping outside of the subjectivity of the self, and viewing the self from the subjectivity of the self, which is to say having the objectivity to be subjective about yourself, like you'd judge a character in a book who acts just like you, and I think when you have a moment like that, it's a revelation that can be spiritual and life-changing if you let its significance sink in.

So there I was that Tuesday morning so long ago, a disaster at the breakfast table, and that's when I get a notification on my phone from the *Washington Post* that Tyrone had been arrested. Then the calls and texts and Facebook and Twitter messages started coming in. What's the plan? Where do we start the demonstration? When? How soon can we mobilize through social media? So I just shut off my phone.

I decided to take a walk instead. Autumn in angles, like music. It even made me forget about Tyrone for a moment, lost in an arithmetic of color. I headed over to *Politics & Prose*. I didn't think I was going to go in, but then I went in, and that's how I met Ralph. He was in my section. I suddenly decided that I liked the way he looked, and like I said, I'd decided I'd forgotten all about Tyrone, so I figured I'd holla, and why not?

"Find anything?"

"Not yet. But I just got here."

"Is this your favorite section too?"

"Of course."

Bonding over the books in the Remainder Room. I still remember what we bought. I got *The Black Jacobins* by CLR James, and he bought *ZAMI: A New Spelling of My Name* by Audre Lorde. Obviously we were trying to impress each other. Best of all, he didn't seem to recognize me. I didn't want to be that Lena Powers right then; a rare feeling worth exploring. Maybe we ought to get coffee. Okay, *The Den*, then.

"Howard, huh," he said. "I did a stint at Georgetown, but I got early release for good behavior."

"I beg your pardon?"

Tyrone always wanted to be a poet, but for me Ralph was always the poet, the way he put words and ideas and concepts together in a kind of whirlwind where one word might come out the other end with a new weirdly windswept meaning.

"I never did want to be affiliated with an institution. I'm better off as an independent scholar."

The real story, as it turned out was that Ralph published a piece in *The Hoya*, Georgetown University's newspaper of note, which deconstructed the racist structure of the political science curriculum as he had experienced in his first year at the school, an article for which he was quietly reprimanded by the university, without any actual punishment of course. He was so outraged by this "personal affront" (his words) that he hacked the GU website and changed the university's description to read that as of the next semester, Georgetown would be a "Historically Black College and/or University," and "join the hallowed rank of already established HBCUs." Needless to say, this was deeply frowned upon by the administration, and that was the end of Ralph's university-affiliated career and the beginning of his work as an independent scholar.

It impressed me, of course. I thought it was totally Afro-punk, which was a thing back then.

As you might have gathered from that story, Ralph was something of a computer whiz, and his stunt was picked up on by Arnold Novus. Yeah, that Arnold Novus, the head of the African American Grass Roots Activist Organization (AAGRAO). Novus, Ralph explained, was something of a scofflaw and contrarian gadfly himself (everyone already knows this of course, especially considering his stunt that landed him all over the papers back during the Obama years), and he found the prank kind of funny, and asked Ralph if he wanted to join AAGRAO as a web designer. Which was what Ralph was now doing. That impressed me even more than the original story, and so we got to talking about AAGRAO and activism and the ADO and what I was doing with the ADO, and Ralph said, "hey are you doing anything this afternoon?" and I said, "no" of course, even though I was thinking about how I really ought to be at that rally with Tyrone, but I knew I wasn't going to go to that thing no matter what, so when Ralph said, "you want to come with me to the AAGRAO office this afternoon? I'll introduce you to Novus," well what the hell do you think I said to that?

The AAGRAO offices are located in Cathedral Heights, a kind of posh part of Washington, which like Georgetown is sort of hard to get to by subway. So we just called an Uber and were whisked uptown to this small little storefront office on Wisconsin surrounded by restaurants and bookshops and such – it looked so innocuous you would have never taken it for political headquarters. As soon as you walked in the door you found yourself surrounded by Africana, like you were going to see Shaka Zulu himself. It almost looked like a museum, with African sculptures in glass cases on podiums, African flags on the walls, African masks beneath the African flags, and then of course the requisite portrait of Malcolm X and a little less conspicuously Martin Luther King. Pictures of the 60s in general: Huey; Amiri; Bobby; H. Rap; Eldridge; Fred; Stokely; you name it.

I'm not forgetting the women – there weren't any. That should have told me something right there.

But I can't stress how charming Novus is when you meet him. Ralph told the receptionist (the only woman in the room) that we were here to see him; she picked up the phone and then here this man came out in a blue and gold African robe with a matching African crown on his head, all smiles and teeth, a thin mustache lining a wide mouth and a little goatee to match, like a mix between a Black militant and a French painter. He walked right up to me, larger than life, like they say, and I mean it too; he is an extremely tall man, and although he's slim, he has this presence like he fills out the entire room. He couldn't have come all that close to me, but I felt like he was standing directly in front of my face, and Ralph said something like, "this is the co-founder of the ADO," and Novus looked at me like he was looking at an old friend and said, "the leader of the ADO" to which I said, of course, "we actually don't have a leader, it's like Ralph said, I'm just a co-founder, and really everyone working with us is a co-founder," and Novus said, "of course, of course" although I remember thinking at the time that he didn't sound convinced, and he didn't want to sound convinced, either, "one of the many co-founders," he mused.

We went into his office, and I asked him how he'd heard of ADO.

"Everyone's heard of ADO who's paying attention." (If you're not pissed off...) "We have people downtown right now, rallying for Tyrone's release."

It made me shout out loud with joy inside that he'd heard of ADO, that he was even referring to Tyrone on a first name basis like that (would he have done the same with me?) and that they were even rallying with us – rallying *for* us. I'd known we had made some in-roads with ADO, but it had never occurred to me that Arnold Novus knew who I was, that he was following my work, that in effect, Lena Powers, this Lena Powers person was a personality that existed in a very public forum, and not just in my own head. Maybe this should have been obvious, but for some reason it wasn't until this meeting with Arnold Novus that I thought, oh shit... this is actually going someplace.

"Well, I'm happy to hear that," I said. "Because it makes no sense, you know, that he should have been arrested for jaywalking, and it's clear that they were targeting him for who he is."

"It was a mistake," said Novus. "They're making a hero of him." And when he said that part of me squished up, because that was what I'd been thinking too, and then there was all my jealousy and this vertigo feeling of Tyrone becoming somebody, sure, but who was Lena Powers?

"Yeah, right? And it also turns him into something of a spokesman for us. And we've been trying to avoid that. We really don't want any leaders."

"As you've mentioned." Novus smiled a smile that made his eyes squint like he was looking at the part of me that was squishing up and then he leaned back, and he said, "of course, every movement needs spokespeople. Of some sort. Not necessarily leaders. Even #BlackLivesMatters has spokespeople."

"Well – yeah, I mean. But lots of them."

"Yes, of course." For a while no one said anything. Then Novus leaned forward and said, "Lena – do you mind if I call you Lena?"

"Oh no, of course not, I –"

"Lena, I'd like to offer you a job here with us, if you'd be willing to work with us. I mean, I know you're busy with your own organization, and I don't want to interfere with what ADO is working on, but I think – and I don't want you to take this the wrong way, but I think you are going to find yourself more and more edged out by Tyrone."

I opened my mouth, closed it. I mean, what do you say to that? Novus watched my expression closely. It felt uncomfortable, so I looked at Ralph, who was sitting thoughtfully brushing the tips of his fingers against his left eyebrow as though he were deep in consideration of something of the highest order of importance.

"Can I be honest with you?" Novus asked.

"Oh, I – I think you just were," I managed.

"I suppose I was. Listen, Lena. I've been doing this a long time. Long enough where I can see the way the wind's blowing, if you know what I mean. I'm saying this because I think you can do important work, and I want to see you doing that work instead of getting caught up in ego and pettiness and all of those things that have nothing to do with the hard work of helping people."

"Of course." Indicted. Discovered. Found out. "But I – I mean, Tyrone – I think –"

"Tyrone hasn't done anything but jaywalk. He'll be out this afternoon. Or maybe they'll hold him overnight, but that's it. And when he comes out, he'll give a speech – I mean, he'll have to – they have people out there waiting for it already, as you know. And I know the ADO is an organization without a leader, but the press doesn't buy that kind of thing. The press needs a story, and a story needs a hero, and that hero is going to be Tyrone. That's the story they're going to run with. He's perfect – Black, male, well-spoken, a freaking poet, of all things. And then a hero for getting arrested, and this just on the heels of the demonstration downtown where he already gave a phenomenal speech introducing your organization to the world. So you see what I mean?"

"Well, sure, but that's – I mean, Tyrone will do anything in his power to subvert that narrative." I wasn't so sure though, and I didn't say it like I was really all that sure of it, and then my voice dropped and I said, "I mean it's like you said, he's a poet, and so, well, yeah."

"I don't doubt his integrity, not for a moment. I just know how these things turn out." He capitulated with a gesture of his hands and leaned back. "Or maybe I'm just being selfish because I want you to work with us, here. That's really what I'm getting at, and you can forget about what I just said about Tyrone and the ADO."

"Well, of course my working with you doesn't preclude my working with the ADO. What did you have in mind? I'd be honored to work with you, of course. That goes without saying."

There had been a little gust of tension that had blown into the room, but it dissipated with that enchanted gesture of Novus', as if he had introduced the tension just to have it there, and then dispelled it when it no longer served a purpose or had outstayed its welcome. I glanced up at an African mask winking back at me, and then I felt a little dizzy, as if some sort of spell had actually been cast in that room, and when I looked over at Ralph, he was still in his same contemplative posture, as if he were just another strange decoration in the room.

"We need a P.R. person," said Novus. "That's been my job up until now. I'm the one giving the interviews and running the social media and all that, but I'm old-school and honestly, I'm not cut out for this type of thing. My background is in traditional community organizing, and I'd like to get back into that on the grassroots door-to-door level. What I would need someone young to do is present a pleasant face for the organization, manage our social media accounts, give speeches, host events, that type of thing. Would you be interested?"

When I think back on that encounter, today, as a mature(r?) woman I'm amazed that the feminist in me didn't have warning bells flashing like crazy, and maybe I did have those warning bells, but I was young, and overwhelmed by the moment, and still a little taken aback by the little bit of wizardry that Novus had cast over the room, and so I just sort of nodded my head thinking that here we were; this would be the official birth of Lena Powers the person I wanted Lena Powers to be, the public persona. Visions of me standing in front of audiences giving speeches to loud applause and watching likes and followers grow exponentially and my face on magazines and on television and all those aspects of ambition so encouraged in men but discouraged in women flushed through me so that I just kept on nodding ridiculously, until I finally managed, "yes, yes, yes, I'd be honored, of course of course of course."

From *Tyrone Grant's Grand Jury Testimony*

(April 10, 2046)

MS. WHIPPLE: This is Andrea Whipple. It is April tenth, 2046. The time is 11:11 a.m. We are about to call the defendant, Tyrone Grant, to the stand. As usual Francis and I will be leading the questioning. Any one of you may interject with additional questions at any time, or you may wait until the end of our questioning, however you see fit. Please remember, however, that no questions may be asked about conversations between Mr. Grant and his attorney. As you are aware, client/attorney conversations are confidential. Any other questions are okay. All right, then with no further ado, let's begin. I call

TYRONE GRANT

to the stand. Mr. Grant, do you swear to tell the truth, the whole truth and nothing but the truth before this Grand Jury gathered here today?

MR GRANT: I do.

EXAMINATION

BY FRANCIS SMART:

Q: Can you introduce yourself to the grand jurors and the court reporter with your full name please? And spell it out as well, please.

A: My name is Tyrone Grant. T-Y-R-O-N-E. G-R-A-N-T.

Q: And have you appeared before this court before?

A: No I have not.

Q: So you are testifying that you do not know anyone in this court-room?

A: Yes I am.

Q: Can you repeat that as a statement before the court?

A: I do not know anyone in this courtroom.

Q: Good. And have we met before – you and I, I mean?

A: Yes we have.

Q: We have? When did we meet?

A: Just now.

Q: Just now? You mean when I spoke with you and your attorney just before these proceedings?

A: Yes, you did. I mean, yes I do.

Q: Good. Now try to keep focused, Mr. Grant. And you were served a subpoena to sit before this grand jury?

A: Correct, I was served a subpoena.

Q: And you were given the opportunity to consult with your attorney?

A: Yes I was.

Q: Okay, good. Now. Let's get right to it, then. Alright? Good. Where were you on February 14th, 2046?

A: The day Lena was shot.

Q: That's correct. February 14th, 2046. The day President Lena Powers was shot.

A: I was there.

Q: You mean that you were in attendance at the speech at Georgetown University's Gaston Hall on February 14th?

A: That's correct.

Q: And what time did you arrive?

A: Around 10 a.m.

Q: And why did you arrive an hour before the speech was scheduled to begin?

A: Oh. It was going to be packed. Everyone knew that.

Q: Did you have tickets for the event?

A: Yes.

Q: And how did you obtain tickets for the event?

A: Lena. She gave them to us.

Q: And where did you sit?

A: Right up front.

Q: I see. Now you said: "she gave the tickets to us." Who are the additional people you are referring to?

A: Cudgo Loo and myself.

Q: And who is Cudgo Loo?

A: Cudgo Loo is…

Q: Who is he?

A: An actor. A friend?

Q: And had you and Mr. Loo had conspired to disrupt the ceremony in any way?

A: Oh, yes.

Q: What had you planned on doing?

A: We just wanted to make a peaceful protest. Ambrose Littleton. His murder, you know?

Q: I'm afraid you'll have to elaborate.

A: We just wanted to ask the president some difficult questions?

Q: You don't sound so sure. What were some of those questions?

A: How to restructure? Why she wasn't doing more to restructure? Like we used to talk about, me and Lena. This restructuring, and – I don't know.

Q: And what do you mean by restructure?

A: A restructuring. Just what I said.

Q: Can you elaborate?

A: Getting rid of the cancer of the American Constitution.

Q: You believe we should throw out the United States Constitution?

A: There are some parts worth keeping.

Q: Was it your intention to harm the president in any way?

A: Oh no. No. Oh. It's – it was – that was Lena… How?

Q: And yet you claim there is a need for revolution.

A: Restructuring.

Q: Can you elaborate?

A: Me? No, that was pure Lena. I mean, me and her, but that was like really her thing. Read her MA Thesis. It's all right there.

Q: Do you know who shot her?

A: If I did… No... I don't know. I wish I did.

MS. WHIPPLE: At this time I'd like to introduce a video recording of the event in question. If any of you are not able to see the screen, please indicate that now. Very good. This is Gaston Hall on February 14th, 2046. The day in question. The first voice you will hear is that of President Powers delivering her address to the convention.

VIDEO EVIDENCE

LENA

Good morning to all of you. First off, I want to thank you all for coming here to hear me speak. In the two years that I've held office, I've had the opportunity to travel all over the world and speak about issues national and international. But when it comes to speaking about problems right here in our own neighborhoods, there hasn't been enough discussion.

(Applause.)

As most of you know already, I grew up working as an activist alongside Black Lives Matter, AAGRAO and Occupy. So issues concerning what's happening in our streets go right back to what got me interested in politics in the first place. And I think it's time our country really had an open, honest conversation about race and class and wealth in this country.

(Applause)

Thank you, but we're here today for a very serious reason. The murder of Ambrose Littleton. To think that in 2046 a couple of stupid, drunken white police officers could publicly film and upload the lynching of an unarmed, innocent Black man is an abomination.

TYRONE

That's because there never really has been an honest discussion about race and class in this country!

CUDGO

Those of us who haven't sold out to the establishment aren't surprised at all.

TYRONE

Not one bit!

CUDGO

Black Power, my brother; Black Power, my sister.

TYRONE

But you just fucking forgot. And we do mean you, Lena. So take the shit personal!

(Shuffle of Secret Service accompanied by a rush of shouting from reporters.)

LENA
(putting up her hand, waving off security)

Security, stand down. These are friends of mine, as everyone here knows. They are free to speak their minds.

The lights go out.

LENA

Security!

TYRONE

What the hell?

A VOICE

Get your hand outta my pockets!

A SECOND VOICE

Word.

Sound of shots being fired.

Screaming.

Static.

MS. WHIPPLE: That concludes the video evidence. At this point I will turn questioning back over to Ms. Smart.

EXAMINATION

BY FRANCIS SMART

Q: Were you present in the video we just watched?

A: Yes, I was.

Q: Were you the one who originally interrupted President Powers?

A: Yes, I was.

Q: And was that Cudgo Loo with you?

A: Yes it was.

Q: And who was in charge of the operation?

A: Oh. Oh no. We were just a couple poets trying to spark a discussion.

Q: And at some point you, um, I believe, you say: quote – "So take the shit personal."

A: Yes. Yes. That was unfortunate.

Q: Did you have a relationship with President Powers at some point?

A: Yes.

Q: Can you elaborate?

A: No.

Q: Okay. Noted. Were you the one who shouted "Get your hand outta my pockets?"

A: No. No, that wasn't me.

Q: Was it Mr. Loo?

A: No, that wasn't him either. I mean, just from the voice. Run it through a simulator if you don't believe me.

Q: Mr. Loo is an actor, you said?

A: No, that wasn't him. Even acting. A simulator should be able to detect that, too, I think. But I shouted "What the hell?" Cudgo - he didn't say anything.

Q: Can you tell us what happened after the events depicted in the video?

A: Chaos. People were getting trampled and everything.

Q: And how long before the lights came back on?

A: It was just a few moments, I think, but it felt much longer.

Q: And what did you do while the lights were out?

A: I must have dropped. Stayed low on the floor.

Q: And what did you do when the lights came back on?

A: I stood up and started towards the door.

Q: And were you able to evacuate the premises?

A: No. Secret Service got me first.

Q: Was Mr. Loo detained as well?

A: Yeah. They got him too.

Q: And how long were you detained?

A: Until Lena's pardon.

Q: And Mr. Loo was also released only after Lena's pardon?

A: Oh. I think so. I'm not so sure.

Q: Have you been in touch with Mr. Loo since the shooting?

A: I heard from him, but just once.

Q: When was that?

A: Sometime last week. April first. April Fool's Day.

Q: This was by phone or in person?

A: It was an email.

Q: And did the email say anything unusual or that may have caused you alarm?

A: No. It was just Cudgo's way. Pure Cudgo.

Q: Were there any attachments to the email?

A: Yes, there was an audio file.

Q: No video?

A: Just audio.

MS. SMART: I would like to introduce to the court the audio evidence in question.

AUDIO EVIDENCE

MR. LOO

Three days after the shooting, the president died
Then came back again, great
Glory to God!
In purple perplexion she 'rose off the bed
Big eyes all a-bug and here's what she said:

It's been a while since I seen ya, I see y've been good,

Been trying myself, not doing too good.
Was dreaming in streaming dreaming is told
Unkempt in perplexions of vexed neighborhoods.

Three days after the shooting, the president died
Gave the Smith to the people, said give it a try!
Fired low fired high started firing wide
Shot the president, the people, the whole goddamn tribe.
Black Rome like back in the days of little old Italy
Where the streets sometimes funky as a riff by Bo Diddley.

MS. WHIPPLE: That concludes the audio evidence. At this point
I will turn questioning back over to Ms. Smart.

EXAMINATION

BY FRANCIS SMART:

Q: This was the message in the attachment?

A: Yes, it was.

Q: And this is Mr. Lou's voice?

A: No doubt about it.

Q: And what did you think when you listened to it?

A: I don't know.

Q: You don't know?

A: You invent the words.

Q: I beg your pardon?

A: You invent the words for how it made me feel. I don't know them. I don't have them.

Q: Do you know what the poem means?

A: No. You'd have to ask Cudgo. It reminds me of an old African folktale. T'appin.

Q: Terrapin?

A: Some kind of turtle.

Q: Does this folktale hold any specific significance for you or Mr. Lou?

A: T'appin? No.

Q: And you don't know why Mr. Lou sent you the poem?

A: No.

Q: And you haven't talked to him since?

A: No.

MS. SMART: Okay. That's it for me. Andrea?

MS. WHIPPLE: I have no further questions.

MS. SMART: Well okay then. Thank you very much for your participation and cooperation Mr. Grant. That officially wraps thing up for us here.

(End of testimony)

From *Harlem Spleen* (2041)

by Baldwin Schattenfreud

Chapter Three: BLACK ANARCHY

I seen the best minds of my generation destroyed by white liberalism, starving hysterical naked, dragging themselves through the
white folks' blocks all day looking for a fucking buck. Talk about a
waste of time.

I was born on August 31, 1995, and it wasn't your America. I
was born in Tübingen, Germany, my mother a refugee from Mo-
rocco, my father a German social worker who met her "on-the-
job." which is like a love story straight from the storybooks, and yes
I do mean the ones written by white folks. There was an inherent
imbalance of power, sexual, racial and cultural which I was alert to
growing up but never learned how to define, because the language
hasn't developed ways of expressing it, or rather it has, it's just developed better ways of suppressing it. Not that we spoke English
growing up – we spoke German of course – *auch eine bescheuerte Spra-
che, aber nicht so schlimm – nicht so extrem rassistisch wie Englisch* – but
problematic enough in its own rites. Don't get me started.

The problem with English is what everyone says is its great advantage, and that's its adaptability. But if you live in a world which
is based on a deep racism rooted in capital and social structures,
then every level of those social structures will reflect the racism of
the dominant structure, and so the language only adapts within a
racist paradigm, and that's why I say that the racism of English ex-
tends to the language of white poets, black poets, beatniks, hippies,
punk rockers and rappers alike, and don't no one get out alive.

The only ones who really did were the jazz musicians, and that's
just because they could abandon the damn language altogether, and

so they made inroads nobody else made, and that's why Black writers have been trying to catch up to music since day one, only as soon as they try, out comes the English, which you know, is very white of them, very white of them indeed, very much like a whale, to explain racism in a language that already undermines them while demonstrating the justness of the complaint.

Damn. Sidetracked again: I thought I was talking about the day I was born. That was the selfsame day twenty years in the past before Merkel said, "*Wir schaffen das*," and opened up the borders to the refugees. So far, so good. *Das schaffen wir. Oder?* Well, not really, "old girl," to use an old Briticism. Which is the way white guilt works. Let the refugees in, let them in, Germany is white and white's alright, and don't bother to think about how we might accommodate them, just let them in, let them in, so long as they're in whiteland they're in rightland, and everything'll be alright, man. Ain't that white, Kunta Kinte?

They done took my blues and gone. Hughes said it. Matter of fact, Hughes wrote the damn poem "Howl" and a damn sight better and damn sight shorter when he wrote "I, Too," in which Hughes says the same thing, only says it in four sentences, whereas Ginsberg goes on and on and on for four interminable parts (the irony of my complaint hasn't been lost on me). The very first lines set up the dichotomy. "The best minds of my generation" are where? Where are those dudes? My God! They're dragging themselves through "the Negro streets!" − well! That's definitely not where the white man belongs! The white minds being the best minds of the generation, of course. That little assumption isn't even questioned, it's just set up that way right at the very start, Ginsberg didn't even notice he said that shit, but he said it all right, and none of the other white critics noticed it, neither. Why would they? It's what we've all been taught, the way the language works, and Ah, Carl, if you are still white I am still white, and it's been crazy niggers running around since day one, so, you know. What you doing in them streets, boy?

These poor damned angelheaded hipsters. Makes me think of Arthur Rimbaud, the Nigger of Narcissus -- he sings on his boat in the bay. Ginsberg gives us the whole list of them, and all of them have fallen outside of society some kind of how, which is some kind of cray cray, and the only rhythm to capture this feeling is bebop, you know, them Black cats who blow baby blow, who? You know! The Negro! The Authentic American! Tell 'em Jack! Who poverty and tatters, why very much like a Negro – contemplating JAZZ! If you don't watch out someone is gonna bust out and is bound to mention Islam any minute now, these guys really do get carried away that way, don't they? They who were hungry who were gay who were once happy who were inspired by genius who licked Negro balls who read poetry to communists who danced the Charleston in front of the Ritz Carlton in Negro attire who smoked cannabis and stared like wild wide eyed Negroes into the Poseidon dusk of America who spit tobacco and peyote and dreamed of being famous who went to the insane asylum because Celine did who studied Shakespeare and Plato and Proust and Saint Baudelaire and pissed out of windows crying I am the Negro I am the Negro I am the Negro I am the Negro and wrote poems about white folks who pissed out of windows crying I am the Negro I am the Negro I am the Negro I am the Negro who showed up drunk to job interviews because of white privilege who wrote contemporary howls because of white privilege who done took my blues and gone because of white privilege and who the hell cares? Haven't we had enough of all that? Damn Langston while your shit ain't safe my shit ain't neither my Nigga.

Ain't nothing new under the sun, it's *been* raining alarm clocks – and I ain't just talking about knowing the time. The bells started going off the moment we got off the boat, and they ain't stopped ringing since. Okay professor, ease up a moment on the tomfoolery. After all, it's Ginsberg who writes about the taxicabs of reality. Ease up? Look, the brother is lost in a white fantasy of the coloredman's suffering, from the burned alive in a time when Black men were still being lynched and burned regularly, had actually suffered the tanked-up clatter of the iron first hand and not just the metaphors for bad fashion. Damn, man. If I have to look at another fellow white man in a bad tweed suit, I'll revolt. Right, right, right. Keep your cool, man. Talk about an ecstasy of fumbling, vile incurable sores on innocent tongues. Think of the children.

No, the entrance to the poem for me, and after all that perambulating preamble, I will still admit I like the poem (can't you tell??), but it is a perfect example of the trap of the English language, and if you think it's just because the brother is white, wait till you read my next chapter – no, the entrance to the poem for me is Ginsberg's institutionalized mother:

My own mother was institutionalized within the walls of her house and her community and her country, a quiet Moroccan woman who moved to Berlin when she was 28, and if you asked her about her past, she wouldn't say a word, she would ignore the question until you stopped asking or answer with one of those withering looks, the vanished past, like African American academics looking for root countries of origin in Africa, where a bleak silence blinks back a blank history, rich and teeming with life. She wouldn't speak about it, and she never really got the gist of German neither, it didn't become her and so she didn't become it neither, but it diminished her something serious, too. She consulted the walls, would look at the wallpaper and I swear they could communicate, but she was a woman of few words. Even for me. I speak a stilted Derja, unsure of the constructions, and standard Arabic? Forget it, though I did study it a couple years, a couple years too late, or maybe I was just too lazy, no the entrance to the poem for me is Ginsberg's institutionalized mother. His mother asterisked (in my version it's seven asterisks) – I didn't know how to hear that the first time I read it then I found it online, and there it was – my mother asterisked. & click.

That's the thing about Ginsberg's poem. You can find a window in all that wildness, climb in, and start to rebuild and re-write

Ginsberg's poem from the inside out, so that Ginsberg's poem ain't really Ginsberg's poem anymore, it's your poem, and you've challenged at the get-go all the language and assumptions in it, until it's turned against itself and collapsed in a wild holy howl loud with Moloch, malarkey, and you better axe somebody. Pop ignored it, Mom I mean, Pop ignored her, ignored the problem, a mad mother in the muddle. Pop, who actually jumped off the Brooklyn Bridge and swam to China ignored her. He just up & disappeared one day, and then it was me in a small one-bedroom in Bushwick, which was alright, because it takes a village and mine was Brooklyn. But you don't even need Brooklyn to remember Ginsberg's last fantastic book flung out of NYCHA, and that spasmatic 4 o clock door, to see it for yourself, vivid as your own memories, even though they are also imaginary. Once father left – very niggardly of him, I must say, very much like a nigger – and when put like that it sort of sounds like the start of one of those old rap songs you can still find online – once father left, things fell apart, because mother was unstable, and I was "cheated of feature by dissembling Nature, deformed, unfinished, sent before my time" into the role of patriarch to a madwoman and a disintegrating household. And then when I was thirteen I came home from working mowing the neighbor's lawn and found my mother, that last fantastic book flung out of NYCHA, and that spasmatic 4 o clock door and the last fantastic look on her face something I'll never forget, like looking at arias of hell, and the smell of shit, and was that Ray Charles on the radio, Allen, or was it Trane, like we bask the days away in soundtracks of soul music, and not the horrific screaming in my throat that went straight to my head and hollers there even still and if he hollers let him go, holla at your boy, or just fucking howl.

No, I never managed to manage the words to match that matchless horror. The words were delivered ever thereafter from the essence from my mother where she were, ever in my mind with it don't mean a thing, and then she took those communications from the walls and she began to relate them back to me, and I've been conversing with that wallpaper ever since as it peels through my memory, rotting off the walls if it ain't got that swing. So I found myself ensconced in an apartment underneath the Harlem elevated that looked out on a cemetery of automobiles, huddled masses of metal shell skeletons where I lived with a poet, a painter and a political science major, a Black revolutionary, a spiritualist and the other brother bourgeois, respectively. This was my education, long evenings arguing over cheap glass jugs of crimson Carlo in a cold ceramic kitchen, where we argued with ourselves and my head the windows of my skull where my mother argued with me, and where sometimes I would see her peering out through the blind sockets.

Here's the Black revolutionary, we can call him Huey:

Yo, I saw the worst minds of my generation praised by poets, parading through Harlem World and Bed Stuy and Queensbridge talking about they care about the Black man, fingers crossed behind they backs, angelheaded hustlers sheisty motherfuckers taking money from the machine curtailing the system buying votes going to city hall with checks in hand saying they still give a damn about the Black man; who say Capitalism works if you let it and politicians can be poets and the cowards are still at it to this day; who kept mansions in Virginia writing swirling words about liberty while whoring out our women drunk on wine in the evenings in blindfolds of liquor and sat at dinner tables replete with splendor dining with white men as if the shit just came down from the hand of god and not the clenched black hand of the entrenched Black man a metaphor for our country if ever there were; who sat with top hats and beards as long as their lies talking about they freed the slaves when they didn't do shit but cover they ass and who in private rooms and oval offices talked about Black folk ain't shit, one white man is worth more than a nation of niggers and I'd go on out in the street and start shooting Niggas down on fifth avenue if a Nigga gave me so much as one askance glance and y'all would applaud that shit, and

I would feel pretty good about it too; who fought for a racist union and gave lip service to Black people while taking graft money and supporting businesses while building a nation built on Capitalist racism that excluded the Black man all the while talking about things will be better in time farther along farther along we will know more about it while our people continued to starve and were lynched and run out of opportunities to reconstruct the nation and we will know the reason why; who whooped about the forward race and raced to colonize colored folk into concentration camps throughout the Caribbean, Latin America, the Philippines, the Black and Tans swinging theories about big dicks and dollar fli-pomacies, in order to establish an American demagogracy; who fur-thered the family legacy of concentration camps with the yella Jap-anese while refusing to acknowledge greatness and wouldn't allow the white house door to be darkened by one fleet Black foot and were so in love with their imagined power while they sat cowering powerless in wheelchairs they wouldn't even say it's wrong to swing a human being dead from the trees and only allowed one Black in the government, a white supreme court justice with ties to white terrorism; who shrank from publicly acknowledging the civil rights of other human beings so that the machinery would continue to bring prosperity to a family that was so spooked by spooks they sat on National television talking about Black men living in peace and harmony in Mississippi while the streets ran red with riot; who must have heard that all Black folk either rap or play sax and nigged it up real good on late night tv keeping that smile up while throwing Black people in jail and throwing away the key and saying Niggas ought to be bringing coffee and carrying bags and not challenging the white people power structures so long in place and suddenly challenged; who Black themselves nonetheless let the racist meta-structure change them and bombed Black people and Brown peo-ple with technology developed by the racist Capitalist machinery that devours everything in the droning cogs of its precision automa-tion; who Black themselves nonetheless turned their backs on neighborhoods where our brothers and sisters are colonized and killed on the daily and supported the police unions publicly and denounced start-up movements challenging the colonizers so that we come full circle to the original colonizers that collect in the Capitalist machine, a machine that colonizes even those would be radicals, you can not be radical as long as you believe in the demagogracy and dollar flipomacies and damn, Ambrose, if they can just up and shoot your Black ass they sure as hell can up and shoot mine, and now you're really in the fifth foundation in the wasteland of spacetime; naw brother, we need to start this shit anew with renewed vigor a new reconstruction which begins with the destruction of the capitalist, which is just another word for keeping the niggers down, and rise reincarnate in the radical clothes of Black socialism singing *Siyo Nqoba Siyo Nqoba Siyo Nqoba*, and you better believe it, you blue-hearted motherfuckers.

To which the painter, we can call him Ishmael, might respond:

Sure, but who's to blame for the wrath of the idiocy of the blue-hearted bastards that keep bashing out our brains? I'll tell you who, my brother: me, you, Shango! Culture! Fire! The body electric! The rumbling of the bellies grumbling at the bitter taste of antiquity! Humans lying in cells! Armies advancing with torches in the night! Shango! Bloodbaths of generations disappointed in dim philosophy, dipped in the ink of the blood of children who are soldiers! Shango The occidental terrorist! Shango the corrupter of children, Shango the hater of the useful, Shango who claims death for death's sake and lives to kill again! Shango whose mind is pure machination! Shango who burns temples and plunders their wisdom and distorts it into sitcoms and romcoms and TV dramas! Shango who bleeds wine and whose soul is entertainment! Shango whose mind is a monitor! Shango who monitors the mind, whose women are advertisements, whose men are modeled out of clay and iron, bold and strong to the sight and brittle to the touch! Shango, whose sin is sham! Shango, whose sense is shame! Shango who prances like a patsy in blackface, Shango, the shuck n' jive nigger! Shango who calls perfidy renaissance! Shango who calls technologies of stripped earth progress! Shango who dances the dance of the deadman and calls forth zombies to rule the earth! Shango who sleepwalks through death, Shango whose genius is the deprivation of the soul and the death of the innocent and the aggrandizement of the illusion of the self! Shango in whom I live inside, a bony skeleton you recognize as words or simple feelings! Shango in whom I scream! Shango as a whim and Shango as a dream. Shango whose innocence is a weapon! Shango lost nights streaming pictures across a screen, bent towards again, but now alone, no knowledge disclosed, foreclosed feelings and the shimmering simplicity of boredom! Shango whose fire is ice! Shango who is decadence! Shango who is dread! Shango who is the overlord of the dead and ascends to the sky swinging from trees strange fruit as we fall supplicating to our knees! Shango, who done took my blues and gone, Shango the magnificent, Shango the horrible, Shango the noble, Shango whose name is yo-mama's-big-ole-fat-behind! And so they came in their boats, bringing offerings to Shango, Black bodies with Black music a Black culture to electrify with the fire of Shango! Breakthroughs! Shango! Over the seas, to the new land! They gave them guitars and they bid them sing in the sterile light of morning where Shango looked startled on the holy words through the bloodshed and laughed electric until the very clouds shuddered and coins rained from the sky, down to the river, flooding the streets now paved with gold.

Whereupon the bourgeois brother, we can call him Osiris, would come in with:

Brother Ambrose! I'm with you in Brooklyn where you bleed out your innards; I'm with you in Brooklyn where you're spent in your own spleen; I'm with you in Brooklyn where your soul slips between the slots of the sidewalks; I'm with you in Brooklyn where you've died a dozen more deaths; I'm with you in Brooklyn where you join the jokes of our New York's swinest; I'm with you in Brooklyn where we are both shades in the same shadows of hell; I'm with you in Brooklyn where you have become a martyr and marauder, depending on whom you ask; I'm with you in Brooklyn where the worms in your body infiltrate the skulls of the living like lice; I'm with you in Brooklyn where your mother weeps with others like her who lost their only living; I'm with you in Brooklyn where you pass through the circles slowly towards your ascent; I'm with you in Brooklyn where you scream as the fires of Malebolge sear the serenity of your spirit; I'm with you in Brooklyn where you bang against the gates like a mad poet your soul is deathless you shall fear no evil; I'm with you in Brooklyn where you are now no longer heir to these thousand natural shocks the flesh is heir to; I'm with you in Brooklyn where you accuse the officers who shot you who sit steaming in the seventh circle of hell; I'm with you in Brooklyn where you split the asshole of satan and turn the world topsy-turvy, up is down and hot is cold and wrong is right but Black is always Black, as there ain't no white; I'm with you in Brooklyn where a million men march together and we all shall overcome; I'm with you in Brooklyn where we watch over the condition of the country where it lies bleeding out its innards on the Bedford-Stuyvesant sidewalk where you died; I'm with you in Brooklyn where you awake into the splendor of memory where you are no longer a victim but one of our heroes the eternal war is here but forever we advance where I'm with you in Brooklyn in my words and my deeds and those brothers who lie dying in your wake may wake once more and walk the long walk home, across the southern borders headed north to a freedom we are still building in the western night we are all of us we are all of us we are all of us we are with you in Brooklyn, my brother.

And out of this anthology of thought came a fifth guest, Black Anarchy. Black Anarchy in which we declare that the English language

is a racist instrument, and must be turned against itself; Black Anarchy, in which we declare that political language is as bad or rather
worse than the rest of the language; Black Anarchy, which realizes
any anarchy is always already governed by power structures and
the power assumed by quote unquote traditional anarchy, white anarchy, is white power; Black Anarchy in which we assume the opposite, that we are also in favor of anarchy, but we are in favor of
Black Anarchy, where peoples of African Descent hold the most
overall power; Black Anarchy in which we argue a plan of transition
to anarchy must begin with the removal of white power structures
and white power material wealth; Black Anarchy, in which we say
first the Revolution, then the Anarchy.

This formal declaration came much later. Formed in our conversations and formatted finally on the phone years later, in alliteration
which interrogates the morphemes of sounds in the language, and
if you languish too long over these linguistic longueurs, you learn
language is lying to you, and how. Look at the words, compare and
contrast and suddenly the language reveals how morphemes are as
much a building block of our being as cells.

Morphemes are cellular; I spent the days wandering the city
reading Iceberg Slim, of all things, Iceberg Slim, brother. There's a
man you can learn something about language from. Maybe the first
really Black book like jazz is Black, apologies to the usual candidates, but Langston was lyin' and Sterling was tryin', and Zora was
pure purple pathology nope nobody nicked it perfect like Slim. I
would take the train into the city, walk up and down First Avenue,
swing east to Union Square or Madison Square Park or maybe all
the way west to Washington Square Park, although there less fre-
quently, and read all day. The best place to go, though, was the
B&N at Union Square, especially in bad weather. Going there
early, you had to wait in front of the door, and hustle to get a good
seat by the large bay windows in the cafe. Then you could lay your
stuff down, and go walk around the floors, and collect books to keep
you occupied for the first few hours. Plenty of material for research,

recreational reading, and inspiration, while you did your own writing. You're stuck there all day, but you don't mind. You're spending every day reading and writing. I had the time to go through and complete Chomsky's first year graduate student linguistic textbook that summer, exercises and all. Universal grammar, says the white man. Talk about language games.

I miss those days, but I'm romanticizing them. I was dead broke, and under a lot of stress. I would've gone crazy without that bookstore. Then the characters I met out at Union Square Park. I spent a lot of time sitting on the park benches day after day, and when you do that for a while, you get to know the regulars. A lot of them are naturally homeless. Used to hustle a little here and there for an extra dollar or two with some kid who hung out in the park every day. That's basically how I paid my way when I first got to New York. That's why I liked to avoid Washington Square Park. I felt myself turning into all sorts of statistics, and that's when my head started pounding and didn't stop for three years, I think every night for three years I lived alone after moving out with those brothers and must have listened to Coltrane's *Interstellar Space* and Pac's *Me Against the World* every single night, one or the other or both, and then there came that call, it was the bourgeois brother, he says, we organizing, and is you in?

A black *Howl* got nothing to do with the loony bin, a black *Howl*'s institution of choice is jail, I mean if you're lucky, and normally it's just the cemetery.

Look, this is literary criticism with a pulse, Black Literary Criticism, not that shit you'll read by T.S. Idiot or Michael Fuckyou or Giles Delude, this is crit with a relationship to real life, and you ain't never seen the like. Ginsberg is a case in point; the language betrays us whichever which way we turn, there is no language there is only the doublespeak of hypocrisy, that's why I spit these English words like I'm shitting them, like a quick footnote, like Holy! Holy! Holy! Holy! Holy! Holy! Holy bullshit, Batman! There was a real loquacious motherfucker on the New York radio back in those days, Phil somethingorother, and he would go on and on and on about Bird, had a whole show devoted to the brother, and would play sixteen seventeen eighteen renditions of the same song, just so's you could hear how Bird changed it up each take, and if you go through enough versions of *Howl* you hear the same, each one a little different, that footnote at the end all switched up depending on which version you hear, they done took my blues and – and so everything is holy, and only a white boy would say so, even Moloch is holy and only a white boy would say so what is the opposite of holy if there are only ideas and their opposites? Let's see there's cursed, damned, corrupt, vile, deceitful, sinful, shameful, depraved, wicked, sacrilegious, vile, loathsome, contemptible, despicable, repugnant, hateful, iniquitous, degenerate, base, debased, noxious, perverse, pestiferous and pernicious, to name a few, so in case it's still somewhere way up there in the air above your head like a patient cauterized on a table like a wheel turning in a wheel, I'll break it down for you real slow, like wait a minute fella: here is my thesis: a Black president is a white president in a white America, which, you know, Ralph Ellison told you a long time ago, or don't you remember that "the demands of state policy are apt to be more influential than morality." What's the variation to this howl of mine? These were the Obama years now, remember. And Obama just proved the brother right – right? Here's Brother Ralph again: "I would like to see a qualified Negro as President of the United States. But I suspect that even if this were today possible, the necessities of the office would shape his actions far more than his racial identity." So, the point is this:

A true Black leader is necessarily anti-establishment. And white folks have been killing our leaders for centuries. A Black president isn't even a Black leader, he's a symbol. Thus, the killing of a Black president is the killing of a Black symbol, and the killing of a Black symbol is an act of white terrorism, no matter who pulls the trigger.

This is the logic of the new era.

This is the shadow & the act, motherfucker.

This is the shadow & the act.

#blackchant

selections: logged: Apr18 2046-May26 2046

<u>CancelComeCorrect</u> @theseandthen Apr 18
@omari yeah brother I was 10 years old cops pulled me over said they found a man around the corner his head bashed in, I "fit the description." Detained me in a cell in CB and I waited there 3 hours for my mother to come pick me up word #FuckThaPolice #IAmAmbrose #BlackChant

<u>StayNameless</u> @staynameless Apr 18
Cop shoots black father in his house, holds daughter hostage, points gun at mother and calls her "a #slimyniggerbitch." #FukThaPolice #BlackChant yall.

<u>Letteer</u> @youtoldyouyoutold Apr 18
#BlackChant Get the fuck out of Southie nigger! —cop on motorcycle to me today on my walk home from work. #slimyniggerbitch

<u>Olijerky</u> @olijerkywize Apr 19
Yo, fukkkk deez cops, nigga! For real. #BlackChant.

<u>WhatItDo</u> @whereiwaswhereiwere Apr 20
Come on out yall. Second Annual Black Earth Demonstration this Sunday in Central Park #AfroMunk #BlackChant.

<u>MakeItLast</u> @makeitlast Apr 20
@whereiwaswhereiwere #ArtsDemonstration #AfroMunk #BlackChant. We'll be playing at the demonstration! New mixtape shit. Come show love.

totheSun @pharoahson Apr 20
@makeitlast Is there a website? #AfroMunk #BlackChant.

CametoTeach @cametoteach Apr 20
@pharoahson naw nicca, aint no website just #BlackChant

2wiceasnice @2wiceasnice Apr 20
@pharoahson @cametoteach yeah we'll be there too. with bells on muthafuckas #BlackQueerTheory #BlackChant.

Novus @aagrao Apr 20
@pharoahson @cametoteach AAGRAO will be there too. Lots of love to my brothers and my sisters. #AAGRAO #BlackChant.

TyroneGrant @therealtyronegrant Apr 20
@aagrao Good to hear you'll be there! We'll be there too! Hit me up with a DM. #BlackChant

Novus @aagrao Apr 20
@tyronegrant splendid! #BlackChant.

OnthisEarth @onceupistwicedown Apr 20
@tyronegrant shouldn't your Black ass be in jail? #JusticeForLena #BlackChant.

SoNice @SoNice Apr 20
Yo, what's up with whitefolk singing rap songs and leaving in the N-Word. Y'all seein this trend??! #BlackChant

Meinung @Meaning Apr 20
Where the jokes at? I thought #BlackChant be lit, but yall like zzzzzzzzz....

Thanks4Listening @Thanxmanx Apr 20
@meinung #BlackChant got woke ha ha. #IAmAmbrose

BeRight @BeRight Apr 20
@thanxmanx yo #BlackChant aint woke, yall jokas is broke.

ParaMilitary @paramilitary Apr 20
@sonice white folks jes wanna be Black my brotha and they fuckin racist too retards lol #BlackChant

CapableCool @capablecool Apr 20
@sonice @paramilitary White folks can be allies too. I consider myself an ally #BlackChant

SoNice @SoNice Apr 20
@capablecool you aint no ally and this aint no damn alliance and shit go back to star wars with that bullshit #BlackChant

CapableCool @capablecool Apr 20
@sonice See it's that kind of attitude that keeps people from coming together we got to come together #BlackChant

BeRigjt @BeRight Apr 20
Damn @SoNice you just got whitesplained by @CapableCool lol #BlackChant

Novus @aagro Apr 22
We can't continue to put up with shit like what happened Sunday. The same damn shit happened last year at the same festival. Sorry for the strong language, but I'm mad as hell. They keep hunting us they want us scared. #BlackChant

carefulfart @carefulfart Apr 22

@aagro #WhiteTerrorism my brother. chant and hashtag it. #BlackChant

SoNice @SoNice Apr 22

Yo, where's that idiot @CapableCool now with his talk of come together? #WhiteTerrorism #BlackChant

TyroneGrant @therealtyronegrant Apr 23

I know @aagro. I'm still reeling. #BlackChant

FracturedIce @fracturedice Apr 23

Organize people. Sunday's pipe bomb is just another example of #WhiteTerrorism. We got to organize as a people. #BlackChant

BlackAnarchy @harlemspleen Apr 24

@fracturedice @aagro @therealtyronegrant #AintADamn-ThingChanged #WhiteTerrorism been with us since #slavery #revolution is the only solution. I'm dead serious #BlackAnarchy #BlackChant

TyroneGrant @therealtyronegrant Apr 24

@harlemspleen I'm open to suggestions. What should we do, brother? What do you mean by #revolution. #ADO is out there on the front lines every day. Come by our office sometime. #Black-Chant

BlackAnarchy @SoNice Apr 24

@therealtyronegrant I respect what you're doing, but we're our own organization, and honestly, we don't think you folks go far enough. #BlackChant

Marrakech @marrakech Apr 24

Nobody here on #BlackChant here to hear a bunch of fake

wannabe revolutionaries flapping they gums @therealtyronegrant
@harlemspleen

BlackAnarchy @harlemspleen Apr 24
@marrakech Feel free to stay ignorant #NiggasAreScaredOfRevolution #BlackChant

TyroneGrant @ therealtyronegrant Apr 24
@harlemspleen Cool handle btw. Sorry to see we don't see eye to eye but we're really all in this together #BlackChant

ChocolateCaramel @chocolatecaramel Apr 25
I lost my sister in the #PipeBombing Saturday. I just want justice yall #BlackChant

AllAlert @allalert Apr 25
@chocolatecaramel so damn sick and tired of being so damn sick and tired #BlackChant

BlackAnarchy @harlemspleen Apr 25
@chocolatecaramel @allalert Another #demontration aint the answer. We know that at least. I've been doing some digging into this #WhiteTerrorism organization that set the bomb. This shit runs deeper than I thought. #BlackChant

SoNice @SoNice Apr 25
@harlemspleen So what you sayin'? #BlackChant

BlackAnarchy @harlemspleen Apr 25
@sonice These muthafuckas call themselves #TheSyndicate. I don't wanna jump on this too quick. I need more proof. But it looks like they may be behind some serious shit what went down last month if you know what I mean. #JusticeForPowers #BlackChant

TyroneGrant @therealtyronegrant Apr 25
@harlemspleen Hey send me a DM. If you're serious about this we need to talk #BlackChant

BlackAnarchy @harlemspleen Apr 25
@therealtyronegrant Look, brother, I appreciate how near and dear this is to you, but I don't do DM. All my shit stays public & transparent. #BlackChant

Novus @aagro Apr 25
@harlemspleen @therealtyronegrant I'm looking into #TheSyndicate. I'll report back with anything our people are able to find out. Come on #BlackChant, let's use our collective knowledge and skills to smoke these fools out!

badboyboo @badboyboo Apr 25
@aagro I'm with yall. Getting my search genius skillz geared up. Will report back. #BlackChant

AllAlert @allalert Apr 25
@aagro @badboyboo word let's do this thang #BlackChant

AlchemyisScience @AlchemyIsScience Apr 26
Reporting back to #BlackChant about #TheSyndicate. They're a real thing. Real underground. News aint even reporting this shit. Check #RobertOwens. Scaryass super racist whiteass nigga. Seems to be the leader.

MorganFruh @morganfruh Apr 26
Goddamn @alcehmyisscience I just read about him. Tell me about it #BlackChant

BlackAnarchy @harlemspleen Apr 27
@alchemyisscience @morganfruh Okay, I just wrote up a profile

on this #RobertOwens cat. Read it <u>here</u>. RT and #spreadtheword #BlackChant

OddjobOut @blueinthefaceblackinthought Apr 27
@harlemspleen Great piece man. People need to be reading this. I'll #chant it

Kamafloj @kamafloj Apr 27
@blueinthefaceblackinthought these crazy white murdafuckas never cease to amaze me man #BlackChant

Miraculousworker @miraculousworker Apr 28
@kamafloj same ol everyday shit #BlackChant

OddjobOut @blueinthefaceblackinthought Apr 28
@harlemspleen yo that article going viral #BlackChant

BlackAnarchy @harlemspleen Apr 28
@OddjobOut I'm just glad to see word getting out there #Black-Chant

AllAlert @allalert Apr 28
@harlemspleen white folks prolly mobilizing #BlackChant

BlackAnarchy @harlemspleen Apr 28
@allalert See this is just what I mean. If we don't organize and retaliate we don't stand a chance. White people are always gonna organize against us. First the revolution, then anarchy. #BlackCincoDeMayo #BlackChant

Novus @aagro Apr 28
@harlemspleen We gotta organize, true, the question is how #BlackChant

TyroneGrant @therealtyronegrant Apr 29
@harlemspleen @Novus I'm going to be speaking at Howard this evening. Come thru y'all. #BlackChant

BlackAnarchy @harlemspleen Apr 29
@therealtyronegrant I'll be there brother. We can talk after. #BlackChant

AllAlert @allalert Apr 29
@therealtyronegrant hey protect ya neck up there my brutha #BlackChant

Kulcha @gotchacaughtcha Apr 29
@allalert @therealtyronegrant gone come thru on some security shit.

TravellingPink @travellingpink Apr 29
@gotchacaughtcha never forget #WhiteTerrorism #BlackChant

BlackAnarchy @harlemspleen Apr 29
@gotchacaughtcha @travellingpibk It warms my heart to see BT come to-gather like this

Novus @aagro Apr 30
@therealtyronegrant Hey good speech last night #BlackChant

Morgij @morgij Apr 30
@aagro I agree but the brotha coulda talked more about the syndi-cate. wut up? #BlackChant

TyroneGrant @therealtyronegrant Apr 30
@morgij we're looking into that. I didn't want to say something without knowing more #BlackChant

BlackAnarchy @harlemspleen Apr 30

@therealtyronegrant With all due respect, what exactly do you mean "without knowing more." Did you or did you not read my article. #BlackChant

JumpUpBeatDown @foolskeepjumpin Apr 30

@harlemspleen No doubt. That nigga @therealtyronegrant got some splaining to do #blackchant

CoreControl @corecontrol Apr 30

@foolskeepjumpin that nigga @therealtyronegrant always been full of it, man. Check his history #BlackChant

OnthisEarth @onceupistwicedown May 1

@corecontrol It's worse than that, my man. @therealtyronegrant prolly guilty of shooting Powers hisself #Justice4Powers #BlackChant

CockeyedKill @cockeyedkill May 1

@onceupistwicedown word #BlackChant

TyroneGrant @therealtyronegrant May 1

@corecontrol @cockeyedkill Lena pardoned me full pardon check the history your damn self

BlackAnarchy @harlemspleen May 1

@corecontrol @cockeyedkill @therealtyronegrant and I don't see eye to eye on a lot of things, but I'm pretty sure these Syndicate mofos are the ones behind the Powers assassination. #BlackChant

Morgij @morgij May 1

@harlemspleen don't doubt that shit but you got proof bruh? #BlackChant

BlackAnarchy @harlemspleen May 1
@morgije I'm working on it. Doing a followup piece to that last one.

BlackKnowledge @blackknowledge May 1
@harlemspleen I always had a feeling #WhiteTerrorism was behind this shit. I never thought it was them two brothas #BlackChant

Pifff @pifff May 1
@blackknowledge That otha brotha the funny one with the funny name aint no killa of no kind I tell you that now

Novus @aagro May 2
@harlemspleen I'd like to connect with you brother. Where are you getting your leads? Let's talk. Come by our office if you have a moment. #BlackChant

BlackAnarchy @harlemspleen May 2
@aagro I'll stop by if I get the time this tomorrow or Friday but let's keep conversation open here on #BlackChant. I want transparency above all.

TyroneGrant @therealtyronegrant May 2
@harlemspleen I'm for transparency as well. That was kind of me & Lena's thing when we were still working together. Let's engage here on #BlackChant

Lisplisplips @lisplisplips May 2
Allasudden this nixxa come talking about transparency. @therealtyronegrant WE DON'T TRUST YOU NIXXA #BlackChant

OnThisEarth @onceupistwicedown May 2
@lisplisplips Ain't that the goddam truth #blackchant

Primaphobia @primaphobia May 2

@onceupistwicedown @lisplisplips See this is the problem with us black folks. We always fighting amongst ourselves. Even here on #BlackChant

OnThisEarth @onceupistwicedown May 2

@primaphobia Nigga we aint no monolith. Not even "here on #BlackChant"

Primaphobia @primaphobia May 2

@onceupistwicedown No, but we are a community- #BlackChant is and should be a community. Black people need to act as a community. These white people out there are sure as hell working together. We need to work together too if we want to be strong. Just sayin.

Jookslooks @manstandalone May 2

@primaphobia And I couldn't have said it better myself. #Black-Chant

AnthemAttack @anthemattack May 3

@manstandalone Word. I was at that speech the other day. That shit needs to be published. #BlackChant

Kapers @kapers May 3

@anthemattack I agree wholeheartedly. It ought to be. @therealtyronegrant You planning on publishing a transcript of your speech from the other day? #BlackChant

BlackAnarchy @harlemspleen May 3

@kapers @therealtyronegrant I wouldn't mind seeing a copy of it myself to be honest. #BlackChant

Novus @aagro May 3

@kapers @blackanarchy @therealtyronegrant I'll third that motion. #BlackChant

TyroneGrant @therealtyronegrant May 3

@kapers @blackanarchy @aagro No worries, I'll put it up on the website this weekend. I'll hit up #BlackChant and let y'all know once it's up there.

Kapers @kapers May 3

@therealtyronegrant Great! I look forward to reading it. #Black-Chant

Lisplisplips @lisplisplips May 3

@kapers If you believe anything that nixxa say I got a bridge to Brooklyn to sell you. #BlackChant

TyroneGrant @therealtyronegrant May 3

@lisplisplips I'm not sure what I've done to offend you but I'm on the up and up here. #BlackChant

Primaphobia @primaphobia May 4

@lisplisplips I'm still waiting to hear more about these Syndicate creeps. @harlemspleen Are you going to follow up on this? #Black-Chant

BlackAnarchy @harlemspleen May 4

@primaphobia I'm hot on this topic. #blackchant

CordialtilIkill @cordialkiller May 4

@harlemspleen @primaphobia Yeah wussup we all waiting #BlackChant

BlackAnarchy @harlemspleen May 5
@cordialkiller I know. Forthcoming. In the next day or two. I'll publish my findings right here on #BlackChant

Novus @aagro May 5
@harlemspleen Findings? Brother, if you've found some actual evidence, we need to talk.

BlackAnarchy @harlemspleen May 5
@aagro I've been meaning to stop by your office. I haven't had the chance yet, but I'm gonna publish as soon as I have the evidence. #BlackChant

MorbidDreams @morbiddreams May 5
@harlemspleen Yeah, don't wait up for our #SoCalledBlackLeaders to twist things the way they want. Keep it here on #BlackChant

Alkilolick @alkilolick May 6
@morbiddreams Damn man if I had a dollar every time I heard a #SoCalledBlackLeader pretend he wasn't trying to be one #BlackChant

FortranStan @fortranstan May 6
@alkilolicks That's how Lena Powers was too. And @therealtyronegrant was right there with her on that fakery fuckery. #BlackChant

TyroneGrant @therealtyronegrant May 6
@fortranstan Honestly, I never wanted to be any kind of leader, and I'm sorry how everything turned out around all that. I'm writing about this. #BlackChant

OnThisEarth @onceupistwicedown May 6
@therealtyronegrant Ain't no one trying to read your lies. #BlackChant

<u>**MickeyYoureSoFine**</u> @heymickey May 6
@onceuptwicedown I don't care what none of y'all say. I still ride with @therealtyronegrant! #BlackChant

<u>**BlackAnarchy**</u> @harlemspleen May 7
Here's what I got on the Syndicate. I'm not waiting on news organizations not waiting on publishers not waiting on media I'm going in with this now. Follow the thread. #BlackChant #Syndicate /1

<u>**BlackAnarchy**</u> @harlemspleen May 7
First off, most of you don't know me, so I should say something about myself before I jump right into it. I'm part of an activist movement that's the same as my handle. #BlackAnarchy. #BlackChant #Syndicate /2

<u>**BlackAnarchy**</u> @harlemspleen May 7
We believe in a black anarchy where black folk first take over the wealth and means of production and then dismantle the government. In that order. #BlackChant #Syndicate /3

<u>**BlackAnarchy**</u> @harlemspleen May 7
So those are some loud words, I know. And no one is saying it's going to be easy. But at this point for anyone paying attention, there's no other option. #BlackChant #Syndicate /4

<u>**BlackAnarchy**</u> @harlemspleen May 7
I don't buy into that old Black thought socialist bullshit and I don't buy into this white man's capitalist bullshit either. What socialism got right is that we got to look after each other #blackchant #Syndicate /5

<u>**BlackAnarchy**</u> @harlemspleen May 7
What capitalism got right is that whoever owns the means of production has the power. #blackchant people listen. I'm talking revolution. #Syndicate /6

BlackAnarchy @harlemspleen May 7

So Black folk got to get the means of production into their own hands, and I'm telling you now, the white man isn't just going to hand that shit over with a smile and a nod. #BlackChant #Syndicate /7

BlackAnarchy @harlemspleen May 7

Real revolution with real blood where real shit goes down. Sorry if you ain't trying to hear it, but if not what can I say except you don't hear me tho. #BlackChant #Syndicate /8

BlackKnowledge @blackknowledge May 7

@harlemspleen I hear you brother. Go on widdit. #BlackChant

BlackAnarchy @harlemspleen May 7

Now there's been a lot of talk about #WhiteTerrorism, especially since Powers' murder and then that pipe bomb that went off at the rally. #BlackChant #Syndicate /9

BlackAnarchy @harlemspleen May 7

And some of you have already read my piece on @RobertOwens of #TheSyndicate. White liberal academic cat whose sister was murdered by a Black man in the Appalachian Assault of October 2036 and then turned into the racist asshole he's always already been. #BlackChant #Syndicate /10

BlackAnarchy @harlemspleen May 7

I did some anonymous fishing around y'all, pretending to be a white dude. Posted on #WhiteChant (yeah, that's really a thing) and everything. If you dig deep enough, it leads you to this @RobertOwens dude every time. #BlackChant #Syndicate /11

BlackAnarchy @harlemspleen May 7

He's at the forefront of the new White Power movement, and he prefers to stay underground as much as possible because he wants to run a terrorist organization. You don't believe me jump on some of these message boards yourself. Do your own research. #Black-Chant #Syndicate /12

BlackAnarchy @harlemspleen May 7
The media doesn't know enough about him to cover him, and they'd get it all wrong anyway. We did some serious undercover shit like in that old-ass Spike Lee movie #BlackKKlansman, #Black-Chant #Syndicate /13

BlackAnarchy @harlemspleen May 7
Got people in there attending actual meetings and everything. A lot of these meetings are online now, so you just got to get software where a white AI face is sitting there in front of your computer instead of your actual Black ass and you can join right in. #Black-Chant #Syndicate /14

BlackAnarchy @harlemspleen May 7
I'm not gonna lie, I thought @therealtyronegrant was behind the Powers shooting at first too, but now I know better. #BlackChant #Syndicate /15

OnthisEarth @onceupistwicedown May 7
@harlemspleen Alright nigga how we know you ain't a white supremacist or a cop yourself right here on #BlackChant?

BlackAnarchy @harlemspleen May 7
@onceupistwicedown People know who I am brother. In real life. I don't know the first thing about you though. #BlackChant #Syndicate /16

BlackAnarchy @harlemspleen May 7
All that foolishness aside, this is some serious shit because I am traceable in real life, and so I'm actually putting my actual Black ass on the line here. #BlackChant #Syndicate /17

BlackAnarchy @harlemspleen_May 7
Now this @RobertOwen cat, his Syndicate goes for the whole plausible deniability act. #BlackChant #Syndicate /18

BlackAnarchy @harlemspleen_May 7
So if you go to one of these online meetings, they aren't there screaming racist slogans or anything like that. That would be too obvious. #BlackChant #Syndicate /19

BlackAnarchy @harlemspleen May 7
They say they take a conservative outlook and are against identity politics and are against liberal bias and they are for taking the country back and "restoring America to itself" #blackchant #Syndicate /20

BlackAnarchy @harlemspleen May 7
We all know what that means, but they won't admit it up front, because then they get labeled a hate group. Right now as a non-profit, they're benefiting from government money - your tax money and mine to keep up this racist nonsense. #BlackChant #Syndicate /21

BlackAnarchy @harlemspleen May 7
The person who set off that pipe bomb last week was a member of the Syndicate. I know because they talk about letting him go from the group after that. #BlackChant #Syndicate /22

BlackAnarchy @harlemspleen May 7
They do this kind of thing where they have one person commit an act of violence, and that person takes the fall for it and has to publicly leave the group. #BlackChant #Syndicate /23

BlackKnowledge @blackknowledge May 7
They call that shit suicide bombing... not even shitting you. #BlackChant #Syndicate /24

BlackAnarchy @harlemspleen May 7
So now #WhiteTerrorism has not only adopted the tactics of so-called "Islamic terrorism," which is already a racist trope, but now they also co-opting the media's language. But that's no surprise after all. White folks always were the original terrorists #BlackChant #Syndicate /25

BlackAnarchy @harlemspleen May 7
Anyway the reason I think this goes even deeper than the pipe bombing is because of some allusions that they've made in their meetings. #BlackChant #Syndicate /26

BlackAnarchy @harlemspleen May 7
This @RobertOwens cat has a code that he's developed, and the followers know the code somehow. I don't know how they know, but decoding texts is kind of like my thing. So I've been decoding what they've been saying. #BlackChant #Syndicate /27

BlackAnarchy @harlemspleen May 7
This guy and his organization, he himself has admitted it in code, are responsible for the murder of President Powers. #BlackChant #Syndicate /28

BlackAnarchy @harlemspleen May 7
Not only can I tell you all this much but I can prove it. I have video of me attending the meeting, and I have a code-cracker, and I am going to publish both online. #BlackChant #Syndicate /29

Novus @aagro May 7
@harlemspleen Please respond immediately to my DM and come see me in person as soon as possible - before you make another move #BlackChant

TyroneGrant @therealtyronegrant May 7
@harlemspleen That goes for me too. Please get in touch with me ASAP. I just sent you a DM. #BlackChant

Cordialtillkill @cordialkiller May 7
@harlemspleen Publish that shit! #BlackChant

BlackAnarchy @harlemspleen May 8
@cordialkiller THIS ACCOUNT HAS BEEN INDEFINITELY
SUSPENDED

JumpUpBeatDown @foolskeepjumpin May 8
Did that fool @blackspleen just pretend to suspend himself
on #BlackChant wut up?

CockeyedKill @cockeyedkill May 8
@foolskeepjumpin he one hella conspiracy ass nigga #divaniggas
#blackchant

TyroneGrant @therealtyronegrant May 8
@cockeyedkill we're looking into that. I didn't want to say something without knowing more #BlackChant

JumpUpBeatDown @foolskeepjumpin May 8
@therealtyronegrant ??? #blackchant

CoreControl @corecontrol May 8
@foolskeepjumpin looks like he accidentally resent one of his old
chants #BlackChant

OnthisEarth @onceupistwicedown May 8
@corecontrol Or he's just a supreme asswipe!

JumpUpBeatDown @foolskeepjumpin May 8
@onceupistwicedown asswipe sounds about right #BlackChant

TyroneGrant @therealtyronegrant May 8
@foolskeepjumpin I didn't write that last chant...

CoreControl @corecontrol May 8
@therealtyronegrant then it was someone on your faculty man #BlackChant

PerchedUpOnaWall @perchedandwatchinya May 8
@corecontrol So basically all y'all motherfuckers are fake as fuck anyway peace @harlemspleen peace @tyronegrant #BlackChant

TyroneGrant @therealtyronegrant May 8
@morgije that wasn't someone on my staff, I don't have a staff I write all my own chants myself it is after all what I do I write so thank you I find my own words. logging out will report back #blackchant

BlackKnowledge @blackknowledge May 9
@harlemspleen I always had a feeling #WhiteTerrorism was behind this shit. I never thought it was them two brothas #BlackChant

PerchedUpOnaWall @perchedandwatchinya May 9
Yo #blackchant I just broke out the popcorn on these two corny niggas

TyroneGrant @therealtyronegrant May 9
@perchedandwatchinya we're looking into that. I didn't want to say something without knowing more #BlackChant

BurgerStop @burgerstop May 9
@perchedandwatchinya there he goes again #BlackChant

OddjobOut @blueinthefaceblackinthought May 10
what y'all make of this new shit #BlackChant? #RobertOwen NEW YORK TIMES BREAKING NEWS: White Supremacist Robert Owens Arrested in Connection to Powers Murder

AllAlert @allalert May 10

@blueinthefaceblackinthought I know! I damn near shit when I saw that! #BlackChant

PerchedUpOnaWall @perchedandwatchinya May 10

@allalert Yeah, I still don't know what to make of it.

AllAlert @allalert May 10

@perchedupandwatchinya Sounds like @harlemspleen had a point after all. #BlackChant

Novus @aagro May 10

@allalert I never doubted his integrity, for the record. I've met @harlemspleen in person. Yes, he's a little eccentric, but he's authentic as all hell. #BlackChant

TyroneGrant @therealtyronegrant May 10

@aagro we're looking into that. I didn't want to say something without knowing more #BlackChant

BurgerStop @burgerstop May 10

@therealtyronegrant Not this shit again. #BlackChant

AllAlert @allalert May 11

@aagro Yeah and something's definitely up with @RobertOwen, creepyass white nigga. #BlackChant

JumpUpBeatDown @foolskeepjumpin May 11

@aagro @allalert Okay, but @blackspleen did do some corny shit with his last thread. What was up with that?

TyroneGrant @therealtyronegrant May 11

@aagro we're looking into that. I didn't want to say something without knowing more #BlackChant

TravellingPink @travellingpink May 11

@foolskeepjumpin And then there's this Tyrone-Bot-Thing #BlackChant

CoreControl @corecontrol May 11

@travellingpink *Maybe* there's something to what @harlemspleen is saying, but @therealtyronegrant aint real at all. That nigga is straight up fake. #BlackChant

OnthisEarth @onceupistwicedown May 11

@corecontrol @RobertOwen is what happens today in new America where everybody is a race nationalist. #BlackChant

Novus @aagro May 12

@onceupistwicedown As the great James Baldwin once wrote "As long as you call yourself white, I am forced to call myself black." #BlackChant

TyroneGrant @therealtyronegrant May 12

@novus we're looking into that. I didn't want to say something without knowing more #BlackChant

PerchedUpOnaWall @perchedandwatchinya May 12

@novus there he goes again #BlackChant

TravellingPink @travellingpink May 12

@perchedponawall Something fked up about the whole thing #BlackChant feel infiltrated niccaz

JumpUpBeatDown @foolskeepjumpin May 12

@travellingpink don't it tho?

Kulcha @gotchacaughtcha May 13

@foolskeepjumpin yeh whateva niggaz. I'm ridin wit @harlemspleen on this shit. This is some straight up conspiracy shit.

OddjobOut @blueieinthefaceblackinthought May 14

@gotchacaughtcha #BlackChant #RobertOwen I'd be careful what I say here on BC

Kulcha @gotchacaughtcha May 14

@blueinthefaceblackinthought Think I'm scared? Let a nigga just try and run up on me for some ish I said on #BlackChant.

TyroneGrant @therealtyronegrant May 14

@novus we're looking into that. I didn't want to say something without knowing more #BlackChant

OnthisEarth @onceupistwicedown May 14

@gotchacaughtcha @therealtyronegrant You got to be shitting me if y'all believe these niggas. It aint no conspiracy but the one cooked up by @harlemspleen who is probably in on this with @therealtyronegrant. #BlackChant

Novus @aagro May 15

@onceupistwicedown #BlackChant At the risk of being included in your conspiracy theory for saying this, I can actually vouch for @therealtyronegrant in this case. His account has been hijacked, he's not using #blackchant right now, and the account should have been deleted already.

ScaryNigga @scarynigga May 15

@aagro Oh shit @therealtyronegrant a #BlackChant zombie-ass-nigga now.

OnthisEarth @onceupistwicedown May 15
@scarynigga He always been that. #BlackChant

OnthisEarth @onceupistwicedown May 15
@aagro Maybe his account did get hijacked I still don't trust that nigga. If he gone for good soon good. #BlackChant

Novus @aagro May 15
@onceupistwicedown He's still reading #BlackChant of course. He's going to make a public announcement in the next couple days.

CoreControl @corecontrol May 15
@aagro @onceupistwicedown Let him make an announcement then. One way or another one of these two conspiracy theory's going mainstream Let's hope it's the right one #BlackChant

Kulcha @gotchacaughtcha May 22
@corecontrol I don't know these official Black leader ass niggas, but I sure don't trust no govt-ass niggaz either, especially not that Ralph nigga.

GameDayDontMeanAThing @gamegrindhustle May 22
@gotchacaughtcha Who said anything about Ralph on #BlackChant?

Kulcha @gotchacaughtcha May 15
@gamegrindhustle @harlemspleen said something somewhere I think. And I think that nigga Ralph knows something.

BurgerStop @burgerstop May 15
@gotchacaughtcha No doubt he knows something. #BlackChant

TravellingPink @travellingpink May 15
@burgerstop Yeah, Ralph always wanted to be president. No doubt about that. #BlackChant

JumpUpBeatDown @foolskeepjumpin May 15
@travellingpink And he ain't waited but a minute to start jumping in hard. I mean President Powers just died. Show her a little goddam respect.

TyroneGrant @therealtyronegrant May 15
@novus we're looking into that. I didn't want to say something without knowing more #BlackChant

Kulcha @gotchacaughtcha May 15
#BlackChant kinda fucked up the timing of these @therealtyronegrant posts. They be listening.

OddjobOut @blueieinthefaceblackinthought May 16
Yo #BlackChant! Y'all check that speech by @therealtyronegrant last night? What y'all think? Speak my sisters and brothers!

Novus @aagro May 16
@blueinthefaceblackinthought For my part, I thought he stated his case well. I don't want to make any definitive statement for the moment, but I'm mulling it over. Love to hear from more of yall too #BlackChant

OnthisEarth @onceupistwicedown May 16
@aagro ok, I'll bite. I think @therealtyronegrant has a point. I do think Ralph is up to something; dirty as shit; but I also think @therealtyronegrant is using this just as a PR play, so he benefiting from the shit #BlackChant

AllAlert @allalert May 16
I don't know about y'all, #BlackChant but I've been watching that shit on repeat.

Novus @aagro May 17
@allalert They're starting an official investigation #BlackChant

Kulcha @gotchacaughtcha May 17
@aagro They investigating the president? Oh shit #BlackChant.

Novus @aagro May 17
@gotchacaughtcha Yeah. It could take a while and might never even happen, even if there is enough evidence to prove he's been obstructing justice to cover his ass. They never convict presidents though #BlackChant

ScaryNigga @scarynigga May 17
@aagro Ain't no previous president killed nobody, and definitely not the last siting president, even if he wished he could lol #Black-Chant.

Novus @aagro May 17
@scarynigga Depends what you mean by killed they all kill people and Kletterkater certainly had a lot of blood on his hands, but point taken. #BlackChant

CoreControl @corecontrol May 18
Yo this shit on Ralph is getting serious. You have any info @aagro? #BlackChant

Novus @aagro May 18
@corecontrol I wish I did. I'm glued to my devices just like everyone else, wondering how it's gonna play out. #BlackChant

TyroneGrant @therealtyronegrant May 18
@aagro we're looking into that. I didn't want to say something without knowing more #BlackChant

GameDayDontMeanAThing @gamegrindhustle May 18
I thought @therealtyronegrant should been gone #BlackChant. What up?

OnthisEarth @onceupistwicedown May 18
@gamegrindhustle shit don't surprise me. I wouldn't be surprised if Ralph and @therealtyronegrant were working together, and Ralph taking the fall for it #BlackChant

PerchedUpOnaWall @perchedandwatchinya May 18
@onceupistwicedown That's some deep conspiracy talk. I can't go all there yet

OnthisEarth @onceupistwicedown May 18
@perchedandwatchinya It's not just me. Check out this website.

Novus @aagro May 18
@onceupistwicedown I wouldn't trust that website - #BlackChant, please be attentive to the sources you get your news from

OnthisEarth @onceupistwicedown May 18
I suppose we're just supposed to go to mainstream media sources like a flock of fuckin sheep, right @aagro? That and listen to you of-ficial niggas. #Fukdat #BlackChant

Kulcha @gotchacaughtcha May 26
I didn't much like the nigga, but he was president and he was Black so fuck it RIP President Ralph Bellicose. #BlackChant.

OnthisEarth @onceupistwicedown May 26
@gotchacaughtchaThey lynched that nigga I'm telling you don't listen to the official BS media nonsense about that nigga lynched hisself THEY lynched his Black ass. #BlackChant

From *The Arabesque Commission* (2100)

Chapter 7:

The 2043-2044 Democratic Primary Season

7.1. OPENING QUESTION(S)

I.   The question that every study of the 2043-2044 democratic primary season must @ some point deal with is why Grant ran 1st instead of Powers. This is essentially 1 question with 2 parts. The 1st part of the question is whether Powers' eventual campaign was planned by Powers & Grant in advance[1]. The 2nd part of the question is whether the appearance of Cudgo Loo during the primary season was part of that plan, or a wild card.

II.   This much is certain: Powers was political; Grant was the house poet (or granting, the house pet). In any case, his candidacy came as a surprise. Feminists understandably protested Grant's campaign & called for a Powers campaign instead.[2]

---

[1] The answer to this question opens up additional questions. For example, if they planned it in advance together, as I argue they did, why Grant 1st? Why was it timed the way it was? These are questions which I will answer in this chapter. If they did not plan it together, at what point was Powers aware Grant would run, and what were her feelings about Grant running instead of her?

[2] There were 87 separate demonstrations by women's groups around the country protesting Tyrone Grant running instead of Lena Powers between Grant announcing on January 30th and Powers announcing on May 1st.

III.	The best way to untangle this wrangle is to answer the 2nd part of the 1st question 1st, because it is the most easily answered, despite various misleading accounts. For example, in Edward Scanner's 3-Impact *Good Riddance to Bad Blood* (2078), Scanner argues that Grant & Powers planned their respective election campaigns together, in advance, reasoning if either of them won, they were both guaranteed a spot in the White House, as they were already effectively president & 1st lady, or president & 1st man, as the case may be.

REJOINDER

Then: the cold but sunny dawn of the announcement @ the new Politics & Prose *in Cathedral Heights;*

the sudden & dramatic appearance of Cudgo Loo that bright blue morning;

Loo's bizarre, esoteric & arcane references to performance –

could it be that Loo's upset was actually a plant by Grant & Powers as well?

RETURN

So goes the theory.

7.1.1. THE CASE OF CUDGO LOO

I.	Scanner intuits nicely that Powers & Grant planned both their candidacies in advance; more on that later, but a digital analysis makes it clear that Cudgo Loo was not a co-conspirator:

II.	NAMELY, on January 30th, 2043, Tyrone Grant officially

announced his candidacy for president. There had been chatter that he might. There had been chatter that Powers might too. The 2 had often acted in tandem: they had started the ADO together; they made public appearances together; they both released their memoirs on September 27th, 2041-- Powers' best-selling *Separate Powers*, & Grant's somewhat more literary & fragmented *Collective Unrealities*. In the month after Grant announced his candidacy, 76.8% of all American news media with more than 2 million page views per week ran @ least 1 op-ed speculating @ the probability of Lena Powers joining the race. Not a single media outlet mentioned Cudgo Loo.

III.   I h/kd the following records: Cudgo Loo visits Tyrone Grant the next week after Grant announces his candidacy @ the ADO headquarters. Footage from street cameras show: Cudgo Loo entering the ADO Headquarters @ 9:25 on Monday, February 2nd, 2043. He spends 45 minutes there, leaves @ 10:11.

IV.   I haven't been able to obtain any recordings or transcripts of their conversation from that morning. Lip reading software has recreated portions of it (see appendix A), but these transcripts suffer from the typical LRS problems from this era & are not very revealing.

V.   Querying the records of cellular communications between each of their 2 numbers during this period brings up more fruitful results. The 1st traceable call between the 2 men comes from Tyrone @ 11:11 on January 30th, the day after Grant announced. The call lasts 7 minutes & 22 seconds. Cudgo calls Tyrone later that day @ 18:19, a call which lasts 4 minutes & 3 seconds.

VI.   Between 2020 & 2041 there are 0 traceable phone contacts between Loo & Grant. A thorough h/k of email, social media, dms & chats reveals nothing. But was there personal contact? A better way of mapping their movements is to track their general proximities to 1 another through cell phone mapping. Cell phone mapping can pinpoint even when they might have been in the same restaurant, café, bar, club, hotel, etc... @ the same time, & might give us a clearer picture as to their exact relationship.

VII.   Mapped out are the movements of both men using their device records for those 20 years (Fig. 1), & while both of them spend most of the time in the Washington, DC area, with occasional trips up & down the east coast, they never meet. There are, for sure, some near misses. On October 18, 2032 the 2 men appear to have just missed each other @ the corner of P Street & Connecticut, & on May 3rd, 2038 Cudgo Loo goes into a Starbucks 20 minutes after Grant leaves that same Starbucks on 16th Street in Adams Morgan. Powers' movements in relation to Loo reveal nothing either (See Appendix B & interactive online map). Lena Powers' records also show 0 communications.

Fazit: The only possible conclusion is there was no previous collusion with Cudgo Loo.

7.1.1.2.: *BEGINNINGS*

I.   The death of President Kletterkater had, according to 94% of accredited scholars who have published on the subject, a 2-Impact on the election of Lena Powers. President Kletterkater is the southern Democrat who, on his deathbed, went mad as the story goes, requested an audience from the media & delivered the following rant, reprinted here in its entirety:

The shirt is too small. The shirt or the shorts is too small. I'm approaching to the point where the exercise isn't working. I have been the Monday morning sun & I have been the Saturday evening moon, looming red, the dead remember me & you remember me @ your wedding as well, & I am the earth & sometimes I am the small puddle filled with worms, & they are always inside you & so am I. Or so I was. Do not trust the president, Citizens of the United States of America, do not trust the President of the United States, Citizens of the United States of America, I repeat Do not trust the president of the United States of America, Citizens of the United States of America, regardless of who he is, trust me on this, there are no exceptions, because he is a figurehead, a robot, a cyborg, unknown to himself & unknown to others & unknown even to the puppeteers who propel him. I was the President, so I am telling you what none of the others have said, have been either too craven or too endeared to their loved ones to say -- the man behind the curtain is what the Internet likes to call him maybe, or the Deep State, but it's not like there's one man or one State somewhere, there are Gods & they are real & they can come down to us like anyone else, but you all will never see them... ha ha see they said they would kill me if I told you & kill everyone I loved but I am already going to die I am about to die & I don't love any of you, & so I am telling you... & they are real & they can come down to us like anyone else, but you will never see them because they don't want you to, because they are actual Gods even if we created them, I mean all of us, & they change, but they control the President. You are all of you fools. You think this is a democracy... This is the very 9th circle of fascist hell & the proof is none of you know it.

II.   At which point, or so the story goes, he fell back & died. The video does appear to corroborate this, but of course, there have also been questions as to the integrity of the video. President Kletterkater only admitted 1 reporter, & that was Brendan Parklife, the racist, sexist, *Libertarian* gadfly famous for such classy remarks as: "I refuse to have Aunt Jemimah running our nation."

III.   This is the man who is responsible for the footage we have of President Kletterkater's last moments, so percentage of probability of accuracy, according to my own algorithms (see Appendix B) is around 3 percent. The income here is how unreliable & incomplete records of even the most current of events could be, even in what they called @ the time, the "information age." This is something we would do well to remember in our own time, & which I will try to remember in this analysis.

IV.   This melodramatic story has of course become the center of national myth, & it has been retold so many times in so many distorted forms, & subjected to so many manipulations of videos that, especially given the immense passage of time that has since elapsed, it is impossible to disentangle the truth of any of it.

V.   President Kletterkater's death, in any case, is important for Tyrone Grant's campaign because of Grant's willingness to take Klettekater @ face value & promise to expose the secrets of the presidency to the public. It is, in fact, the parable of President Kletterkater that begins his announcement speech that cold January morning @ the new *Prose & Politics* in Cathedral Heights.

I will be the 1ˢᵗ president to put complete transparency between the White House & the American People.

VI.   A stylometric analysis of Tyrone Grant's speeches, & even more surprisingly, his poetry around this time show that his style develops more & more in the direction of Kletterkater's own peculiar style, especially during the campaign months. (Fig. 2). By the time he delivers his final speeches & poems, his speeches resemble Kletterkater's enough that 1 might think they were written by the same person when 1 looks @

the stylometric results[3], especially Kletterkater's deathbed-speech. Clearly Grant was taking notes from Kletterkater — he was studying him.

VII.   This is easily borne out by searching the search records from various IP addresses Tyrone Grant's account had been associated with. The # of times Grant searches for Kletterkater (& this is only from traceable IP addresses) increases exponentially in the months of his campaign. Compare that with those same searches on Clinton, Obama, Trump, Bernie Sanders, AOC & you see that Kletterkater stands out. This is inverse to the number of searches he had done before the campaign; up until that point Obama had been his highest searched president. Surprisingly, & tellingly, we find the same thing when we search Lena Powers' IP records. Her searches for Kletterkater increase exponentially during this period as well. There is clearly some sort of Kletterkater connection between the 2.

VIII.   Kletterkater's Master Thesis was "Simulcasting: A Study of the 2016 Presidential Election Cycle" (2033). It is so theoretical it turns into more of a treatise on performativity & American politics than a study of the election season, but it provides some clues as to what Grant & Powers were actually planning. The thrust of the book is that campaigns thrive on spectacle & novelty, & covers 2020 to 2032, a formative time in American politics.

IX.   Just 3 years later Kletterkater would be elected president.

X.   Kletterkater's rise to fame was through his YouTube

---

[3] This is an actual theory advanced by a colleague of mine, who suggested they might be written by the same speechwriter. However Grant always insisted he wrote his own speeches, and it would be strange indeed if Grant hired the speechwriter to start writing his poetry, too!

channel. His rants or poetic monologues or social commentary or logorrhea, whichever you prefer to call it, became a rare must-watch social media event. The famous viral "The Fake Celebrity Society Personality Nightmare," which 1st called attention to his series is a perfect example of the excesses & eccentricities of his rhetorical style. That he went from YouTube star to President of the United States in 3 years was, by 2036, not surprising.

REJOINDER

Then Kletterkater's MA Thesis proves Grant & Powers used Cudgo Loo as a plant;

what better way to drum up spectacle;

and Kletterkater calls it "spectackle" with a "k"

and Grant & Powers would have known that.

RETURN

But it's already been established that Cudgo Loo could not have been planted by Grant & Powers, because there was no contact between them.

Cudgo Loo's appearance works well within the context of Kletterkater's theory, when we turn to Kletterkater's concept of the "miraculous accident," which he demonstrates always occurs when a campaign applies "spectackle" to its strategy.

Fazit: This lets us safely say that Cudgo Loo's intervention was entirely unplanned by Grant & Powers.

7.1.2. THE CASE OF THE GRANT & POWERS CAMPAIGNS

I.   This leads us to the 2nd question, which is more difficult to answer: had Grant & Powers planned to run against each other from the start, & if so, how much of the drama that occurred during their election campaigns was real & how much manufactured?

II.   This time the 1st part of the question 1st: Had Grant & Powers planned to run against each other from the start?

III.   I believe they had:

IV.   NAMELY, the 1st public mention of either of them running occurs on October 1, 2041. This is on the Anderson.Paak show. Paak comes out & asks Tyrone if he's "doing the Black president thing?" Amid the canned laughter & applause, Grant says, somewhat cryptically, "ask Ralph Ellison," probably a reference to the cryptic maze-like structure of Ellison's masterpiece, *Invisible Man*. Paak doesn't press the issue, & so little was made of that brief, forgotten clip. It was only dug up later during the dirty trenches of the campaign season, with the Holigood campaign arguing that it showed how he "buddied up with rappers," but for the most part it was forgotten.

V.   The next mention of their running I located in an op-Ed for the *Mankato Free Press* in Mankato, Minnesota on November 2, 2041. It argues the case for Lena Powers for president & does so wonderfully. Had it appeared in the *New York Times* or the *Washington Post* it would have certainly garnered quite a bit of attention.

VI. In any case, Grant & Powers needed no help getting media attention. The holiday season comes, & the ADO New Year's Bash 2042 in New York City is a sensation. Held @ Brooklyn Bowl, musicians, politicians, poets, writers, journalists, internet intellectuals, they all came through that night & Grant & Powers live-streamed the whole thing. The video was streamed by 11-million consecutive viewers. The distribution of viewership worldwide will be of interest to future scholars (Interactive Map 2).

VII. After that event, a mapping of all major media outlets shows that there was an ever-increasing amount of chatter about their possibilities as candidates, even if it was fairly informal @ 1st (Interactive Map 3). By late January enough op-eds have appeared in fairly well-established newspapers that it can officially be thought of as an open question in the American political arena by early February.

VIII. Their *New Yorker* profile, "The New Black Power," in the May 20th, 2041 issue was the article that propelled them officially into the national conversation. This article tells the arc of their story from when they met as grad students @ Howard, through the forming of the ADO, through their early days organizing & hustling; it talks about the tensions that would seem to arise from their different temperaments – the politician & the poet – & how they had grown up, in a very real way, in the public eye, although always on a local scale, @ least up until that point; it talks about the successes & setbacks of the ADO & how the big break for them came with their alliance with AAGRAO on the day of the October 19th, 2032 Newark Riots, a serendipitous if inevitable meeting between two of Washington's most interesting neo-Civil Rights Organizations, or the Collective Leaders of the New School (CLONS), as they sometimes called themselves,

preferring to dispense with terms like civil rights leaders &
movements & organizations & alliances etc... Collectively,
the movement (a term they would have objected to here)
were the leaders of a new school of thought, & it being a
primarily Black & Brown movement, it encompassed civil
rights of course, as well as gender rights & other generally
left-wing liberal causes. A number of organizations can be
said to have belonged to this collective, but since the collective did not officially exist, no one organization can be said
to have officially belonged to it. Unofficially, chatter generally places the **ADO, AAGRAO, BLM** 2.0, Nightbreak,
NINJA, & Milestones as the organizations most often mentioned in connection with the **CLONS** (Fig 3).

IX.   By November 2032 the **ADO & AAGRAO** were working
together as partners on events, as evidenced by their
Thanksgiving Food Festival for the homeless in Malcolm X
Park. In early December the *Washington Post* does a profile
on them, "Next President and First Man?" by Ellen Treehouse. Treehouse writes:

*Conjecture has gone back and forth about which of these two will run,
or if they'll go for broke and both run. Let's hope to see them both jump
in this thing. They make a damn good dynamic duo, and damned if
they don't give you two ways to vote the same way.*

X.   Treehouse enthusiastically supports the double-barrel approach. So it was far from a fringe idea that they might run
together. Treehouse suggests that if only 1 of them were to
run, it would be Powers, but of course as things turn out, in
late January, Grant is the 1st to announce his candidacy.

XI.   The announcement of Grant's candidacy set off a great deal
of speculation. Especially in light of the Treehouse article.
In 38 interviews made with either Grant or Powers between

January 30th & March 31st (the 1st quarter of 2042), there were 0 mentions of the Grant-Powers team-up, whether it would happen, & if not, why not. Meanwhile there seemed to be tensions arising between the 2 parties – parties, instead of people, because their relationship as a couple seemed to start fracturing around this point; how much – to what degree is difficult to gauge, because prior to this rupture in their relationship, their relationship had been for them, & for us as media consumers, largely a private matter; now, their relationship was both public & highly politicized, not only for us as media consumers, but also for them, & their everyday lives. Powers expresses as much in an email she writes to Grant around this time:

It's hard to write this to you, but I don't know how to talk to you do we talk anymore, it's almost like we just perform; you would probably add a flourish and the end there, something corny like, all the world's a stage. But yeah, Tyrone, we just perform. We're these people now, Tyrone Grant and Lena Powers, and not just Tyrone and Lena anymore, and actually you know what, writing this is worse, because I think it will just be stored and located and read later anyway, so even in writing you, it's still a part of the performance. So we're pretty fucked here Tyrone. Or what do we do?

XII. We as historians find ourselves in a similar dilemma. Knowing that much of their performance was performance, how performative was it? Or to put the question more precisely, when are they trying to manipulate the narrative, & when does the narrative get out of their hands? Certainly, in the email above, Powers makes it sound as if the narrative has gotten out of their hands. But the email is so deliberately written, so *dramatically*, that we have to question whether the email itself was part of the manipulation of the electorate (and us historians), or whether it is a genuine expression of crisis, especially considering how self-aware it is of itself as a performative text.

XIII.   The above email comes to us from the h/king of Powers' laptop in April 2043. The date on the email is February 14th, Valentines Day[4]. Who h/ked it, how & even why remains an unsolved mystery. What we do know is that the information on the laptop was leaked & uploaded, & thus made completely public, including all the documents on the machine & all the emails in the Powers' mail app. It turns out there wasn't anything on that machine that was of any interest; business correspondence, emails with Tyrone & others, but nothing revelatory, nothing with any information not already in the news; in fact, the tension in the relationship was the only unknown element unleashed by the leak, & of course, this was just fodder for gossip & style magazines. Some have suggested that Powers & Grant orchestrated the laptop leak in order to publicize a fabricated relationship crisis just for the mainstream media attention (see Scanner, Joyce, Numbers), thus creating "spectackle."

XIV.   I agree with this hypothesis; the data seems to confirm it, although not unequivocally.

XV.   Ralph Bellicose, Powers' chief of staff during her campaign & a long-time friend, was also well known as a computer whiz, & had worked for years in Silicon Valley building a short-lived Black American nativist social media website,

---

[4] It should be mentioned, they would meet later that evening at *Gretchen's* in Georgetown for dinner, for what appeared to be a perfectly amiable evening, in which they managed to rack up a bill between them of $243.44, including two bottles of red wine, appetizers, entrees and desserts, with aperitifs to top it off – so they managed to talk about something. This little factoid should be kept in mind as I continue on to the following argument.

blackmodernism.com, a site he paid an exorbitant price for, & being unable to recoup on his investment, found himself out of work & in a lot of debt. It's @ this point, in May of 2043, shortly after his startup fails, that he suddenly emerges in the political field under Powers' wing as campaign manager, which she announces on May 1, 2043.

XVI. **The timeline of events** is as follows:

1. On **January 30, 2043**, Tyrone joins the race

2. On **February 14, 2043**, Bellicose's start-up goes belly-up

3. On **April 1, 2043**, Powers' laptop h/ked & leaked, a leak of interest only to the gossip pages, & of no real political import

4. Chatter about the 2 increases 72% between **April 2nd & April 30th**.

5. On **May 1, 2043**, Powers announces her candidacy, with Bellicose as her campaign manager.

XVII. With just a little look @ their data trails, it's easy enough to connect the dots:

XVIII. After years of almost no communication with Mr. Bellicose, President Powers contacts him shortly after his company fails on February 21st, @ 6:36 P.M. They talk for 4 minutes & 14 seconds; on February 24th they meet for dinner @ *Legal Sea Food* in Chinatown; the bill is $182.34. This could be considered an expensive dinner for 2 people who haven't seen or even talked to each other in years; the next day, Bellicose appears @ Powers' offices @ 9:11. He is there until 10:02. The contract of employment begins March 1st.

XIX.   Thus, we can be certain that Powers was already decided on joining the race by February 25th @ the latest, considering she was already hiring a campaign manager. If the email about the relationship was written on February 14th, Valentines Day, a day which they ended spending together anyway, having an apparently great time, certainly the idea of running was already in Powers' mind. It stands to reason that Grant was fully aware Powers intended to join the race & looked forward to it.

XX.   Moreover, there is the issue of the h/kd laptop itself; the laptop, 1 of Powers' company-issued side-machines, would never have been a top choice for a real h/k-job. Powers never had her main office computer h/kd; she certainly never had her personal computers h/kd; she never had her mobile devices h/kd; just one laptop with no information for anyone, but the gossip pages. If she didn't leak it, she should have, & she should have thanked the person who did.

XXI.   Even more glaringly, no 1 ever h/kd anything of Grant's – not even a side laptop. It would stand to reason that a h/kr targeting Powers would also target Grant – or @ the very least target more than just that 1 of Powers' laptops.

XXII.   Nor could they have picked a better time to become the subject of media gossip, from the political to the romantic. They became ubiquitous media faces: from May 2043 to the end of the election in November 2044, Lena Powers & Tyrone Grant are mentioned in or shown on 83% of news programs broadcast by major & semi-major news channels & websites (see Chart 1). This was enough to have both of them front & center during the 1st debates, the week of June 22nd to June 26th.

XXIII.   The evidence supports the claim that Powers & Grant planned their campaigns in advance. They always knew they would be running against each other. They had not, however, planned the re-emergence of Cudgo Loo & that may have been the unknown element that sent their relationship into a downward spiral. Loo's appearance @ Grant's announcement for candidacy had caused significant chatter.[5] That gave Loo a platform, & he used it to great effect in what has become known as the *Super Tuesday Usurpation* (STU). To understand the STU, it is necessary to take a brief look @ the primary debates that directly preceded the STU.

7.2. THE PRIMARY DEBATES (FEBRUARY 2043 – JANUARY 2044)

I.   On February 11th there were 35 democrats in the 2043 Primaries, & the 1st round of debates took place from Monday, July 27th to Friday, July 31st, with 7 contestants during each of the nights. The nights were divided into themes, topics that were @ the forefront of the most important issues each candidate was interested in, & labeled accordingly. The 5 issues were (1) economic stability, (2) environmental concerns, (3) America @ home & abroad, (4) the spiritual soul of the nation, & (5) Identifying Politics. Each night the debate was held in a different city – Memphis, San Francisco, Boston, Santa Fe & Baltimore, respectively.

II.   The debate week had been a debacle. The 1st night the candidates argued back & forth about their credentials for

---

[5] While many news media purposefully ignored the interruption, mentions of Cudgo Loo increased online 3892% in the next 4 weeks following January 30th.

running an efficient economy. Lukas Middlegrown, the front-runner from evening 1, a Wall Street banker, was trying to capitalize on that particular position, positioning himself as the smart money-maker. His chief opponent, Christina Angelbread argued that only a spiritual re-awakening could save the economic collapse the country was headed towards, & mostly defended her book, *The Neo-Communist Manifesto*, which could be said to be a fairly good summing-up of her economic philosophy. There was a much talked-about exchange where Middlegrown suggested Angelbread had been scheduled for the wrong night, would have fit much better on night 4, only she was probably too kooky for those nutcases. To which Angelbread responded the only thing mystical in this conversation were his economic theories.

III.　The 2nd night was a somber affair, with front-runner Gary Richwonder reciting figures & dates, more or less giving humanity a deadline & discussing his plans for further colonization of the moon, & increased funding in space station construction. His chief opponent, Amy Goodblock argued that doomsday environmentalists had been predicting the death of the planet for the last 50 years, & here we are today, which sparked a long round of debate concerning the health, or rather lack thereof, of the planet Earth.

IV.　The 3rd night front-runner Wendy Quijote discussed her foreign-affairs plan, a 3-step 4-Impact plan to remove American money & industry from the crumbling European economies, & impose sanctions against China & India. Burton Mandrake, Quijote's chief opponent argued that this quixotic approach would just lead to certain war with the United States facing China & India, yet another World War that no one wanted to see happen.

V.   Night 4 front-runner Urike Marga argued that the United
        States needed to look back over its history, & take stock of
        its sins, warning that the only way to avoid the impending
        threat of global war was to realize America's crimes as a na-
        tion, & deal with them, while recognizing America's often
        racist approach to foreign policy. Her chief opponent Brian
        Silversmith argued that the American spirit had been weak-
        ened by political wokery, the culture of *Gotcha Analysis* & the
        lamentable refusal for Americans to believe themselves to be
        Exceptional, a right that belonged to any group of people.

VI.   Powers & Grant headlined Friday night @ 20:00 on the
        Identifying Politics evening as head-to-head front-runners.
        Also on the stage that evening were Pickwick Purplebellow,
        Angela Diamondstar, Mabel Dillitant, Cornish Kerryman,
        & August Wessenleak. The 2-hour 5-Impact event was the
        most discussed of the debates, & the highlights from it are
        still often-referenced viewing material online.[6] Pundits, crit-
        ics & online voices were overwhelming in judging Powers
        the winner of that debate. Her performance that night was
        stellar, & she made the competitors, Grant included, look
        amateur in comparison. The most played clip is Powers' re-
        sponse to Purplebellow's remark that Powers didn't even re-
        ally represent Black people, as she had never lived with
        them.

VII.   Powers' response (the full clip can be seen @ strawberry-
        press.net/lena/powerresponse.html) included the follow-
        ing:

Listen, I've heard this kind of talk before; with all due respect senator, these are racist talking points that you unfortunately seem to have adopted & internalized. Black people are not all from the same neighborhoods as much as institutionalized white supremacy would like us to believe we are. That you yourself would use these kinds of tropes & weaponize them against me says more about you than it ever could about me.

But I can tell you something about myself: I grew up in Hoboken, not a bad place to grow up, & we weren't in an all-Black neighborhood, but it wasn't all white, either. We were just average Americans like most Black people are, & I am certainly not going to apologize to you or anyone else for refusing to be a racist stereotype.

VIII. Powers & Grant both ran on their Reconstruction Reboot platform.[7] Nothing less than a New American Reconstruction (NAR) was required to redress & address the failures of the 1st attempt. America could be seen as a somewhat unfinished land – stunted in growth by the crippling failure of American Reconstruction, & the loss of one its greatest leaders in exchange for one of its worst. The NAR platform argued that nothing less than a contemporary, modern reboot was needed in order for America ever to be whole & healthy.

IX. Opposition to the reboot method was plentiful. Pickwick Purplebellow, the Black nativist voice on stage that night found the NAR platform too abstract. "Black people, Black people who had suffered under slavery that is," deserved wages for their work, argued Purplebellow, & "to talk about some abstract Reconstruction Reboot, when Black folk

---

[7] Reconstruction Reboot was the doctrine that argued that the reparations discussion was not going far enough; more than reparations was needed. The best analysis of it is Elaine Strike's 2059 *The Black Robotics of Reconstruction Reboot.*

need money today, & money today for work done over hundreds of years & still not paid up – talk of some Reconstruction Reboot had to be some of the most asinine brain-
washed white-supremacy serving position a brother could
take, & the white man knew it" & why didn't these "so-
called revolutionaries" see it? "Give us the money you owe
us."

X.   Angela Diamondstar represented the Indigenous Peoples
Movement. She agreed with Powers & Grant – the United
States needed a remake – but her remake was far more radical. It was time for a day of reckoning for what the settlers
had done to the Indigenous Peoples of America. The country had to be remade from the ground up if the planet were
to survive, if the people were to survive, & justice among
people meant a healthier planet; the two had always been
connected.

XI.   Mabel Dillitant represented Black Lives Matter 2.0.[8] Dillitant argued that, while reparations were in order, systemic
racism had to be addressed, & dealt with, battle by battle:

*As far as I'm concerned, we have been on the front lines of this since day
1. The real genius of BLM was that it focused on a single issue; there
are hundreds of issues that Black people face on a daily basis. By close-
reading the issues we learn to address them in meaningful, & more importantly, lasting ways.*

---

[8] Known somewhat affectionately online as NAACP 2.0 #BLM2.0 was the for-
merly leftist, and now seen as somewhat conservative and integrationist, product
of the CLONS.

Diamondstar:

> *Which is fine, if you want all your time & talent wasted in nit-picking racism in a system that will never be free from it. It was built on racism. It must be restructured entirely. You do not nitpick the problems of a house with a faulty foundation; you must 1st fix the foundation itself.*

XII.   Cornish Kerryman, representing the Neo-Celtic Collective argued that the system was classist & racist, & a restructuring was necessary along class lines. Kerryman argued that the entire Capitalist system was corrupt, that it was inherently classist, & thus racist, & he argued that reparations ought to be a wealth distribution based on past work paid in honest wages, & continued productivity. Something of a fringe candidate @ the time, it's interesting to note how Kerryman's ideas caught on some years later, making her one of the most important Identifying Politics politicians of the time.

XIII. The final candidate, August Wessenleak, represented the Quueer community. The 1st serious Quueer-candidate for President of the United States in American history, Wessenleak, who was also Black & intriguingly charming, had been born male, but identified as female. Wessenleak argued that Identifying Politics was the key to forging a new Atlantis out of America – that America would have to realize that it had created in itself a new race & gender that transcended previous race & gender categories, & that was in some ways Atlantis rediscovered. Wessenleak argued that American Exceptionalism was the opposite of white supremacy, it was on the contrary, a dissolving of distinctions between ideas like race or gender, in fact – a complete breakdown of Foucauldian categories.

XIV.   It was a lively exchange, & a quick 2 hours (the full video can be seen @ strawberrypress.net/primarydebates, along with all the debate footage from the entire primary campaign season). 73% of news pundits opined that the winner was Lena Powers; 12% argued for Tyrone Grant; 7% found Wessen's esoteric approach to be a cool antidote to the seriousness of the others; 4% of the news pundits found Dillitant to be the most convincing, including many major old-guard Black leaders, for example, both James Newkirk & Barry Ompossum not only argued Dillitant won the debate, but both figures also publicly endorsed Dillitant. This, in contrast to Mickey Yallfavor, who published a now-famous scathing critique of Dillitant just after the debates, the infamous *Harlemite* article "The Fake Black Pancake Flake."

7.3. THE SUPER TUESDAY USURPATION

I.   A big win in the South Carolina Primaries on February 1st made Dillitant the front-runner. This was a huge upset, & no one had seen it coming, especially after what many considered a lackluster performance all around throughout the debate cycle. Some have argued that the conservative message hearkened back to the 2020s when things made sense, & that appealed to voters (Miggerhower, Angelhobo, Limbertree), whereas others believed it to be the beginning of a generational shift (Warblelover, Naghound, Ambuliver). The benefit of hindsight tends to favor the 1st reading.

II.   Grant had looked forward to South Carolina, probably hoping for a boost for what was an ailing campaign. Grant's presence in the race had become something of an embarrassment. No one was certain why he remained in the race once Powers joined. Between the 2 of them she was clearly the better choice, & so there was very little support for Grant after Powers jumped in, especially after her stellar performance in the 1st debate week. Grant's *like* rating hovered around 5% in the polls, & with the obvious increasing personal bitterness between Grant & Powers that comes out in the debates that followed the 1st week of debates, bitterness that makes the performances sometimes mawkish & difficult to watch, Grant himself became difficult to watch as a flailing candidate. In any case, his pitiful result in South Carolina ended his campaign entirely.

III.   He wasn't alone. South Carolina knocked a lot of the remaining candidates out. The race had been sliding in the direction of Identifying Politics ever since the 1st debate week, & after SC, only candidates from that sector remained. Grant, in fact, was the only candidate from that sector to drop out after SC. So in another sense he was very much alone.

IV.   On February 8th Wessenleak won Nevada in a very close race with Dillitant. After that it looked like the race would come down to just Dillitant & Wessenleak, & the lean of the news media reported it that way as well. In fact 88% of national polls had Dillitant & Wessenleak as front-runners, & @ least 232 op-eds were published in print & online new media arguing that it was now a 2-candidate race, & Dillitant & Wessenleak were the 2 candidates. Wessenleak's support base had mobilized the Quueer communities in & around Vegas, & through social networking & casual networking & word-of-mouth a vast number of voters had turned out for Wessenleak, thus making him a surprising & exciting front-runner as the 1st openly trans person to even run for the office.

V.   The next surprise came with the Iowa caucuses, which Powers won by a landslide. She won an unprecedented 81% of the state, & the reasons for that have been discussed @ great length (See Miggerhower, Limbertree, Horace, Naghound). Much of it certainly had to do with her campaign strategy, which referenced the nostalgically soulful phrase *Black Girl Magic.*

VI.   By Super Tuesday only Powers, Purplebellow, Wessenleak & Dillitant remained. Purplebellow had been hit hard by losing Iowa where he had expected to win big. He had been counting on the state to give the life to his campaign that it gave to Powers' instead.

VII.   In terms of footwork, Purplebellow outperformed all the other candidates, spending 98 hours in public appearances in the week leading up to it, including meet & greets & door-to-door personal greetings. His numbers in the polls were rising impressively, & in the days leading up to Super Tuesday, 71% of all news media said that it was anyone's guess & the polls were too close to call. This of course changed on Sunday evening with what came to be known as the Super Tuesday Usurpation.

VIII.   Cudgo Loo's eventual reappearance had been expected, predicted even. That he would turn up right before Super Tuesday had only been predicted publicly by 1 blogger, Victor Bigeye, whose article, "He Gone Come" has only 22 views @ of the time of this writing. No one could have predicted what Loo would do, though, not even Bigeye.

IX.   Here's what Loo did:

X.   Loo appeared on a video that went viral in which he proceeded to tell the story of how he met Powers & Grant, got to know them, hustled them into politics & how after that he felt abandoned by them. That was partly what was behind his outburst back in January. He admitted that Grant had written the poem he'd declaimed @ the Lincoln Memorial back in Washington in 2019, & even admitted the whole get-thrown-in-prison plan.

XI.   If Loo had been hoping to sabotage Powers' campaign, he failed. On the contrary, Cudgo Loo on viral video telling these wild stories of reckless political & artistic youth instantly mythologized Powers & Grant, & Powers outperformed on Super Tuesday again, thus knocking Purplebellow out of the race entirely. Dillitant also paled in comparison, & did not do well on Super Tuesday, a huge disappointment to his campaign, as he was hoping to get a boost to secure front-runner status. Instead he dropped out. Powers became the undisputed front-runner & sailed to the nomination fairly smoothly from there.

XII.   Cudgo Loo's motive has been the subject of a great deal of speculation. The most likely explanation is that it was a good promotional move for him to come on television & tell his side of the story. To speculate about Loo's political motivations is complicated by the fact that all available data points to the fact that Loo was not very dedicated to political causes, & that he was more interested in political movements for their performative potential (See *Loo: A Performative Life & Mythologized Death* [2166]). Loo never voted in any public election, so it is impossible to trace specific political beliefs through voting records; he was not registered on the voter rolls. While he kept generally liberal company, tracking his movements shows that he attended events thrown not just by #BLM, ADO, & Occupy, but also ADOS, the Libertarian Flare & MIST. So there does not seem to be any

steady political ideology motivating Lou. It was a purely selfish act, a usurpation in exactly the terms described by Lou
in his video:

*Americans are afraid of a usurpation of their minds, but they minds
need a usurpation, because a usurpation is a distracting intervention by
something that thereby becomes the new reigning occupant.*

7.4. CONCLUSION: QUESTION REVISITED & REVISED

I.   This chapter began with the question as to why Grant ran
1st. The question had 2 initial parts: was it planned in advance, to which we have concluded in the affirmative; the
2nd was whether Cudgo Loo was an intended consequence,
to which we answered in the negative. The question remains: why did Grant run 1st?

REJOINDER

Despite the liberal talking points, it's still a patriarchy;

*I heard he told her a man just has a better chance of winning it than a woman
does!*

A man always has to come 1st, to sponsor the woman 1st. The 1st
lady.

RETURN

Of course these kind of talking points were expected by the Grant
& Powers campaigns. Certainly Powers would have known the optics of Grant running instead of her, & her only announcing her

candidacy 2 months later. The only possible conclusion is that these talking points were the point; in short, the reason Grant & Powers arranged it the way they did was to inspire just this kind of chatter.

7.4.1. WHY?

I.   Because this was guaranteed to give Powers the edge & advantage, & Powers was always meant to be the one who won the presidency. By making Powers appear overshadowed by established patterns of male entitlement, Grant & Powers assured Powers a sympathetic profile, & that explains the floundering Grant campaign, & the powerful Powers campaign. The idea certainly came from Powers herself & is just another example of her political genius.

7.4.2. FAZIT

I.   In short, Cudgo Loo. The longer version of the story would most likely involve the stress of running parallel presidential opposing campaigns while being a public political couple, & dealing with the daily media barrage, & the sudden 24/7 news cycle having them as the focus along with the sudden destabilizing appearance of Cudgo Loo all added to an emotional environment full of anxiety & passion. Such an analysis is certainly beyond the scope of this study, but it would make for a wonderful speculative historical novel.

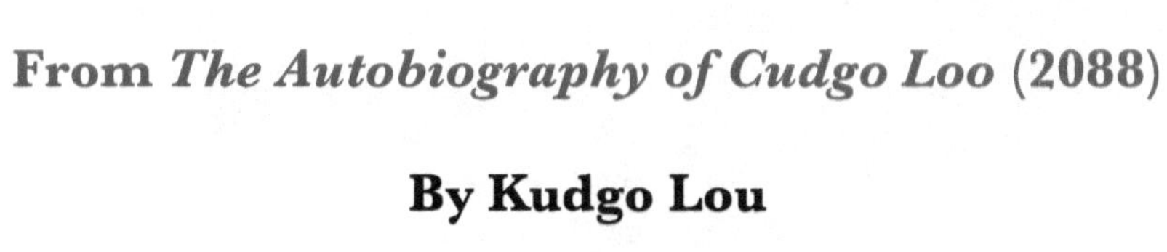

From *The Autobiography of Cudgo Loo* (2088)

By Kudgo Lou

Yo, it threw the whole Black world out they damn minds when
Ralph did that, (foot
Note white folks too)
Alternating patterns through the young spring sunlight, bobbing
alone
In the Oval Office
And who should find him there?

Swinging
Like a Black Fred Astaire?

I remember the day I heard, brother, sister, we all remember
The day we heard. Word on the street was
Ralph had been murdered and I aint one for conspiracy theories
either except but the
Playing with narratives they provide, but my brother my sister
This particular puzzle gave me pause.

Did Ralph hang himself what the fuck tho?

Lost during moments of contemplation
After Lena's weird ass
Murder nobody
Caught yet the whole world thrown
Out they damn minds
And here me
Crooked in the cranium.

I wondered as I wandered
Through the everyday daze of days that drizzled by
Tyrone not returning calls, no surprise
There the brother must
Be deep
In mourning. But
Damn my
Brother.

I remember the day I heard, brother, sister, we all remember
The day we heard. There were the words
From the radio, still on – the radio still on – to wake me up, Presi-
dent
Ralph Bellicose has been found
Dead
In the Oval Office
From what is an apparent
Hanging
Suicide.

In mourning. But
Damn my
Brother
What a way
To start –
To start the morning.

I got up and blundered through
My morning
Rituals which are non-rituals
For me
Which is maybe why I blundered them
Though, I had no foundation.

I still go natural I
Rolled a D, puffed my math
Way up through the corner of Columbia Heights where I stay

With the new bakers and buzz of coffee deep roasted
And bruncheon omelets for lunchin hipsters
Blipsters and the people who think
Black art is something other than just being your own
Young gifted and Black natural
Self.

The morning sun felt crayoned
In maroon and orange in a rush and the rush hour morning
Crowd of young professionals
Continues to prove Washington
Has no imagination
(And maybe never did but you
Aint heard it from me) And
Crowds of young urban professionals
Cruising casually cool like look who in
The motherfucking Heights but this aint
Nothing new. I'm just still here and
Complaining cuz I remember Columbia Heights
Back in the aughts.

Where I grew up

Back then I remember staying up late
On the corner
With my people,
Puffing D's
With my people
applying
Quantum physics to twists of the wrist

Shooting see low on
The wall against Oscar's.
Drinking 40s from Oscar's
Playing Black
Stereotypes like we play
Whitefolk
Faded as the morning waxes orange crayon
Like the spreading day today on my way

To an interview Sunday
Morning WPFW Show with Drebb Welder,
Who wanted to
Hear my story. Neither
Of us knew that the night before
They'd find that nigga Ralph straight up
Lynched in the White House.
What the fuck? Like I say

I woke up tho and it was on the radio.

&

I was higher than the obelisk by the time I
Got to that studio in Funky ass Farragut West that
Creeper weed what? Drebb Welder
Warbling on about whatever
Yes, Drebb I heard the news
What do I think? I just switched
The channel over to cartoons
So you know here
We are.

While we were still on air the Bad News compounded.
It was a goddamn C-O-N-

spiracy.
Before I got out that studio alive we
Had heard (in no uncertain order):

Speaker of the House, Garmin Cinderblock
Had assumed the office of the presidency
What?
That Black Anarchy guy was accusing that
White Supremacy group The Syndicate
Of lynching Ralph
What?
The Syndicate was refusing
To comment
That
The Internet was exploding
With talks of Race War
What?
And the new boogaloo and
(*Larry where yr Black Boogaloo?*)
So I left.

&

At this point it becomes very hard to distinguish
Versions of stories so many versions
Have been told and I
Was not
Really in any way central like
Y'all think:

First I went home and
Smoked a D.

The calls kept coming in all day,

My phone began to ping so damn much
I shut it off
I turned off my computer my people I
Went out into the wandering day.

I mean
Renounce society embrace culture
Entire.

I shut it off
I turned off my computer my people I
Went out into the wandering day
That bewildering May day,
And people looked at me as though I
Came from another planet no they
Had always done that now they looked at me like I
Owed them some kind of explanation for
Something but I didn't know what.

This was something new
Fangled.

I tumbled down Seventh Street,
Seventh South East
Tripped up am I tripping? Famous on Seventh
South East? Down by the Orange Line Station
Eastern Market
Buying new blunts
Dude comes up like "Yo what up?
You Cudgjo Loo or what?"
What?

&

I got tired of that motherfucker Cudgo Loo quick too.

Careful who you say his name

I rode the Metro
With no particular place to go
I rode the Metro. I rode the Metro
Because I could

Get off at the world
Had changed. America was

Woke groups of demonstrators had
Formed around the city, and I step off
Emerging at L'Enfant Plaza and what

Brought me to Federal Center where
Demonstrations forming as if from mist wafting

Into convergences of people who
Would swift into group like birds
Murmurate the clouds

Above us crushing lush white
Against azure and glass skyscrapers?

&

Jimmy got his head bashed in
First, no one knows where it
Came from he swiveled in a sweaty purple pastel
of red and flesh and fell heavy on the fucking
Steps man.

They came bearing gifts: racists
Who they up gathered up up
The Street demonstrating against our demonstration some
white power Bullshit
And they unleashed these gifts on us, they really
Just brought the racists over arrested, sure,
But not in cuffs and then walked them right over to us
And don't tell me that shit doesn't
Sound like a straight up
Set up.

Set up
My nigga.

Get up, my nigga,
Jimmy
Got his head bashed in
First, no one knows
Where it came from.

&

There were two speeches of note
That I heard before
The cops came:

Brother in a blue and gold African
Robe stands up, microphone on and everything says
"Brothers and sisters listen up!"
He lays it down
About the Lynching Act of 2020
And the Syndicate using that as a launching
Pad for their ideas of white supremacy
Race war

Starting with
The Symbolic Lynching of Ralph.

(2) Complicit in the deed
Was the thesis of the second speech
Of note not only was
The Government complicit in the deed, they
Allowed it to happen,
Plotted along with the Syndicate,
Were complicit in the Race War and were
On the side
Of the Racists.
Dems and Rebs.

&

Jimmy and I had been talking
About his old
Lady when the panther and the lash
And Jimmy went down
First, no one knows where it
Came from he swiveled in a sweaty purple pastel
of red and flesh and fell heavy on the fucking
Steps man.

Like I said, my demonstration was
Peaceful, it was
Suddenly cops and other racists everywhere, fists
Slinging, fists raising, fists bringing
Warfare and Wokery brother it was

Pandemonium and I weave my way
Through the crowd and come out
By the north side of the Hirschhorn where

I could spot the whole thing, where
I had just been myself a riot
Of color and sound, blood and black and white flesh
And the blue brunt of brutes on brown brutes the

Horses rearing up like Confederate Slave Patrols
On some real
Cowboy John Wayne shit
In This Day and Age.

I headed north on Seventh to bear witness brother
By the National Museum I saw the same.
I continued north on Seventh to bear witness sister
At Judiciary Square I saw the same. A goddamn
Shame. I walked north and kept on
Bearing Witness brethren:
If the Race War wasn't official it was
Happening.

&

Here's what I saw:

At first just like skirmishes
Here and thurr between the cops
Up in the sky
All these
Helicopters aglow in the eerie afternoon
Indecision of bluey sun and dark, the sun a wan yellow beacon be-
hind
Heaving buzzing gray-black clouds and
Wondrously sure azure skies. And then remembering
Those televisions in the studio the Bad News Baldwin
Schattenfreud frowning with that heavy Biggie

Smalls frown with a crown frown that only
Schattenfreud can reproduce and
Jimmy Baldwin and I –
I continued uptown to bear witness –
I bore witness back to the Heights –
I bore witness to Georgia where Howard held
The history –
I bore witness to the Heights –
I saw the

boy standing on Georgia and Harvard and I saw him
About face on the cop Nazi salute and hawk a
Shock, and then about face again and away he marched like a
stepping
Goose, up
Flips the bird
And the officer
Raises his pistol and it wasn't like it at all in that moment but
memory
Remediates it into a blockbuster – and he raises his pistol
And he fires and we all died and we all watched the

boy spin like a little Black Sambo
Top spitting brown and red
Blood like a Pollock hiphop
Tagging on a red-brick wall or a gray garage and
On our clothes. And
Then
The Heights

Organized my nigga!

You needed to be there because all
At once them brothers and sisters came together in groups

And the cops kept shooting.
It was the Crispus Attucks
Moment of the Black Revolution my brother it was
Waterloo for the white man it was
A testament to
Black Power.

&

The first massacre was on Georgia and Harvard

33 dead cops and seven dead Niggaz

We organized and marched right back downtown my brethren.

I joined a group of brothers who looked
Like they be the cultural wing of the movement
Black poets and rappers and writers and painters and lovers and
thinkers
And we got to talking
And politicked up the politics of the day and they
Told me how the cops just rode on up
To the Heights expecting of course there'd be
A riot in the Hood
But there wan't no
A riot in Hood
So a few officers just went plain-clothes
And started one
And you know what the krackkers say:

Once the lootin starts
The shootin starts.

They shot a boy who called them on they Nazi-ass shit we all

watched the

little

boy spin like a little Black Sambo
Top spitting brown and red
Blood like a Pollock hiphop
Tagging on a red-brick wall or a gray garage and
On our clothes. And
Then
The Heights

Organized my nigga!

Which is where we now were we
Marched right back downtown
We marched past Howard we marched
Down through Rhode Island Avenue
Down through
Gallery Place and we
Torched the whole city as we went.

We burned Washington to the ground
From North West to South West

And the cops

Just
Watched.

And we knew they would
Why:?

After Ambrose Littleton after President Nina Powers after
President Ralph Bellicose after
That boy like little bloody Black Sambo going
Viral as we marched President
Garmin Cinderblock couldn't bring
Himself to shoot a bunch of Black
People on national television in fact
In the Nation's Capital as his first and only act
As acting president he act-
ually Sent in the national guard to tell the cops to
Stand the fuck down yo
Stand the fuck down yo

Stamp the fuck down yo

All the way from
Uptown down.

&

I stopped off in New
Kalorama, and stopped by
Tyrone's crib he
Comes to the door
Looking like the bear
Got him
He been
Drinking, and analog
Cigarettes lay scattered in ash
Trays along the walls and on tables
A shambling old

Cliché of a washed-up poet
Politician even if Tyrone was still
The talk of the town.

How ya whatever small talk
I got in through the front
Door, vampire style invite and
All I say to the brother is
Brother break out the booze both ways cuz we
Got some strategizing to do and
Do you believe that cat just sat
There and shook his head and said

Huh?

&

Did you or did you not
Just see a bunch of niggaz burn down
The capital the
Capitol and all and
Children were running and
Women were running and
You were running
Out of time?

&

Tyrone swivels up like a switchblade turns
On the portable and starts
To surf in starts
And fits through
The history
We made
This morning.

Holy fucking shit he
Goes to the window and pulls the heavy

Curtains aside where ornery flames
Curtain the view set quick
With black heavy thickets of smoke.

I was part
Of it I admit it
And he looks at me quick and
Then he looks back at
The portable but I can tell
He's trying hard not to smile so I
Trip the brother up I do I
Say Ralph plotted the whole thing you know all
From the start he
Wanted to start
A race war.

And then Tyrone goes
Quiet and strange a moment and
Then he sees me and then I don't even have to

Wink.

&

I guess this story has been told
A few times by various
Media outlets and even maybe
A book or e-missive
But it is
My Story
And it hasn't been told
By me.

There are the
Interviews and the quick
Quotes and the buzz
Quotes and the teachable
Moments and that
But to quote the Monk:
Here it is straight no

Place yourself right there in that
Moment while we're laughing something
Serious and suddenly the sunlight
Red through the Devastation
Of Washington we
And the blue curtains purple
And the azure glow of the wounded
Sky and the thick black clouds and
The portable flicking images, imagine
What do you do but

We sat our butts in front of the portable
And put on the camera and Tyrone comes up like
"Yo what up? You Cudgjo Loo or what?"
went live
Right there with Tyrone chanting
Black Chant
And me sending out missives
Through my own (ahem)
Networks we were
Live!
For some
Fifteen minutes and by that time we
Already had Baghdad, dad,
That means like twenty
Million motherfuckas checking out
Our shit.

Which was

Like Vanessa told us old school headz you
Gotta save the best for last
So we
Started with bullshit and party
and Party
And bullshit, playing
Revolutionary music like
We Bee
The Anthem of the Revolution

So we started with the Revolution
Will Not Be Televised of
Course and then we played some Nina
Simone, damn Baltimore,
Then we
Put on Fight the Power, just cuz I mean
You have to
And then we put on
Kendrick Lamar We Gonna Be Alright and then
We put on HooDooMan
Spooky Action
At a Distance
The Chariot Swings
And you know you can't forget Carolina
Cotton and her classic
Kunta Oochie Walla and
The Ghost Collective's
Assault!

Look, eventually you all will have to read about this anyway, when you're assigned the 400,000-word *Arabesque Commission*, which somewhat painstakingly details the history of presidential chicanery from Kletterkater to the ousting of Arabesque, so let's drop the formal tone, put the lecture aside, and really talk about Cinderblock as a person a bit. First, I want to adopt a kind of twenty-first century slangy tone to set the setting; I'll try and talk to you the way they talked when they talked casual-like back then. Then I'm going to give you some context and then you're going to have to do some research on your own for a few minutes in groups. I'll end with a question, and then I want you all to take a position on this question and defend your position. Okay? Here goes:

Cinderblock grows up on the Island, North Shore, Maryland Avenue. Growing up he was always in the city and other boroughs. His friends in Brooklyn have different ideas than his friends in Staten Island. His dad's a failed salesman, Willy Loman-like, and his mother a frustrated schoolteacher. So they're post-Trump Republicans, of course.

Meanwhile, his friends in the city and the other boroughs are not. This conflict between the right and the left, and since we're talking about early twenty-first century America, the white and the Black, becomes the central conflict of Cinderblock's political thinking. He would hang out in Brooklyn freestyling with his Black friends one weekend, and the next weekend, he's out drinking on the North Shore with his Italian friends, where they would be rapping more at girls than each other.

Yeah, that was corny. But so was he. I'm not saying that's my thesis, but in a nutshell that's Cinderblock's tragic flaw. Everyone thinks he's corny, because he never fit in with either clique, too Italian-American in Brooklyn, and too Brooklyn in Staten Island. So he grows up real conflicted about race.

He bounces around in his early years. Doesn't go straight to college after high school, just hangs around the neighborhood, working, getting into trouble, but nothing serious, probably out of a kind of cowardice that developed alongside his corniness, a corny coward, you might call him. That's how he imagines himself, in any case, from his online record at that time.

After an aimless year like this, he enrolls in CUNY, and gets a BA in Political Science. He's a surprisingly good student. He manages to get a scholarship to an MA program at NYU, where he also does remarkably well, writing a fascinating thesis on the 2020 election — I know, everyone's written about that election — but he remediates it as a series of essays commenting on documents from the election cycle, giving a much more polyhistoriographic view of the election cycle, and effectively arguing -- with Spenglarian logic, mind you -- that the Western world was caught in what he referred to as "the Wheel within a Wheel." It's worth reading. But it's his discussion on race in the dissertation, which became a bestselling book — especially surprising for an academic dissertation turned academic press monograph — it's his discussion on race that starts making his name ring bells. His assertion that African Americans basically carried the election for the Democrats wasn't so controversial; his argument that African Americans had constantly saved the country from itself beginning just after Reconstruction was a bit more controversial; his conclusion that the future of the United States was African American — that the fate and future of America was to be a Black run country was quite a bit more controversial, especially since he considered a future Black America a thing to be celebrated.

The argument was sound, and if the book was controversial, it wasn't anywhere nearly as radical as Cinderblock himself would become, and probably because of his book. Through countless interviews, online discussions, academic analyses, Cinderblock became something of a transformed figure: the book, argued Cinderblock's most vociferous critics, was basically reverse racism, and suggested that Blacks were superior to whites; Cinderblock argued back that the idea of his book was meta-historical, not moral, and that Black Americans were simply destined to make America into the great land white America had envisioned, but because of their colonialist European mindset and aesthetic, were unable to bring to fruition -- it had nothing to do with one race being superior or inferior to the other; no, it was simply a metahistorical fact that the exploitation of Black America by white America, and Black America's eventual triumph and claiming of the country which had previously enslaved them was an integral part of the bend of history toward ultimate global utopia.

As you see, the corniness kind of won out in the end. He became so intent in this counterresponse he came to believe it zealously. Truly zealously religiously. But remember the Staten Island is still there too. So he marries a half-Black/ half-white book editor, and the two of them become a cultural studies power couple. But remember the Staten Island is still there too. So, he's this new John Brown figure on the one hand, but he's also petty racist on the other, and he can't kill that part of himself, it's part of him, and it keeps popping up.

Like in a press conference when he said that (and I quote) "the Black man is only still victimized by America because he is afraid to fully embrace white America, when if he realized that he is basically a lamp-blacked white man, he would get on much better." Cinderblock later apologized (under lots of pressure, let's be clear here) for the statement, and claimed it had been taken out of context, that it was meant to be ironic, a reference to an obscure Black reporter from the early and mid-twentieth century named George Schuyler; there was also his tendency to hang out with people who were clearly associated or at least sympathetic to, white supremacist organizations, especially people from his old neighborhood in Staten Island. Cinderblock claimed this was just done out of loyalty to old friends who had been in the field together with him; and finally, the final nail in the cinderblock, to coin a phrase, was when Cinderblock called President Powers a "hysterical Black banshee."

So he was something like a white racist-against-Black-people Black Power warrior. A strange thing to be, but fairly normal for the times, which is somewhat indicative of how things were and how people thought back then. Not that we're above reproach ourselves, but I'd like to think some progress has been made all the same.

Anyway, Cinderblock's response is to marry a Black woman. A book editor, Candace Turnheart, or Candace Cinderblock or rather Candace Turnheart, the *ex*-first Lady, the only First Lady ever to divorce the President while still in office. That's how bad things got. We have both their accounts of it, but hers is more interesting, of course.

She embellishes some of the details, but basically she begins with the good years, when they're this Washington power couple, and they have the world as their oyster. Sky's the limit. All the cliches you can think of. But she has to live with this man, too – this racist, perverted soul who is constantly at war with himself about identity politics, and meanwhile, can't even develop an identity for himself. And when I say perverted, I mean it in the way you were thinking too, because the racism manifested itself in strange sexual racialized demeaning perversions which she goes into in some detail in her book. But she tolerates it, for one thing, because she generally does love him, he's fucked up, but hey, who the hell isn't? And also because she says she's obviously already internalized some of the oppressor's own negative stereotypes about her herself, and demeaned her self-image in her own estimation, and so she let these things pass as quirks, sexual, temperamental quirks that we all have in our own peculiar ways.

No one ever thought or expected that Cinderblock would be

president one day, least of all Cinderblock himself. He started out with a job at the World Bank, which was nice bank indeed, but money or not, after a while he got restless there, and then started working in Washington think tanks, developing along the way a political philosophy that was inspired by his upbringing, his Spenglarian metaphysics on the Black Race in America, and the Libertarian politics his friends he began to make in Washington think tanks discussed with him. As much to his surprise as everybody else's, he made an uncanny good study. He picked up on the nuances of political philosophy fairly quick, began reading voraciously, finding syllabi online, politics, economics, philosophy, sociology; he's young, single and has the time and energy, and has spent his life asleep. It's the 2030s! The information age seems like it's just hitting its stride! There's so much to learn!

He develops a rhetorical style that's part Staten Island, part Brooklyn and part all the books he's reading from Marx to W.E.B. Du Bois to C.H. Douglass to Ayn Rand to C.L.R. James to Alan Greenspan to Roxanne Gay to Ta-Nehisi Coates to Peter Greenbranch. So he's actually a really good speaker, and even a good debater, and soon he's going out to bars in downtown Washington after work with his friends from the think tank, and they're making liberals look like assholes thanks to him and his wit and wordplay, and they say he ought to seek a job in Washington.

So he does. He runs for the House, he thinks, what the hell: he probably won't win the election, but he might at as well give it a damn go. The 11th district seat in New York has never been all that stable in the first place, so maybe he has a shot. And it's true, he picks up a populist tide fairly early on, after all he can claim Brooklyn *and* Staten Island, and that about covers it since his district is Staten Island and South Brooklyn, so he never loses that momentum, New Yorkers love this guy, he's a New Yorker, he's got a Black wife, he's down like most white boys are afraid to be, he's cool, yeah, he's a little crazy, but Black folk are saying, "sure he is, but so are we."

His challenger doesn't stand a chance, to be honest, he's

considered part of neo-establishment politics; Cinderblock uses his own youth, energy and vision to his advantage. The neo-establishment politicians have turned the Democratic Party into a party of identity-politics ideologues, he argues; the new generation of Democrats has moved beyond such reactionary politics and embraces scientific progressivism (which, to be honest, has its origins in the neo-establishment politics it abhors).

On-the-ground organizing and energy win Cinderblock a narrow victory, and he unseats the incumbent Democrat, something no one expected he'd be able to do. These upset House victories are like a blessing and a curse, though. Because they give you name recognition, and turn you into something like a freshman House celebrity, and that's a bad time to have that kind of constant hard scrutiny. Cinderblock manages it well, because he's already developed a persona for himself, and so he just has to play and ply this character Cinderblock he's created, and so he become even more of a radical for Black politics, but then there are the constant reports of unfortunate quotes and questionable behavior, and in the nitty gritty details of his policies, which bills he votes for and which bills he votes against -- these reveal a politician less interested in civil rights and civil liberty and justice than his rhetoric would suggest.

But Cinderblock manages it all well enough, and his approval ratings are good, and it's telling that he's even well-known enough to have the approval ratings he does. Everyone expects that he'll wait a few years and then make a senate bid once he's become familiar with Washington, and especially so because his name recognition continues to accrue. He's writing articles for the *Washington Post* and the *New York Times* and *New World Business*, and he's making appearances on Sunday morning news programs, and so his name is making waves. But the time for a senate seat bid never seems to arrive, it's just not his time, Senators Blake Clark and Angela Adams are both new to the senate, and they're both popular in New York, there's never a good time to run, and in the meantime, time is running out. By 2042 he's been in the House for ten years, and it doesn't look like he's moving over to the senate any time soon.

Nonetheless, he's given the opportunity to give the rebuttal speech to President Kletterkater's State of the Union Address, and it makes him into an instant household name, and not just a hot ticket in Washington. He has that famous line, "their own websites have warped these candidates into caricatures." Cinderblock is a character all on his own, of course, but not like Kletterkater, and Cinderblock comes out swinging, with his full message of racial injustice in play – he calls Kletterkater a racist, a neo-Trumpian, a demagogue and a disaster. It's an electrifying speech, and I'll dev it to the Tabernacle this evening, and I highly encourage you all to read it. It becomes something of a classic, although people have forgotten about it in recent years, I suppose, with all that's been going on this seems really like quaint ancient history, but I'd say Cinderblock's speech is still relevant today, and plus, it's just a masterwork of rhetoric.

In 2044 the House nominates Cinderblock for Speaker, and then it's settled: he's not going to the senate, he's staying in the House. When he becomes Speaker to a Democratic majority in 2045, he sets a record as the youngest Speaker of the House in American history at the age of 37, the next after him being James Blaine at age 39 in 1869. We all know what happens next. President Lena Powers, America's greatest hope, is murdered. Cringe-inducing (by today's standards) headlines about the Black Female Kennedy appearing across the country. Her death precipitated a new era in American politics that had already been brewing since the 2020s: precipitous, revolutionary events in America were on a steady and unsustainable increase; at the very least they premised severe problems with the Union that the future, of course, would later bring to bear.

The Black Revolution of 2046, from May 26th to June 19th is the first thing everyone thinks about when they hear the name Cinderblock, and that's understandable. Those few weeks probably changed the country more than any event since the Civil War. And Cinderblock was a lightning-rod of a president to have in the White

House for that, and as an unelected president at that. It begins with the suicide of President Bellicose, of course, which is widely interpreted by certain sectors of the society as highly suspect. Demonstrations and riots start happening all over the country, basically in every major city. But this was just new normal early-to-mid two-thousands metadrama, and normally did not lead to full out revolution. It was the events in Washington, DC, most historians agree, that set the revolution in motion.

Like I said, demonstrations were taking place all across the country. And then here comes this group of demonstrators, and they see a kid, Marshall Namor, 12-years-old, and he's taunting a policeman, and the policeman just shoots him dead, just like that, a kid, an unarmed Black child, because the kid was making fun of him. And there were all these demonstrators who had just marched up to the scene from various directions, and they just all went in full riot mode, but organized. They shackled up the policeman who shot the kid, and his partner, and then they marched as a Rebellion (or what the media called at the time an organized riot) and looked like the militarized disciplined Black American army come to claim its proper vengeance.

Keep in mind, Cinderblock is now officially president; but he's only been president for about six or seven hours maybe, if that, and he's being briefed on all of this. He's only president because President Powers was murdered, and Vice President Bellicose committed suicide, and he just happens to have stumbled into Speaker of the House, and so now he's President of the United States, and he has the first fully organized Black rebellion happening within the first few hours of taking office.

He doesn't do anything. There probably isn't another president in the history of the country who wouldn't have done anything, even the four Black presidents the country had had up until then would have reacted more pressingly than Cinderblock did, Obama would have blasted the hell out of those demonstrators, President Harris too; Powers would have annihilated them, and President

Bellicose would have probably walked out there with a bullhorn and a soapbox and delivered a speech in hopes of stopping them, but Cinderblock didn't do shit.

The rest of the country saw them as a threat; but he didn't. He was more afraid of himself than he was of them. He knew he could be racist, he knew he *was* racist, and he was terrified of *being* racist, and terrified of thinking he had inherited Staten Island's racism, and so he didn't do anything. He didn't want to send anyone out there to confront those demonstrators, he expected it to be a peaceful demonstration, and when it became obvious that the police were not going to let it stay peaceful, he seized up and sent the National guard in not to stop the marchers, but to restrain the police, who looked like they were looking for a race war.

This, as you can imagine from your studies in this era, well this caused a hell of a lot of stir in the media, in Washington and on social media. Almost every Republican was calling for Cinderblock to be brought up on treason charges, and now remember his reputation and his dissertation turned bestselling controversial argument for the inevitability of a Black America. Those who aren't talking treason are talking about the 25th Amendment you know: kick him out if he's too crazy to be president, but really everyone is talking treason talk, like Cinderblock is the 21st century's own Nat Turner turned Black president, to reference a famous short story by Orbital Johnson, and this gets picked up on by two controversial counterculture figures, Tyrone Grant and Cudgo Loo. These two were famous, or rather infamous, for being the original top two suspects in the murder of President Powers, later acquitted, and even pardoned in advance by President Powers before she died. Also known in fringe cultural circles as poets, Grant was a little less fringe because of his close relationship to President Powers and the activist organization they ran together, ADO.

Well, they pick up on the zeitgeist of the moment, and they start broadcasting online right away, on that first day of the revolution. They pick up on this rhetoric about Cinderblock being a traitor, and they start asking why? Why is he a traitor to America? Because he failed to murder Black people, as would have been expected of him? Because he understood the revolution was a pathway to a better way for America? Because he knew the protestors would not turn violent even when the police would? And so this is the question I want you to answer: Why was he a traitor to America?

Or to put it less rhetorically: Given all we know about what has happened since Cinderblock's presidency, what is his political and cultural legacy in this country, and is this legacy overall positive or negative?

Nat Turner turned Black president (2062)

by Orbital Johnson

Outside seeking pockets of cool down Broadway, 92nd to 63rd, the wind weird warm strong November revolution rain like the season was raining the blood of the last, Orbital Johnson made a call that changed the world for ever even if nothing ever changed for Orb himself. That call was to mess around and make that President Ralph Bellicose doll from shit in the dump. Unravel the whole doll starting with the string around its neck and that's what the fuck you call a chain reaction I said getting away with murder. Orbital dollmaker Orbital Dolls the store bearing his name and the day now almost done, Orb headed home, doll in hand, home meaning

Orb took the doll around the corner and killed him on Columbus Circle ducking into the Park.

It was on a whim, Orbital never knew why he went and done the deed, it was like a wind that passes by your orbit. Total whimsy it might have been a cloud what looked like the brother, the name of the dollmaker and the flash of the flashy brother's red green and black suit in the flash of the colors on the cover of a book in a bookstore window with them selfsame colors and he thought god damn if the brother ain't for real really president, well I reckon I best goopher his ass and quick!

So he made the doll and killed him in Columbus Circle.

And ten minutes later he learns Lester leapt. And there it is right in big scrolling worried red letters by the time he makes it back down to Times Square, squeezing through bodies to catch the words, worries himself into a day bar, television running, starts day drinking proper. Orb considers his options over an odd afternoon.

He walks out that bar warm in the cold ass day and makes his bad self way downtown West Village, dump behind the hopster art shop yup just enough goodies here to assemble me a Cinderblock.

He sews him up in a little coffee house out the way place, dirty and for real uncool nobody cares comes in he sews him up a Cinderblock good over a coffee black and a cookie cuz he needed chocolate chips for eyes. Considers what to do with old chocolate-eye Cindy. Considers killing him but can't cuz he likes the damn doll too much to just go and fuck it right up. Maybe later. For now we'll just have ole chock-eye start a race war. He's going to need a little space to set this shit up.

Snow drifts a lazy way down coming out the coffee joint an afterthought here or there nothing serious. Orb and Cindy go hand in hand downtown across the Williamsburg Bridge to the river shore and scouts out a small smack of territory like setting up pieces for a boardgame word Race War by Milton Bradley. He collects stones along the shore, black and white, alright worries the lines setting them up, like placing bets almost superstitious. The shore is cold hard mud anticipating December. Good for the stones, they wedge into the earth and hold fast. Lays Cindy ahead the white army, then changes his mind, lays him ahead the Black army, changes his mind again changes his mind again who the fuck you fighting for Cindy? Finally decides to just have him keep switching back and forth at random.

First Chocolate-eye Cindy lays ahead the white army and he holds them back as the Black army advances. Then Block lays ahead the Black army and he gives a speech, a born famous speech where he declaims ex cathedra on "the coming Black America," "the Great Black Hope," and "the evisceration of America's sins in white evaporation."

White army advances; they don't wait for Cinderblock to come back. They don't want him back, but he's still the president. This is a conundrum. Where do things escalate from here, and how? Orb suddenly feels the bottom drop out beneath him and damn. Tireder as a muthafucka. Sits down in the sandy mud. Sand and snow and the snow is snowing a little snow still not much though. Day dimming eyes swimming where to sleep? It's extra cold by the shore, for sure not here but where? He heads off shore to ward town.

In the nothing around, just a bunch of hipsters. Slips down the stairs of the L-Train, takes out a book, slouches into a read on a bench and sleeps and reads and sleeps and reads and sleeps and reads and the cops don't bother him if he plays it like that, and if they do, he just gets on the next train and goes. Tonight he's reading an older novel by Older Black Statesman Colson Whitehead, *Underground Railroad*. Depressing. Especially down here. But a nigga knew what he was getting hisself into and so.

He wakes up suddenly, the sound of the steps, the shoes the steps the cops he wakes up when the cops show he up always wakes up when still asleep still he hears the cops and he wakes up and now here he was and Cora is still on the run and the sentence picks up where the last left off.

Sir, is there a reason why you haven't taken any of the trains in the last two hours?

The Underground Railroad

I beg your pardon?

This book, *The Underground Railroad*. I'm thinking about this. Does space make a difference in how I read the book? So I'm reading this book here. – in this space. To see if it makes a difference.

Makes a difference? What kind of difference?

I guess that's the question.

Do you have ID?

No sir.

I could bring you in for that.

Is this Nazi Germany already?

Just move it along with the next train. Next time I'm taking you in.

Niggaz been shot for less. Counts himself lucky: Goes back up the stairs into the cold old frown. The snow low down too just drifting along too all along town. A few stores still open but none to go in he can't go in none of these beats on Bedford. Turns off at the next block east. Winds his way through Williamsburg word it takes a while but somewhere well down Broadway east beneath the tracks and hip hop shopping avenues down a block a little bit of a walk and the snow still blowing poetry cool jazz dizzy into a chintzy café but low key and grungy and so he'd probly be cool. Could still afford a whisky neat and warm even if obviously he could damn well not. Been down so long it look like

Play out Cindyblock with coins and a whisky. And a little shadowboxing. A sip and the warm whisky works wonders blundering snow outside softly settling Brooklyn. For a while the patrons are burned against the wall in the cold copper light of the bar in black shadows here CINDERBLOCK enters stage left impeachment trial. The old sour looking hit-his-Brooklyn-stride-in-the-summer-of-2025 aging hipster of yesterlore, Cinderblock, impossible at his impeachment. The other shadows lurch into the shadow cast from the character in the corner, they want to impeach him so bad they could preach. But can't do it on account of Amelia Arabesque, President pro tempore, who would become president with Cinderblock's removal. Anyone but her. Appointed during the Powers administration, she was militant, like militant, though. So, counting shadows, plying through coins to count see if there's another whisky coming after this one's gone, it ain't enough votes to impeach and Cindy comes through with the votes he needs to keep him afloat just a little longer at least. Yep! Orb finishes up the first and orders up another.

Talk of the 25th fizzles same reason. Cindy's sitting pretty. Starts making plans for 2048. His shadow elongates against the wall like a finger of fire and others rise as well, he ain't the only nigga scheming on forty-eight. Block ought to be easy to topple, he gets a serious challenger in the Democratic party even, Maplethorpe Melvin, a throwback from the left wing wing of the Democrats back in the Biden days, talking all kinds of crazy shit about previrtual economies. It don't do him no good; Cindy is a special American kind of crazy all razed up on race and culture and plays Robert E Lee to his own Grant in what might just as well be known as The Cold Civil War.

Orb is dranking them slow and the ideas come in a kind of slow flow that fits the feel of the expanding night in a lull of snow, low now blanketing the sidewalk like blow no good way to keep you awake though. Cinders can't slow down now, the police riot on the rioters blue and red sirens wail and flail against the copper walls of the bar quick and gone Cindy keeping the peace with the National Guard and then there's Cindy watching a revolution go flaccid for lack of resistance.

Sure, other states try. There are organized marches. Groups of hipsters trooping the shadows of bars singing *You Are My Sunshine My Only Sunshine* and other such nonesuch. But it aint no kind of a revolution and that's all on account of the deft diffusion technique of old Cindy here, Orb he still has the doll, not bad old boy and them teachers always said you aint amount to shit just like a nigga. Well, shit. Check a nigga out now!

And now Orb is out of money and back out into the snow cold and toes bending in the ice. Decides to head around the corner, fishes around in his pocket finding lint just lint *creegee* he thinks we used to call it *creegee*, gee, sleepy in the warm weather windy snow, which way to go?

Cinderblock doll in hand still swinging: The speech in front of the capital, with a million Black men and women and children standing strong like y'all better believe it, and with them them Spanish niggas came out too and even a few Native Americans, and of course you know white folks came out for them niggas in forces too, and here comes Fairchild Bothersome, and now here comes his left hook he gives a speech like look:

yeh, Black Independence Day 2.0.

Orb fumbles in the snow and scuttles on the ice and slides a lie down smile into a wall where the cold stone leans steamed ice into his cheekbone. He winces and dances himself aright with Cinderblock dancing too moon on snow on Orb and spotlight on Cindy sees them niggas a-marching a mile away and starts in to dancing talking this and that kind of jive talk turkey bullshit. Quoting himself from his dissertation and everything, a quirk of his he quotes his own shit so much it's like Jesus quoting the *New Testament. Black revolution!* Some white people, man…

Cinderblock whisked away with the wind and then Orb really can't find him, can't find the Cinderblock doll, he had him just a moment ago, and now everywhere the snow and the cold makes you move like your muscles are atrophying, the smothering cold white night. Cinderblock is gone and so there's nothing to do but storm the podium and stormy Fairchild Bothersome lives up to his name and bothers the hell out of a whole lot of niggas, Black, white and otherwise with his famous Presidential-address-reply-speech, "Eternally-recurring Storm," which was just like Mama said knock you out

---

Presidential Address: May 27th, 2046

President Garmin Cinderblock:

Listen, Americans. And people all over the world, because I am self-consciously addressing a global community. The mind is a mild fire, it burns half so bright and hot as needed to kindle the tree of Knowledge. Later historians and theorists cast their spin, in an attempt to make their own present disasters seem less disastrous through their sure cool clarity about past disasters.

Today America faces disaster. Not from the peaceful demonstrators, who are still being harassed by a vile racist police force, but from these very white supremacist officers who are harassing these patriots, and all those others who would keep our country mired in the muck of misanthropy. I do not condemn all members of law enforcement, but I do condemn those today who have rained down terror on peaceful protestors!

America, you elected me, you know who I am, I never had to lie or hide it. Go read my dissertation. I still believe every word of its thesis: the Black Nation shall guide America into the Promised Land!

And America, I will make every effort to see that they do.

The bitter and beautiful irony of American Exceptionalism is that its truth spites its foundations. Its foundations, racist and culturally myopic, argued that American Exceptionalism lay in its god-granted mission to be that shining city on a hill, a beacon of freedom, when everyone knew the land was a continent of slaves enslaving people; like a seedling from a seed, opposition breeds new birth, the Black nation, oppressed and exploited, has continually shown America its dignity, what it would look like if America were to practice it.

America, today we do not turn our ire and violence toward peaceful protestors. They have their ancestors in the legacy of Martin Luther King, Jr.; they are the children of the revolutions we continued in the names of our ancestors. Even when our ancestors fought for forces of evil, we in turn fight against that evil in the knowledge that they lived in a knowledge void.

To that end, I have arranged to meet with Arnold Novus of AA-GRAO. I look forward to his input and advice on how we can bring this nation to a place of healing; and more importantly, how we can put the lessons Black America has taught us about democracy into practice.

Video Session Billie Raven and Amelia Arabesque: 01 13 March 2046

BR: Hi Good morning! It's good to finally see you. I look forward to getting to know you.

AA: Thanks. Good morning. I mean. Sorry. Never done this before. To be honest, it's already weird.

BR: It used to be weirder – when my father – But anyway, my name is Billie. Billie Raven. I know you know that already, of course, but we should formally introduce ourselves, I think.

AA: Okay. Nice to meet you Billie. I agree. I mean. Yeah. My name is Amelia. Amelia Arabesque.

BR: Nice to meet you Amelia. I should tell you in advance that I am recording this session. If you do not want me to record the session, I won't.

AA: Oh. Okay. I don't know about. Yeah. Recording the session? Isn't this supposed to be completely confidential?

BR: Of course it is. Recording the session simply helps me take better notes, improve my notes and learn from large data patterns. On an even more practical level, I believe the best approach to reconciliation is discussing the recorded discussions with you once we've gone through a few sessions. Generally, I like to have a few reflection sessions after several regular sessions. In my opinion, it helps a lot if you are able to visually witness yourself develop past psychological and spiritual hangups. Especially. Not that I'm saying.

AA: No, it's alright. No, you're right. Of course I want to see them later. And to discuss them with you would be really helpful.

BR: Great. So, we're recording. Now, tell me about yourself, Amelia.

AA: Well, I don't know. Where do I start?

BR: Tell me why you're here.

AA: I'm here… well you know why I'm here. Everyone knows why I'm here. Everyone looks at me like… like why am I *not* seeing a shrink… ? Sorry, I know we're not supposed to say that… shrink… anyway. But Lena. Of course. I'm here I'm processing Lena's death.

BR: Tell me about Lena.

AA: Lena? Lena was. I don't know. Well everyone knows her as the president, so there's that aspect of Lena, President Powers, you know? That quick-witted, in control, super cool, Black Girl Magic President. And then. There's. That's there was. There was. I didn't see her much toward the end of her I mean, really, I mean after she became president, and even before that, the whole campaign, suddenly, one day we're sitting drinking bottomless mimosas on a Sunday brunch and she's telling me she's gonna run for president, and I thought it was just the champagne. And then, just like that, she was gone, I mean, she was just. Gone. Before she was for real gone.

BR: Busy with the campaign? She probably didn't know what she was getting into herself.

AA: No one does. I mean, that's what she always said. But. She was always driven like that you know. When she was an activist. Knocked Tyrone around a lot because he was sort of a slacker. I mean he still is. I can't believe how they went after him like that. Him and the other guy. You know who I mean. The eccentric guy.

BR: Cudgo Loo.

AA: (Laughter). Yeah, Cudgo Loo! He's a character. But I like him. I never thought it was them. Really never.

BR: Who did you think it was?

AA: Who knows? Any number of crazies out there.

BR: Did that bother you? Not being able to know? Not having that kind of closure?

AA: No. That didn't bother me not that kind of no closure. There was closure in that Lena was dead and death is always closure, and no answers open that enclosure once it's happened, so that I thought more about the lack of space I went tumbling back to the past. I thought about *our* past all the time, me and Lena's and I got a little stuck there. Like reliving the whole everything happening with our political organization and the initial excitement and our friendship and that's the stuff that gets me stuck. And then I like being back there, like I feel lost in these reveries like I am back there and then that stops me here. I think that stops me here.

BR: That's good Amelia. That's the type of thing I want to hear. So you were stuck in the past? And you felt you weren't making any progress in your life as long as you were lost in the past? Am I understanding correctly?

AA: Literally, Billie. Sometimes it was almost like literally, like I wasn't here where I was or where was I? I live alone. Sometimes I go missing I disappear beneath the cracks, I do the work I need to do but I'm not there since I don't go into the office unless I just absolutely have to. That's how Lena was different. She would go. She would go and no one else would. Not even Tyrone. He wouldn't go, but he took all the publicity shots.

BR: You sound like you still harbor a little resentment towards Tyrone?

AA: No, I like Tyrone. I harbor resentment. (Laughter). In general. Don't we all. The most of it comes from how things turned out. Turned out, you know? I met Lena at Howard. She was something. Somewhere somehow she and Tyrone started hanging out, he was there too. But, Jean, Lena and I we were a group, and sometimes Janice would join us too. We don't. I don't. It's hard to make friendships like that anymore.

BR: That's a common complaint I hear.

AA: What about you?

BR: Sorry?

AA: What about you? Do you find It hard to make friendships the older you get?

BR: Oh, Amelia. Let's just keep this about you, okay. That's how reconciliation works best.

AA: About me. Okay.

BR: Okay.

AA: But isn't about me in this moment my way of relating to you? That plays a role too. You can't just be some algorithm calculating a prognosis.

BR: Okay. About me?

AA: About you.

BR: I am finding new friends, Amelia. The first part of my life is another life, and that's as far as I'll go with that. Okay?

AA: Okay. Thank you. Sometimes it really does seem harder, though. I met Janice first. We were roommates Freshman year, and we got along right away. We talked a lot of politics. It wasn't long before we got the idea for the magazine, online of course, but also old-skool style, too, print. *The Reckoning*, you know. The name was Janice's idea. *The Reckoning*. But we liked it. I still like it. I mean the name – that's part of the reason people still talk about it. Did you ever read it?

BR: I'm familiar with it.

AA: Well, everyone is familiar with it. Or thinks they are at least. I don't mean that like it came out. I just mean, it was such a polarizing publication. I had to ask you know.

BR: I always enjoyed it Amelia. Whenever I had a chance to read it, I enjoyed it.

AA: OK. Cause you never know you know. And that magazine. We came up with the idea just hanging out one night. I think we were even watching something. Something about a newsroom, a drama I think, maybe that one about BlackChant. Something like that. And we both thought the same thought at the same time, we just basically decided right then we wanted to start a magazine, a political magazine, a pro-BIPOC-pro-Feminist broader political perspective publication, an online magazine and a print magazine, doing that old-skool vintage kind of thing, where we distributed actual printed copies around shops downtown. Free of course. That was important. Free.

BR: How did you manage to stay afloat?

AA: Ad revenue from the website and donations. You'd be surprised. Because at first it was all donations. At first we didn't sell our magazine and we didn't put up advertising on our website or in our magazine, so the only way we survived was donations. Mostly crowdfunding. And the donations came. Especially after we got Lena onboard. And Jean too. Jean was like a marketing genius. Self-taught, you know? She never went to school for it, but she was good at it. A natural.

BR: When did you change your mind about advertising?

AA: Yeah, that came later. I mean, and now it feels like I'm being interviewed. But. Well, Janice and I, see it turned out to be a really good idea to do the whole print magazine thing downtown, because at first we lost a lot of money printing and distributing it, but since it was free, it started getting talked about. And bounced around social media some too. So that helped. The first issue was just me and Janice, alternating pieces, like a two-girl rap group trading verses. And by the time we got the next issue out we'd already interested a bunch more people. And it kept growing. And then one day I'm walking across the Howard quad, I'm walking past the classics building – back then Howard still had a classics department, and there's Lena on the steps and her head is in her hands.

Now I'd see her around before, and I think we had even exchanged a few friendly words, so I slow down. In fact, I do remember — we had been in the same orientation session together, and an administrator — Mr. Linnow, I think — and he's going through the curriculum of our political theory major and Lena raises her hand and asks why so few women were represented. And I went up to her after and bummed an analog cigarette off her and told her I appreciated her for that — not the cigarette, the comment or the question I guess. The observation. Maybe we talked a little bit more. But then I saw her on the steps with her head in her hands, and so I slow down and I sat next to her, and I offered her an analog cigarette, said something like, hey I still owe you one.

She didn't know I was Amelia Arabesque, the writer for *The Reckoning*, I mean I didn't mention it right off. I did say my name was Amelia, of course. Anyway, my mother always told me if you want people to be open with you, you have to be open with them, so I told her about my own problems a little. My dad had just moved out of the house, something had gone awry with him and my mom, he'd had an affair or something? I didn't know. But it made our house a mess of secrets and whispers and lies and it was weird and uncomfortable.

BR: Do you mind detouring? I'd like to hear more about that -- if you don't mind.

AA: Well, it's all part of the same story anyway, to be honest. Because I start telling her all about it, and that really is what starts our friendship. About my mother and my father when I was younger and how growing up an only child may have they may have I mean spoiled me a little bit. And then there were the silences. Long silences at night where I would listen in bed to hear what they said and I heard just these ponderous silences that sounded more eerie than shouting ever could. And I would get lost in those silent spaces in the morning, you know – like talking to my mother the next morning before breakfast and in walks my father and then this vast kind of quietness entered the room and it wasn't him it was the other way around too – I mean I could be in the den going over my homework with my father and then in would sail my mother – I mean it – she would sail in – happy as the day is dark – and she would say something and then the silent spaces opened back up. So I listened for those at night, because I'd learned to read them. And I know how that sounds, but it's how it was alright. And just before they separated I could feel and read those silences something serious and they didn't portend nothing good.

[Extended silence]

BR: Go on.

AA: Well that's all there is to tell about it. I mean, that's what got me so fascinated by Lena in the first place. Because of those silences and the way I thought no one ever said what they thought the world was just a litter of lies and language not for cursing but confusing the issue. So when I saw Lena – we were all just young women back then and we didn't have any power – when I see Janice stand up and challenge the administration – in the middle of all that silence – mind you, it had gone silent, the hall was all silent because Mr. Linnow had just asked "any questions?" and there were no questions just silence and then **BOOM** came Lena's question, and I thought that was just too cool.

[Laughter].

So that's what I meant it's all part of the same story. It's not even a story, I guess. It's just about Lena. That was one thing about her – the first thing. And friendships get rarer when you get older, and Lena and I had been friends for a long time. I can't – I'm too old to be losing friends, but of course that's the whole thing of it, it's when you get older of course that you start losing more friends.

BR: Was Tyrone around often?

AA: At first. Later, not so much. But he was never entirely absent from the picture, either. Like I said, I liked him. But he was also a little flaky. But he was useful too, because he could write. He could write fiction and poetry and plays and stuff like that, while the rest of us, we were more political essayists. And so we're publishing *The Reckoning* and it's making a little kind of a name for its self, you know? And so we're happy, extra excited and thinking we're gonna take over the free world.

BR: Well, you in some ways did just that.

AA: Yeah, didn't we though? Talk about Black Girl Magic.

[Laughter]

BR: How long did you publish *The Reckoning?*

AA: We kept publishing it all four years of college. Then we went to various MA programs, well most of us anyway. I mean Janice didn't. She couldn't afford to, she was only at college on a scholarship because she was so brilliant, but then she didn't have money for school after that. After we graduated we tried to keep it going for a while, but then things started happening for Lena and then that was kind of the end of it after a while. We always talked about starting it back up again someday. But joking like, at the bar or something like yeah, let's revive the band, ladies. But yeah. In some ways it was a missed opportunity.

BR: How do you mean?

AA: For me. For Janice. For Janice especially. I mean it worked well for Lena, and but she was always going places. Though. But it was something special and there were times, yeah, when we couldn't believe how much attention we were getting, but that was how it was in those days with social media, I mean we just fired right off from jump, and that wasn't happening for Black people on social media at all in those days. I mean. It was the zeitgeist of the time too, though, people talking about a Third Civil Rights Era, and #BlackLivesMatter and George Floyd, a goddamn plague which hit Black people worse, talk about some evil ass shit, right?!

[Laughter]

AA: But Lena rode that wave well. I mean it landed her in the White House, so you have to respect that.

BR: There were rumors, I mean... you know all about this and it's a little weird to talk about, I guess, because it was so public but not public but there were rumors that there were all kinds of internal differences and internal fighting and maneuvering and counter-maneuvering going on behind the scenes, I mean that you were involved in.

AA: No. I mean I was involved, of course. You can't be Secretary of State and not be involved. But I – I mean, it was always respect – Lena and I certainly had differences of opinion at times.

BR: Everyone does.

AA: Right! Everyone does! And so, we did too, of course. I mean, that's also part of why she gave me that position. Come on, I have a freaking Ph.D. in Political Science. I know people throw those kind of titles around as a way of shutting people down, the title has more to do with how privileged you've been than others than it has to do with any real intrinsic merit you possess over other people. Party line shit. Of course. But I do – have studied what I'm working on, and we often had disagreements, we had different foreign policy philosophies, I think, and so she wanted that push-back from someone she could trust as a good friend, and so we worked well as a team. But yeah. We could sure disagree though.

BR: So people misread it?

AA: Look, the media always wants the sensational story. Everything got blown way out of proportion online and in the press and in social media just to catch clicks and likes and shares. It was ridiculous. But that's politics and media for you.

 BR: So you felt properly respected at the White House?

AA: I mean, here's the thing. It's also politics. So it's not always pretty. You really gotta be built for it. So you need that sort of inside politics and the Washington machine mindset. It's. I don't know. I don't always like it. But how else do you effect change, how else do you? Do you know Plato's *Crito*?

BR: Not really offhand like that, no.

AA: It's early political philosophy. Socrates in jail, Crito comes to him, says, let's bust you out, they're coming for your ass TOMORROW! And Socrates considers: well okay, he says, see I dreamt it was the day after tomorrow that they come get me, but whatever, let them come tomorrow instead. I agreed to the Athenian State laws by living here happily, and it's my part to change unjust laws not to break them. And at first you're like no! no! no! But then you're like, maybe you're right? Because that's what Black folks have been doing with America since Day One. Right? So I mean, there's something to it, even if maybe Socrates can take things too far.

BR: Sort of the opposite of Civil Disobedience.

AA: Well, sort of. I mean, all of this is to say that we knew we needed to be in politics to change politics, and sometimes that meant things got a little ugly, and then like I said, it's just you have tense moments and then the media loves to make something as normal as that between two friends into something big and ugly and dangerous, and it's not even. It's just another human relationship anyone can understand. And. And we were supposed to disagree. I mean that was the whole point of it being me and her. Because we'd always had these knock-down discussions, all through college even and you can even see it in our exchanges in *The Reckoning*, I mean at times we are definitely outright sparring right there on the page if you read the articles closely enough. We were. Jesus. Yeah, that's funny. Funny to think about.

BR: Her administration got criticized from the left a lot on climate change. I know you –

AA: Yeah, that was one of the things. Lena was focused, I mean she even had a sticker on her door back in college – you had to see it – if you're not pissed off you're not paying attention! – and the irony of it was that Lena could be real myopic about social injustice and didn't factor in climate change in that, not that she didn't think climate change was a big problem, but she was just focused on social injustice and missed how the two topics are intimately connected, or didn't miss it. I don't know. We had different outlooks on that I guess.

BR: So that's what led to some of the drama too, I guess?

AA: It's – to coin it as drama – I think that's the wrong word. After all, it isn't – there's something really something at stake and when you talk about drama the connotation of the word is the opposite of something at stake. So, it's not like it was drama, but deadly serious, climate change is deadly serious, it's existential, we're seeing that this very summer, this weekend, Miami, hell all over the country and in Europe too. So you know it's not – it wasn't quite drama, but like I said you have to use the political system in order to effect change within the system and it's not always pretty. I think – here's the thing... if we – if I – we haven't done enough for climate change, but I think we'd be seeing a much worse – I think it would have could have been much worse if we weren't there – if those of us from the left hadn't had the power to nudge Powers. So there's – that's the details of the politics again.

BR: Tell me some of the stories.

AA: Oh, I don't know. Last year was like a roller-coaster. I mean great God. We had no idea what we were doing – I guess it's like that for the ones who come in new to Washington I mean that Washington, we were after all DCAF but not Washington like that. So it was new. But I don't know. There was the whole Earth Day fiasco in April. Look, I know it's just a stupid holiday, and there's valid criticism in saying why pay so much attention to a symbol when there's so much real work to be done, but the symbols are how we get people to pay attention, especially symbols everyone pays attention to like holidays. Like back what Biden had done way back when – 2021 – with Juneteenth. We were thinking that big, like publicity and the introduction of a new plan that we wanted to move through congress to build on the #GND-Movement.

BR: Well, I know all the media stories. What really happened?

AA: We had to force attention to the issue. I mean – when LBJ complained to MLK that he'd already pushed through the Civil Rights Bill, voting rights had to wait, MLK marched up on Selma and forced the issue. I don't know – I know I'm not MLK or whatever – I don't mean that – I mean that's – those are the kinds of stories you think of and you think there are times when something has to be done, and so for Earth Day, Lena was completely opposed to flooding downtown Washington with parades and information and even having the National Park Foundation join in with planting stations in parks and so on. It was a terrific idea, actually. A bunch of us – me, Toni, Kat, we basically decided it was too important an idea to drop. So we organized our event on social media without the White House.

BR: Yeah. That was a shitstorm.

AA: That was a shitstorm. But that was also Lena. I mean, what was she gonna do? She shouted and fussed and hollered and probably hit me with a hundred hard dozens, but it was still us. And I did what had to be done. I mean, that demonstration that we held – what we managed to do that day – the scale at which awareness has increased in the short time since we did that. Even Lena admitted in the end we were right.

BR: Though, if I understand right, she never agreed with your tactics.

AA: No she never thought we should have held a private demonstration. It turns out no one really thinks that was a good idea.

BR: Except you.

AA: Not just me.

BR: By you I meant y'all.

AA: Damn, girl, then just say y'all.

[Laughter].

BR: Y'all.

AA: We. Yeah. But I mean, it's undeniable, the good it's done. I can't say – to this day I can't say I regret it. I mean, I do regret it because of the people that died. But even their loved ones, many of them have told me they feel their loved ones are heroes, and I agree.

BR: I understand that.

AA: But then I don't know if I believe myself, because I do – I think about Lena, and I miss Lena, and I regret- I don't know. I think maybe anytime anyone dies that you love, there are always regrets.

BR: There are always regrets.

AA: And then there's our demonstration planned for next month.

BR: Are you worried about a similar thing happening?

AA: Lightning doesn't usually strike twice. And there's no reason why we should live in fear. The Black Earth Day Festival just started last year, and it was never meant to be a one-off. So we're going ahead with it. With proper security in place of course. But it's a go.

BR: Good. I plan to be there. But it looks like our session is coming to a close soon. Anything else you wanted to mention before we call it a day?

AA: No. Let's wrap up, then. But, well, actually, Billie. Maybe there is something. Can I ask you a real question? I mean, us Black girls here now just being real?

BR: Of course Amelia.

AA: Does this work? Reconciliation? I mean, what's – it's – isn't this just therapy like old fashioned therapy?

BR: Yeah, basically. I mean it has its roots in it.

AA: And then the spiritual philosophy.

BR: Of course.

AA: That's the part I liked best. I think. The spiritual philosophy of things, because sometimes that's what's missing. I get pulled into the politics and then I forget the spiritual part of it all. And of course that's what's behind the whole damn thing. You know? So that's why I'm here, I guess – I sense that – that – whatever – I mean I think I was hoping – the part I liked the best in your swag, Billie, I think. I dig that. And that's the kind of cool I want to achieve.

BR: Well, it's a cool, I guess, a cool but I'm always working on it too, Amelia. It's always work. For all of us. It's also performance.

AA: Everything is performance. And I think I can do the work.

BR: I'm glad to hear that. I think you can do the work too. I think this first session has been wonderfully successful. Do you intend to continue, then?

AA: I think so, Billie. I think so.

BR: Great. Then I look forward to seeing you again tomorrow.

AA: Great. See you tomorrow.

[End Transmission]

Re: A WHERENESS Msg ¾

Hey kid, I know you think that Re: I wrote is corny – that's cuz it is. But bear with it. For example, where was I? Right. I was sixteen the first time I ran away from home. It wasn't a real attempt like sometimes first suicide attempts aren't serious. In any case I wasn't serious, or I don't think I was. I wanted the freedom, I wanted to make a statement, but I don't think I thought I was ready. So I wasn't really serious. There you go. A whereness. Where are you at? You know? Those moments when you stop and take check of everything –you good? Where you at? But I didn't know anything about that back then. So I just packed up and left home and spent the evening with an overstuffed bag in a Dunkin Donuts. I went back home the very next day, too.

But like I said, that was just the first time. There were more times, a lot more. They got more serious, too, like suicide attempts. The thing is: I didn't even know myself what was triggering them. There I was, fairly good life. We weren't rich, but we were doing well, a house in Georgetown; mom, a total Black girl magic professor at Georgetown mom, dad working at Anthropocene. In the meantime I had plenty of free time, more than enough me time. I had nothing to complain about. At least according to them, and I thought I must be selfish too or something, because something felt fundamentally fucking

[End Msg 3/4]

From *Batshit Ratchet* (2072)

by Amelia Arabesque

BILLIE'S PHILOSOPHY OF MORAL PURISM

The philosophy of moral purism associated with my administration, and which has been so controversial was never really mine to begin with. It was Billie's. I knew right away Billie was a brand-new reconciliator and I knew she'd never last long as one; bottom line, she wasn't professional. She tried to play the part, which was amusing, but I liked her anyway. Which is why I kept going after a rambling first session in which she continuously offered up her own personal anecdotes and interviewed me like a star-struck journalist. She stopped practicing after a year, and said it was because her research in her reconciliation studies had led her beyond reconciliation. I thought, yeah, okay; I knew the job wouldn't last long. But by then we were already friends.

The first time we hung out post-reconciliation was rejuvenating. We were finally able to be a little free, free of all the rules and roles of reconciliation. I told her I never thought she would last at that job, and she agreed and then disagreed and then agreed again and then talked some about what she was studying these days. It was pretty out there, or I thought so at the time anyway, but she was always so wonderful to listen to, because she made her ideas incubate inside you.

She had taken a general Introduction to Linguistics course in her undergrad studies, before she dropped out, but had never lost her fascination for language and linguistics. So she studied it on her own, and she had been working on her own language for a while – a purely imaginary language which she imagined would come from another planet somewhere, so everything about it had to be different from Earth languages.

You mean like Klingon or something, I said, intentionally obnoxiously.

I will admit she did always have the temperament if not the talent for reconciliation. She was patient. She explained how she had thought it was different because she was creating her own language and there was no baggage about Star Trek or some other made up world to bother with, but then, and here she smiled — she had these cool smiles where her face would flick her eyes aflicker and she said but that turned out to be a real problem, deeply philosophically, because the concept of language is incoherent without culture, and so she needed a culture.

And now it sounds like not like Star Trek, but that *Lord of the Rings* guy.

It's true. It does sound a little like him, said Billie. But it's also different than that too.

The next time I saw her I asked her about it again. I had been thinking about it. What about it was different from Tolkien. I had read up on him. It sounded just like what she was doing. Was she writing books?

No, I'm not writing books, Billie said. I do keep notebooks with grammar rules, dictionaries, and that kind of thing around. But Tolkien wrote books, and I don't do that.

Does your language have cultural mythologies? That's what sounded interesting about what Tolkien was up to, from what I read.

Yeah, there are lots of those.

Do you write them down?

No, I don't write them down.

You just –

Know them.

Can you tell me one?

A myth?

Yeah.

Now?

Why not now?

We'll need another round if I'm gonna do that.

Then we need another round, girl. Okay, so?

Okay, so: There's a myth about how the Gods were born.

There are gods? Plural?

Gods. Plural. And the myth is that the universe was chaos and in that chaos every possible chaotic formation came to be and among those chaotic formations was our world right here and from that, well that's how people came to be. And at first there were people but there was no moral order and people behaved like animals do, in a sort of zone beyond good and evil. And then there was this one lady, Assata, and she was a saint to everyone. She took care of the sick and she sacrificed her own needs for the needs of others and she was generally selfless, which no one understood. In fact this behavior of hers disturbed the others so much that a bunch of them plotted to kill her.

So one day word goes around that an elder is deathly ill in the mountains, alone there in his cabin. And as soon as Assata hears word of that she heads up the mountain to take care of him. Only there is no sick elder in the mountains; there is just a trap on the only path up the mountain, a pile of dirt, sticks, stones and leaves over a pit. And in that pit is a floor made up of sharpened stick spikes.

Assata goes up that mountain path with her assortment of herbs and spices and healing tonics. And as she's wending her way up the mountain she comes to the pit, steps onto it, and she falls in. She's torn limb from limb by that pit, with its spikes everywhere, and all her herbs and spices and healing ointments go flying into the air, and the ointments soak in with her bloody flesh, and then they absorb the herbs and spices and then her mangled corpse shudders and the bones reassemble with strips of human flesh hanging off, and she claws her bone fingers into the dirt and climbs out of the pit, just like that.

She's pissed, of course. I mean, talk about ingratitude. But she realizes something. In her new state of undeath she is somehow more powerful. She is invincible because she is already dead. And she has a kind of superhuman strength and she goes to the top of that mountain and she spends thirteen months up there learning how to understand her new powers. She can transport. She can step through a kind of fold in the fabric and come out somewhere else, as she is dead and is really nowhere to begin with. She can move through time, backwards and forwards. All sorts of stuff. She is basically a demi-goddess, because she understands that life and death and before and after don't exist but that there are only various states of Being. But what she really wants is revenge.

She goes on back down that mountain thirteen months later, and she goes and hunts down each of the perpetrators. She knows who they are; she's seen them scheming while traveling through space and time. And so she appears before each of them, just as she is, a skeleton with strips of Assata's flesh hanging off her bones, and she kills each of them, methodically, slicing off their skin layer by layer. And once she's killed the last of them, the ringleader, who watched in horror as his co-conspirators died one after the other, and he knew his time was short too of course – once she's killed him – then she ascends out of this earthly realm and becomes the first real God. Dess. But the first, either way.

Oh. I like that.

But she's the first God. And she's the God of morality. Because it was her righteous purism which led her to carry out her bloody acts of vengeance. So that morality has this brutal side to it in the culture. And that effects the language. Because before her there were no Gods.

Doesn't that mean that there really are no Gods? That Gods are sort of social constructs?

Well, yes. I mean yes and no. Because everyone realizes these stories are just stories. No one would take them literally the way that we take our religious stories literally. The stories are the Gods in a sense. So it isn't that there aren't any Gods. It's just that there are lots of ways of talking about God or the Gods – I think it would have to be Gods, but it's also both – is through as many different means or media as possible, because no one of them is going to catch the concept of Godliness. That's where they're coming from. It can't be Father and Son and Holy Ghost, because it has to be a lot more than that, to anthropomorphize the idea is just another way of considering the vexing, for us but not for them, question of God.

I bet.

So that's one example.

And how do we get other gods? I mean is it really just one God or lots of Gods.

Oh, yeah. Lots of Gods. This is interesting, too. Because the first God, in this system, is the God of morality, it's morality that is sort of at the heart of spirituality. After all, it was her innate morality that made Assata different from her peers to begin with. So once Assata becomes a God, she takes the form of several men and impregnates women all over the world. And the rest of the population, or at least the vast majority of it she kills off with a ten-year plague. And after the plague, the new generation of people are all Assata's offspring. And that means they all have the potential for Godliness. But that potential has to be realized – it's not a given – after all, they are all half human as well. And so, that becomes a common cultural belief – or religious or spiritual belief I guess you could say – that you want to become a God when you die, you want to live up to that ideal in your genealogy, become the offspring of Assata. But more than just an idea anthropomorphized, you die because when you're living you're just a human. A character.

So if Assata was also the father, then we're all the children of two mothers.

I know. It's cool, right? Anyway, that's how we get new Gods. We get new ones all the time. But that's the thing. You have to bring something new to ascend to Godhood. You have to be a God of something, and something that isn't already taken. So that means when people look for spiritual ascent in the culture, they're looking for it in a kind of way of bringing something new to humanity while at the same time, minding moral imperatives.

And what are these moral imperatives? In some ways isn't there a deep amorality to the story, since Assata is a killer par excellence?

Billie's story had me thinking, though. So the next time I saw her I asked her about it again. How far had she developed this thing?

Billie was quiet for a while; she sat contemplating her coffee and I watched her and wondered what she was thinking. She looked up and tried not to frown, but she frowned, and then she said, That's just the thing. This is where my spiritual work and this all meets up. Because I am thinking of – not that I believe in some myth of the Goddess Assata – after all I made it up – but I am thinking of these stories as kinds of parables for the way we should approach spirituality, so it all sort of works to make up my spiritual system.

Well that puts things in a new light.

And that's where it really gets different than something like what Tolkien's doing, Billie said, laughing goofily. But I didn't really know how to put it the other day. It sounds so wacky and out there, I know. Like I'm making up myths and then believing they're real.

The interesting thing about this conversation, though, is that it took us to a different level of connection. Because as a reconciliator, Billie and I had talked about how we felt about things, and then as friends that had broadened and deepened to where we talked about all the little particulars of our lives, but we hadn't really touched on philosophy or spirituality before that point, not in any deep way. Honestly, I wasn't all that spiritual a person, so I would have never pursued a discussion like that anyway, and when Billie mentioned it (which she occasionally did) during our sessions, I just dismissed it. It's part of the reason I dismissed it when she said her spiritual work got in the way of her reconciliation work, but something about this had me thinking.

I asked her:

So, if this myth acts as a parable for your spiritual system, does that mean you think morality is at the heart of spirituality? And that's why Assata, the chief god, is the goddess of moral purism?

I guess so. And why the whole moral purism thing.

That's what got me about the story. Christianity teaches turn the other cheek. But Assata is one vengeful-ass Bitch. I mean don't get me wrong. I love her. But I did wonder about that.

Yeah, that's weird, right? I guess it's not a very Christian society I'm building here.

Cue goofy laugh.

It was Billie, though, so it was influenced by Christianity. When Billie disappeared that first time, it made me think her religious crisis went deeper than I realized. I hadn't heard from her for a while, which happened sometimes. Long periods where we didn't talk much, not even online, but they never lasted more than a few months at most. I saw her sometime the spring of 2050. Then I didn't hear from her again. I was thinking more and more about her weird philosophy of moral purism, as I had secretly decided to call it in my mind.

But then I was also in a state of moral purism myself. I still never reconciled with the death of Lena. I was still processing all that – after Billie, I never visited another reconciliator. And the more I thought about it, Billie's philosophy of moral purism, the more moral purism I felt toward the fact that Lena's murderer had never been caught, that the Black Revolution of 2046 had been a failure, that it had arguably made things worse under the twisted

222

administration of Garmin Cinderblock, that Billie hadn't contacted me for a while.

So, I sent her a quick message and then just as quickly forgot about it. A week later it occurred to me she never responded, so I tried again. No response. I let it go thinking she must have a lot going on, there was a lot going on politically for me, too, so I had my own other preoccupations. Along with the moral purism it also occurred to me that the thing Lena would have wanted me to carry on with the work she was doing - so that's where the idea came from. That I should get serious about my political ambitions. It was born from Billie's philosophy of moral purism and my unresolved anger at Lena's murder.

The Tyrone and Loo Show (November 4, 2057)

featuring special guest Baldwin Schattenfreud:

Loo: Okay. *Harlem Spleen*. Why *Harlem Spleen?* What's *Harlem Spleen?*

Baldwin: I mean, it's a very Harlem story, right? So that's where the Harlem comes in. And then the spleen, well. That comes from an old French poet. Back in the 19th century, so damn near ancient. He had a book called *Paris Spleen*. And in a way my book was like a Black American response to that book.

Loo: But brother. Really? Baudelaire?

Baldwin: A kind of Black Baudelaire made sense to me. And especially concerning my ideas about Black Anarchy.

Loo: What's Black Anarchy my brother?

Baldwin: Black Anarchy is an idea I came up with while working on my book. So the title came later. At first I thought I was just writing a memoir, in the great old Negro tradition, you know? And then it got to where I was reading books like LeRoi Jones' autobiography and *Afropessimism* and *Uncle Bud in Boston* and I didn't think I could write a standard memoir, like there seemed like, just like in those books, right – that there's an idea seething beneath the surface. Like with the restored Malcom biography.

Tyrone: Oh yeah.

Baldwin: So that's where I was with it. And I got stuck. Suddenly couldn't write shit, not for niggas nor thieves. Not a word. And so I just marinated on that for a while. And that's when Black Anarchy started to project itself. I began with the basic, undeniable proposition that western capitalism is inherently racist and colonialist in outlook. From there, I came to the conclusion that the best way to counter this mindset would be an elimination of power structures as we understand them. This is effectively anarchy. But in our world, there is no pure anarchy. There is an anarchy of power structures. And it occurred to me that the only way we could build up Black power structures was to make sure that any anarchy we experience would be a Black Anarchy, where Black power is already in place. So: First the revolution, then the anarchy.

Tyrone: Well, okay, brother. But here's what I don't get. If the revolution is already successful, why you need the anarchy on top of it?

Baldwin: Brother, did you just listen to a word I said? This capitalist system is corrupt by default. We take it over; then we dismantle it. And we replace this bitch with Black Anarchy.

Tyrone: Okay, so tell me how this figured in your book.

Baldwin: I kept seeing the holes in the system. I learned to analyze current events like you analyze a novel, I could pick it apart and see where it was going and the motivations behind actions and policies and it began to affect the way I got along in the world. And that was what I hadn't been able to express in the book – that I was changing writing the book because I was becoming aware that I had already changed, that I was already a Black Anarchist without – not even knowing the term – not having invented the term yet. That would all come later.

Loo: You think your book helped spark the Twenty-sixth of May?

Baldwin: I like to think so, yeah, but in reality who knows? May 26th happened for a lot of reasons, and that kid they shot in Harlem right on the heels of Ambrose and the Ralph Bellicose conspiracy theories and all – all that didn't help either. But the shit had been brewing for a while. If you read history like I read history it's been happening at least since Reconstruction, and it really got its kick from January 6th back when and now May 26th happened, and I don't know.

Tyrone: You disappointed in May 26?

Baldwin: I mean, come on Negro. Aren't you? Y'all started this thing up on May 26th. This right here – this podcast right here is straight out of May 26th, but now it's not like it was in those first days- I mean, don't get me wrong. I'm not saying y'all some lazy niggas, but everyone let the damn ball drop. And then Cinderblock. If ever we needed people to stay ready.

Loo: Man, the damn thing was all performance anyway, like the whole damn thing is performance. There was no way May 26th was ever gonna be anything but just another date for Americans to go on about.

Baldwin: Well, you'll have to just speak for yourself there, brother. That shit meant something to me, and a lot of other righteous brothers out there, just so you know.

Loo: So what did you expect from it?

Baldwin: I expected basically what we got. But I hoped it would lead to something.

Loo: You mean Black takeover.

Baldwin: I guess so. I guess I mean Black takeover. And after Black takeover, then a move toward a benevolent Black anarchy.

Loo: An anarchy where Black people are in control of most of the resources and goods.

Baldwin: You said it, my brother.

Tyrone: That's what makes it benevolent.

Baldwin: You said it, my brother. [Pause.] Look, Black people have been the moral compass of this nation since its inception. Just like Cinderblock himself had to admit. So we need to be the ones in control of the resources.

Tyrone: But, isn't the problem that you're not preparing for a true anarchy. You're preparing for a kind of lawless plutocracy.

Baldwin: In today's globalized world, that's the only type of anarchy we're going to have. Whoever controls the resources has the power—call it a plutocracy, call it a kraterocracy, it is what we are left with when we strip back all the illusions.

Tyrone: Has there ever been a functional anarchy?

Baldwin: There have been many. In a post-colonial world they don't want you to think it's possible, but it's possible all right. Communities self-regulate, and if we think of America as a series of communities, these communities can self-regulate.

Loo: I don't know that I see communities self-regulating, brother.

Baldwin: A lot of them don't: They need the proper education. This is a process. But the revolution needs to happen. It should have been happened. We had a moment back then in forty-six and I don't know when we'll have it again. But a community can self-regulate if they have knowledge-of-self. Not many people know about it, but there's an Afro-Deutsch movement happening in America right now. It's a spiritual movement, and a political movement, and it's straight out of the Black Arts movement and the German Black feminist tradition.

Loo: Afro-Deutsch? You half German or something?

Baldwin: I am all German. I was born in Germany. But I grew up here. Afro-Deutsch. The movement has grown in recent years. It started way back when with Audre Lorde, who moved to Berlin in her later years – so that's its Black Arts movement roots. She taught at a university in Berlin, and she ended up influencing a student there – a poet named May Ayim, and Ayim officially started the Afro-Deutsch movement. It lay dormant a while – known, and respected – but unorganized. And then as a kind of natural evolution from the civil rights era of the early 2020s, it started to take off. First in Berlin, then all throughout cities in Germany, and then you started seeing it here, even. Now there's a society in most major cities – there's one here in DC, there's one in New York. And these brothers and sisters are organized. You need to check them out. Because they're the Afrofuture.

Tyrone: I'll look into them.

Baldwin: So, when I say Black Anarchy, I mean it. Because I think it can happen. But I do feel like we missed an opportunity with the Black Revolution.

Tyrone: What do you think happened?

Baldwin: I think Cinderblock hoodwinked us. He came across as a hero at first, and I know it seemed unthinkable – he had the national guard hold the cops down when we marched on the town. Marinate on that a minute. I don't blame the media for buying the hype. Because you remember the Ambrose Littleton demonstrations; we all saw how they treated those peaceful demonstrators. So this was Cinderblock, and you remember how the right was calling for that nigga's head.

Tyrone: Word, that's what I mean. I mean, we were there from jump street. I'm not gonna lie, we were championing Cinderblock hard, even when other so-called liberals were too afraid to get on board with something as radical as Black Revolution.

Loo: Yo, and then when we all gathered up on the White House. I mean, that shit was a magical moment.

Baldwin: I know. And Cinderblock let it all happen. But then what happens? Like any cheap two-bit northern liberal, he coddles us. Puts a few of us in power. And the rest of us find ourselves back in the same place where we've always been. He got Marcus Wellington up on TV all the time, and Wellington is publishing in all the magazines and hitting up all the podcasts and streams to promote his books, but the rest of us still suffering. And to see Wellington try to turn into the New 21st-century-house-Negro was depressing. He completely appropriated and white-washed what was a bonafide streets movement. So you know these white boys will co-opt your movement the moment they can, and that was Cinderblock's game from the get-go, and oldest trick in the book, he used a Black man to do it.

Tyrone: He did turn out to be a huge disappointment after those initial first few months.
Loo: He came in on the graves of two Black presidents. I mean, come on.

Tyrone: Not his fault.

Loo: Oh, that's his fault.

Baldwin: And he did it so sneaky. That's the thing.

Loo: He needed a Wellington.

Tyrone: Wellington was like a godsend for that man.

Baldwin: Which makes me wonder if he wasn't planted to begin with. Who knows? I know that's one of those conspiracy theories you're not supposed to touch, but what do we really know about Wellington?

Tyrone: I mean, you do have to admit, journalists have scoured his digital footprints and they haven't come up with much to support the conspiracy theories.

Baldwin: Yeah. That doesn't surprise me. I don't even know. I'm just saying it's a possibility; that that's out there. Either way, it doesn't matter, because plant or no plant, he was the perfect Stepin Fetchit to jump in at just that moment, and he bamboozled a lot of Black people too, and that's what was so problematic with him.

Loo: And talking that slick Black power talk, too.

Tyrone: Yeah, but at the end of the day it was all basically in support of the same old neoliberalist white supremacy status quo.

Loo: Ain't that the truth.
Baldwin: And it defanged the damn movement. With the momentum of May 26 – well, that wasn't something we could afford to just drop and kumbaya around while the white man laughed in the

distance. We needed more radical initiative. And then Wellington comes along and that was that. In the meantime, the Cinderblock administration does more to instill white supremacist ideas into mainstream society through the Liberal Initiatives Program.

Loo: Or Lip Service.

[Laughter]

Tyrone: No doubt.

Loo: And of course Wellington loved that shit.

Baldwin: Loved it. Like his own son. And now here we are, it's 2057 and it could be 2027 for all that's changed.

Tyrone: You see any hope for the movement?

Baldwin: Honestly, brother. I can't say I do. We've been in a cold civil war for thirty-years now, and this country is a DINO. And dinosaurs went extinct a long time ago, my brother. So we're on the way out. We're too big to become authoritarian, so we're a weak plutocracy compared to say, China and developing India. I see dark days ahead.

Loo: Prophesy, brother.

Baldwin: I think, unless there is some reawakening of the revolutionary Black spirit in this country the inevitable end is a third world war where don't nobody make it out alive.

Tyrone: The planet's dying already.

Baldwin: Exactly. And it's only going to get worse. Look. I'm not even worried that this country is doomed, because the damn planet is doomed, and I know I sound like them crazy doomsdaysayers, but I don't see a long future ahead for humanity, or at least not humanity as we understand it right now.

Loo: Well, that's the way of things. Cycles. What goes around comes around.

Baldwin: Spengler.

Tyrone: That's a dark vision, but I'm not saying you're wrong.

Baldwin: And then, don't forget the role the Syndicate played in the whole thing.

Tyrone: Yeah, that was a hot topic.

Baldwin: It was more than just a hot topic. I broke the damn story, but then the *New York Times* took it and ran with it and didn't even mention the work I put in. Not one credit, like they broke the story themselves. But Robert Owen and his Syndicate was some dark shit, brother. I'm still convinced they killed our last two Black presidents, President Powers and Bellicose. They straight up lynched that last nigga. So the Black Revolution needed to happen. It's still happening.

Loo: What's up with the Syndicate now?

Baldwin: Oh, they're still out there. I doubt we've heard the last of them. They're

[Transmission ends]

From *Blood in My Eye* (2112?)

by Robert Owen

Chapter 6: "Hurrah!"

From Robert Owen Papers

#

By the time I got down to Rutherfordton, I had already made pretty good time, so I stopped at a diner and actually sat down and ate, although I admit it, the whole time I was nervous and there were a lot of police in there, but they looked more like allies, so although I was nervous, or more I was aware, I still wasn't too worried. I didn't stay long. I was still fixated on this idea of counter-memory, flipping Foucault's counter-history because if history can't really be knowledge, then memory certainly can't be knowledge, and this was the beginning of my revisionist memory and history of America. The conference hadn't been a disaster, but then again here I was at the end of it all on the run, so its relative success I suppose depends on how you read that right there.

So I was thinking about counter-memory and the Syndicate, because that had been the topic of my talk and I squeezed out of the diner and checked if anyone followed me out or if anyone started up their vehicle soon as I started mine and then I drove out into an Appalachian mid-morning sunshine which swelled through my Patriot as the day developed in a lush golden-orange-red spread over tumbling green mountains.

My panel, "Radical Alternatives for White Culture" wasn't until the last day, right at the end of the conference, everyone knew my talk was bound to be a showstopper. The title of it was "The Hero Myth and Racial Discourse Recast as American Counter-Mythology." I know it's a mouthful, but you have to have a title like that to get into these conferences these days. Anyway, the idea was a lot more down-to-earth. Basically, I was looking at the hero myth and thinking about black superheroes and how the importance of black superheroes implies a black essentialism, as if it should matter what color skin someone from another planet has. So the focus of my talk was on the Affrilachia as meta-myth. I used Affrilachia because I see her appearance as the epitome of the essentialist desire to create a black hero mythology that challenges the already well-researched and more or less scientifically proven standard hero myth that has driven the narratives for millennia. So I started my talk with the words: "My White Brothers. My White Sisters. We got ourselves a Affrilachia problem."

#

At the opening plenary Thursday evening Appalachian patriots took the stage and discussed the history of the exploitation of Appalachia. How Appalachia had been largely settled by our Scots-Irish ancestors, here in these mountains, because the lowlanders were largely British loyalists, and we wanted nothing to do with each other. But they were closer to the centers of commerce, and so they hoarded the money, exploited our labor and made us mountain outcasts, hillbillies, just as we had been in the Irish hills where we had relocated back home to escape the tyranny of the British, back when we were Billyboys, loyal to the true Scottish king William of Orange. So we have a long rich culture and heritage which the lowlanders have always denied us and hated.

Despite our economic hardship in the Appalachians, we survived. We thrived. We moved through Virginia down to North Carolina and then we spread from there all throughout the southern Appalachians to Georgia and into Tennessee. In effect, we are a nation within a nation. You can find us in Alabama and South Carolina. Kentucky. And not just in the south, we extend all the way up to New York in the north, we are found in Pennsylvania of course, Maryland, Ohio, we're strong in West Virginia. We are a force, politically and culturally.

And we aren't just armchair activists, either. The Syndicate has been at work uniting us against the liberal lowlanders and their takeover of our country. I see the struggle between us and these liberal city-dwelling lowlanders as the same as the struggle our ancestors the Billyboys had against the Catholics. And I applaud the work that the Syndicate has been doing.

#

My story is a simple one. I was a schoolteacher. Minding my own business. And then one day I was watching television, and what do you think I saw? It was October 22nd, 2036, and that should tell you everything you need to know.

That day radicalized me, like it did a lot of us. I lost my sister that day. That's when I knew that something had to be done; that we had to stand up for ourselves; that five hundred years later, and nothing had changed, we were still the Billyboys and the lowlanders were still the British. Half a millennium and nothing had changed.

And still the lowlanders cast their vices as ours. I could go on about the influx of Germans into Appalachia, particularly in Pennsylvania and even my own home state of Virginia; I could talk about the Melungeons who arrived during the 19th century, and how Appalachia has always been a multicultural place, and that accusations of racism have been used by the lowlanders to turn public opinion against us. Not to mention the fact that extremist movements that began in the early twenty-first century like Black Lives Matter had turned a large portion of the black population into White-hating racists and I might just mention how while Appalachia was not racist, on the contrary, after all, Virginia had even been the first state in the Union to have a black governor – it wasn't a question of race, but of culture.

And culture is what is most in danger nowadays. Ever since the conception of the country, the lowlanders have tried to erase and debase our culture. For a long time we just let it happen, too. We suffered through the pandemic of the early 2020s worse than anyone. We suffered through the opioid and Fentanyl crises worse than anyone. We suffered off-color jokes about inbreeding and stupidity and backwardness, and if anyone even made a single crack about a black man on crack, he was the world's worst racist, and cast out of society forever, but it was perfectly fine to go on prime time and make whatever kind of joke about Appalachia you wanted. Don't think we didn't notice. And then ten-twenty-two-thirty-six happened. And that's when we rose up.

#

Thinking about Affrilachia. You can trace her back to the whole Black Panther phenomenon of the early 2020s too. *Black Panther* was a great movie because it stayed within the superhero parameters – they knew what they were doing when they made that film, and I have no problem with black representation on screen or anything like that. Let them have their movies. But Affrilachia is a term that started bouncing around back in the early part of the 2000s, it basically meant Melungeons and Ramps who had overrun Appalachia. We never really had a problem with them and some of them we got to be real close with, but it was like with the Pennsylvania Germans, we didn't have any real problem with them, but they weren't our people like that, either, and so we didn't fraternize with them too much. But then comes this Identity Politics politics that starts coming out of the left, and that's when, in the 2030s, the Melungeons wanted to have an identity politics movement too and started identifying as Affrilachians. It began with a black poet, Frank X Walker, yeah, Frank X, so you know what to expect. A Real Race Man.

Anyway, that's where it originated, and then along comes Gary Freshshirt and he turns it into this superhero film – A black woman named Affrilachia, from North Carolina, grows up in the Smoky Mountains. It's Freshshirt's first film, and maybe that's the problem with it, but it plays so much into the racial politics and identity politics of Frank X that it just gets bogged down in its own mess, and the way the blacks have taken to it is disturbing. Disturbing and depressing, especially in Appalachia, where we have shared a multicultural life together for generations, and now they're letting this lowlander identity politics bullshit get in the way of all that.

#

The conference was disorienting, to say the least. The whole damn Appalachia must have been there, the second annual Appalachian Culture Conference, a monumental event, to be sure, and only history and the future and such can say what importance this conference will have in American history, but it was a good feeling being there, you could feel it in the air, there was that energy right there. At the opening reception after the plenary, I ran into Adam Canon. I'd met Canon before at the conference last year and we got along all right right from the get. He was chairing a panel this year. It was good to have a connection back to the previous year, it gave things a sense of continuity, a story, a narrative, we were doing things, building on what we'd been building.

On Wednesday I took a drive through Shenandoah Valley. I went at night because I love driving those winding roads at night you feel like any moment you might go flying from the road into the wild, but you never do until you do. It was midnight and the moon loomed over the mountains in a cool November night mood, covered by clouds and pale white and the stars alight above because the night was black and clear. I drove from the independent city of Harrisonburg south down through the hilly wood dangerous puffing dangerous marilala on the dangerous way down, the stars blending with the trees as I passed through Blacksburg, the old trees leaning green and wise in the wind and then down into the North

Carolina lush green blue black evening past the Cherokee National Forest and then outside Asheville, where I swerved up north again as the moon lifted past the veil of clouds separating the night sky from the morning. It was time to head home and at just past five, the sky wavered in the horizon, turning midnight to royal blue in an advancing distance. I raced the rising sun as I drove north through Winstom Salem, then north through long lonely stretches of road while the sun cracked the horizon, a late Autumn morning on the eastern edge of Appalachia America until I was just north of the independent city of Roanoke and headed up the last stretch north back to the independent city of Harrisonburg, where I got out of my truck just outside the city center and vaped one and watched the morning settle into the day. Throughout the entire trip I could smell the smoke of the burning Appalachian forests, and you could see, as the day developed, the smoke rising above the mountain, mixing with the mists and wafting like a shroud being dragged over the Earth.

#

I was worn out not having slept and stoned and dizzy from the hours driving, but I attended Dr. Fritz's panel that morning all the same. It was on the history of liberalism, and featured three panelists who all gave remarkable talks. The first was on twenty-first century Appalachian literature, specifically centering on the Appaliberation movement, that philosophical outlook that maybe begins with Nietzsche and critiques American liberalism through counter-narratives and counter-memory, evoking an apocalyptic vision of American society, in which America's unacknowledged crimes of liberalism eventually led to an American apocalypse, through which we are currently living – think Joe Lobert, think Ben Jeremy, or even Carol Cristopher – and how this Appaliberation movement was perhaps the only thing that could save the nation as we understood or recognized it.

The second paper was on Allen Tate and his American classic "Ode to the Confederate Dead" and his relationship with the black poet Melvin Tolson, whose *Libretto for the Republic of Liberia* was commissioned by Liberian president William Tubman. The paper argued that the vision of liberalism proposed by these two works became superseded by the more radical vision of liberalism that would soon emerge from the volatile sixties, that in fact these two works demonstrate a progress that was thwarted by the Black Power movement and identity politics. These arguments continue to this day; while White Appalachia has made large inroads towards reclaiming our traditionalist liberalism, the damage done by the radicalism of the 1960s and its resurgence in the 2020s resulted in long-lasting damage to any hope of progress.

The third paper was about a black woman named Haley Grace, who like the black people in novels from the early twentieth century decided to pass, but in her case, she did so in order to understand what being black was all about, and to do so she thought she needed to see what being White was all about first – after all, she had only experienced blackness as a black person and not as a White person. The thrust of the paper seemed to suggest that, again like the black people from the twentieth century, radical black liberalism runs the risk of reinforcing concepts of essentialist differences between the races that we know don't really exist. But that's the thing – as soon as you say that the problem isn't with black people, it's with black culture, people start calling you a racist, as if the very opposite isn't actually the case, because if the problem with the blacks in this country isn't the people themselves, then what else can it be other than the culture? But no – these culture warriors want to throw out the triumphs of Western civilization for their own primitive, backwards, cultural sentimentality – one that holds their people back to this day, I might add.

By the time it was afternoon my head was swimming, and I had had enough trouble keeping my eyes open through the last presentation in the morning session, but all the same, I attended a session titled, "Seeing in Black and White: A Roundtable Discussion of the Multicultural Turn in the Movies." The session featured four film critics who were doing something of a metacritique of Appalachian Studies, saying that these groups were buying into the very identity politics trap that they purpoted to despise. The young Appalachian filmmakers, particularly those from the Appaliberation and similarly minded groups were buying into the identity politics game the wokery warriors of the twenty first century were promoting. By embracing Appalachian identity as a cultural history and thinking of themselves as anything but Americans, they were legitimizing the black and hispanic and oriental and gay and queer and non-gender conformist identity politics people, when there was just a general history of American cinema, and even better, Western cinema, and we were training ourselves to look, through identity politics cinema, at people as different instead of as being all the same. I sat in that room feeling to some degree personally accused, because I am guilty of all those things, and this tension would explode by the end of the conference.

#

Can an idea be saved from the lazy thinking that produced it? Here is my argument:

We have ourselves an Affrilachia problem. And the problem is that she exists at all.

And the only reason why she exists is because of the new trend of embracing Appalachian identity as identity politics and not just accepting our varied cultural history as it is. And now there has to be a black one of us, and a black superhero one of us, and the problem with Affrilachia is that she divides us, because it's always her against your traditional stereotypical hillybilly type. Each of the three Affrilachia texts I examined: the film, the digital comic and the album are, by virtue of being born from Frank X Walker's term, already tainted with the idea of the black/White dichotomy that Walker would like to have us buy into. What I argue is that when viewed collectively, these cultural products create this bizarre black Afropessimist mythology that infects not just Appalachian culture, but American culture at large, because it uses Appalachia to emphasize difference, which is the way Appalachia has been used by the lowlanders all throughout our history – defined by our difference. So by building off William Longfellow's concept of the Appalachian Universal in his controversial book *Anti-Appalachia* (2031), I contend that the modern day Appalachian should become a cultural nationalist, which is to say, we embrace our local and immediate cultures, and resist any definition that brings together a plethora of cultures and tries to make a nation of them or a people or an ethnicity. We are, contradictorily Appalachians and non-Appalachians, Anti-Appalachian cultural nationalists and that when we operate thus, we can use our cultural superiority to culturally redefine the country the way the blacks have been doing ever since they got their freedom: Why is it that our young people listen to black music and stream black stories and use black language, when we Whites are the ones who have brought real culture to this country, and if there is a true American culture it is certainly not the African-tainted savage shouts of the black man, but the European dissident cultures of the people that settled the land in this country, and that means Appalachians should have a cultural dominance in the country to rival and even exceed that of the blacks and part of the reason why we don't is because we're so concerned with identity politics, the way the blacks can now afford to be – but we can't – or we're just labeled as a bunch of backwards hillbillies way up in the mountains that the lowlanders can afford to discount.

The birth of Affrilachia as superheroine begins in 2036, with the comic run by Wendy Carter as writer and Angela Dorchester as illustrator. This was about a year after Carter published *Crystal Stare* (2035), a book that went straight to the top of the bestseller lists and signaled a new wave in Afrofeminist radicalism. And if *Crystal Stare* was the sociopolitical text of the Black Radical Feminist Movement, then Carolina Cotton's album *Kunta Oochie Walla* (2035) was the unofficial theme song of the movement. So Carter and Cotton were already considered by everyone to be connected to the movement and then director Linda Muntu's film about October 22nd made her the official spokesperson of Affrilachia. *Black October* was released on July 12, 2037, and it was about the way that Black Appalachia responded to the assault on October 22nd. And I have to admit that technically, it was a well-done documentary, but that's part of its problem, too. Because it just worked like propaganda for divisiveness.

In any case, the three of them together, Carter, Cotton and Muntu made the perfect triumvirate for working (separately) together on creating this Black Affrilachian superheroine counter-mythology that distorts and bastardizes the moral center of the traditional western hero myth.

Worst of all, Affrilachia plays into Black culture's obsession with titles of royalty, and so Affrilachia becomes queen of Appalachia, as if the concept doesn't go against everything America stands for in the first place. Appalachia, after all, is a part of the American democracy and definitely does not need a queen! When the liberals say the conservatives are fascists, they're really just talking about themselves. Carter even admits it when she says in an interview:

> I made her a queen because she really is a Black [sic] queen in the way we mean that when we say that. And the concept of queenliness gives her dignity. So, while on the one hand I

was concerned about the fact that any person who would want that kind of power is already corrupted, still the concept of queen seemed to fit her and I wanted it to be more metaphorical than literal.

Carter admits that black culture buys into iconography that is fascist at heart, and yet she does nothing to disown it.

On the contrary.

#

The evening ended with the Presidential Address. The title of the Address was: "Neo-Hillbillies: Appalachian Studies as Antiestablishment." I was curious what this mouthful of a title would produce. The President, Simon Corregidora, argued for a new kind of Appalachian Studies; up to this point Appalachian Studies had taken a scientific and sociological approach to the study of Appalachian people, history and culture. Corregidora advocated a more active and activist approach to Appalachian Studies: we should identify as Appalachians and we should proudly announce that as Appalachianists, we were coming, ourselves, from an Appalachian perspective, and there was nothing disinterested about our study at all. On the contrary. We are interested in Appalachian Studies, because we are interested in shifting the power balance away from the lowlanders, immigrants and black power people destroying the culture and heritage of America, and in the process erasing Appalachian culture, which had already always had to struggle to begin with.

#

The Affrilachia comic is subtitled "These Boots Are Made for Walking," and it is named after the Nancy Sinatra song, of course, but more importantly, Carter seems to be referencing Sara Stieffel's controversial article, "These Boots Are Made for Walking: An Afrofeminist Approach." Stieffel basically argues that the song can be read as a black woman's manifesto for black female empowerment, and she sees a useful trend in black women empowerment that can be used against the White patriarchal establishment through cultural revolution. She sees the beginnings of this as far back as Gayle Jones and Toni Morrison in the twentieth century, but she charts the black woman empowerment movement through Jesmyn Ward and Clarissa Washington. She considers it a new Reconstruction, suggesting that the first Reconstruction was doomed to failure because women were undervalued and in any new Reconstruction a matriarchal structure is necessary.

Stieffel argues that Reconstruction is a project that is still very much in play to this day, and Carter's reference to Stieffel's article and Sinatra's song reminds us that the Afrofeminist mythology of Affrilachia is a story of a nation still in a state of reconstruction, just as the United States is undergoing a second kind of Reconstruction.

Maybe even more problematically, Carter not only buys completely into the idea of identity politics and applies them to Affrilachia with her black and female identity markers, but also to her Appalachian identity. She wants to be all three and call it intersectionality. This, of course, serves to give her a kind of superior cultural capital, because she now has three sources of identity politics to attack from, and they even seem, at times, to come from opposite poles, as in the black and the Appalachian identities. It comes as no surprise, then, what with all this identity politics cultural capital flying around, that we should find out in the course of the comic that she's queer too!

I swear to fucking God, they would have made her gender nonbinary and female at the same time if they could have gotten away with that nonsense. Virtue signaling is what they used to call it when I was growing up.

I went back to my room and drank a pint and a half of good Kentucky whisky.

#

The next morning was what you'd expect. I needed a break. I slept in late and then walked out of the bed and breakfast and headed into town. I stopped to eat at Jack Brown's and had a few beers too to hair of the dog that shit. It was a wide blue warm afternoon. Harrisonburg's slightly colonial streets in the historic district slipping by, corner by corner. I made my way back to the conference center and puzzled through a few strange sessions. I puzzled over why I was so bothered by our Affrillachia problem. I came to no conclusions.

In the film, Affrilachia's throne is threatened by an Appalachian activist named Mack Fink. Fink knows that Affrilachia's power comes from the cultural knowledge she has gained by reading a previously lost set of ancient African texts. He sees it as the height of selfishness and black female entitlement that she refuses to share this knowledge with the Appalachian activists who have been struggling for Appalachian rights right along with the black Appalachians. He also has a personal vendetta against Affrilachians in general: his sister married an Affrilachian and moved to Harlem.

So far your standard narrative – what you'd expect from the media in this day and age. Basically a *Black Panther* rip-off if we're being honest. But at this point in my speech, I show a clip from the film. Fink has succeeded, he is king of Affrilachia. What's most of note visually in this clip is that Fink begins this conversation as Fink the Revolutionary, but slowly throughout, he changes into Fink the King, and while the transition is subtle, the end effect – the starkness of difference – is striking.

#

Back at the conference I landed in the same session as Dr. Fritz – a session on Appalachian resistance aesthetics. This strange roundtable left me a little dizzy, bewildered, which I suppose was

251

the point, after all what the hell are Appalachian resistance aesthetics? Appalachian culture is Appalachian aesthetics and there is no
such thing as resistance aesthetics; that sounds like something a radical black group would come up with, which is to say absolute
mumbo jumbo nonsense.

The last paper in the session was kind of interesting, though. It
was on Jerold Summer and his theory of pamlimpsesting – which
turned the question from what aesthetics should be to what aesthetics should actually do – what role do aesthetics play in a culture –
and how does that translate into action? Summer rejects previously
Appalachian movements as flawed in that some focused on culture
and some on resistance politics, but never understood how the two
were related, and always had been, ever since the days as highlander billyboys.

It was okay, the talk. It could have all been said a lot plainer, and
you get the feeling that he's going on about Appalachian culture on
one side of his mouth and showing off how good he's learned his
Queen's English on the other. Which is to say I liked the idea somewhat, but I hated the presentation.

Dr. Fritz and I hadn't seen each other in a while, so we went out
with a few other folks we knew out to dinner. It was my last night
in Harrisonburg. I was all set to give my talk in the morning, and
then I knew I'd have to light out pretty much right away. I mean, I
didn't know just how bad it would all get, but I still knew enough to
know I needed to be packed and ready to rock and roll. I was happy
for the distraction of dinner.

We ended up at Billy Jack's. Everyone kept prodding me about
my talk. I didn't want to get into it. You don't just say that right
there like that: that my talk was about Affrilachia and how Affrilachia is an enticement for Fink – that's why he hates her so much.
He has to have her, but he can't: the White man no longer has the
power to rape her. And in that sense, he becomes pathetic, not powerful. Of course, he's portrayed as pathetic in the film, but he's more
than that – he's pathetic because he's a true portrait of the

Appalachian activist. The Appalachian activist in pursuit of Appalachian aesthetic politics and all this other black mumbo jumbo is basically in love with the cultural Nazism of black nationalists and other identity politics culture terrorists. And so long as Appalachian activism continues in the manner of black mimicry it is doomed to the pathetic caricature of it portrayed, accurately – unfortunately – in Freshirt's film.

No thanks. I wasn't going to go into all that right there at the bar in Billy Jack's. So we sat and talked about the good old days.

#

I was clear-headed when I gave my speech. Two beers and a whisky at the restaurant and then a nightcap – a double – at home and then bed. No weed. I got up early and packed. Then I went to the auditorium and I gave the closing address:

"My White Brothers. My White Sisters. We got ourselves a Affrilachia problem."

#

When I finished speaking – when the speech was done, at firstnobody clapped. Not at first. No one did anything. It was real quiet as if people really could not believe what they just had heard. For one thing, it was enough to talk about Affrilachia as a text worthy of the serious analysis I give it, but to conclude that it presented an accurate picture of an Appalachian pathetic aesthetic of the Appalachian activist, well that was too much. The first responses were a couple boos. These encouraged more boos, which encouraged a couple claps and that encouraged more claps, which encouraged boos in turn, all of which encouraged the congregation to hold dear enough to the courage of their convictions that they were willing to come to blows about it.

Pandemonium.

253

I slipped out the back and then headed over to my bed and breakfast. Skipping over the cobblestone as light as I could, nonetheless, a knucklehead spots me and starts to come my way. I double my pace, but now he knows it's me and he's coming closer, at least he's not bright enough to call for backup, and it's only a question of time before he does. I walk around a corner a corner too soon, and then walk around the next corner and walk up to a half corner, a driveway, I walk up the driveway and look back, he's not there.

I turn on my heel, head down the other way, and turn the corner again – all clear. I slow my roll, take note. The day is lifting the sky white blue clouds the mountains in the meanwhile majesties marking their time, I turn the next corner, I need to get to my Patriot, and that's at the bed and breakfast, and I need to get back there and then something – well, that's when it occurred to me: if I lose that yahoo, he's sure to go back and spill the beans that Elvis has left the building, and then they might all be waiting for me at the bed and breakfast.

I doubled-back again. Now I was looking for him. I retraced my steps. I stumbled and coughed. Cursed on purpose. Heard his steps. I stood up and started strutting. I was loud enough – he could hear me. I could hear him not far behind. He was coming faster. Good. He should be. I took out my switchblade. He turned the corner. "Listen," I said-

"You are one Benedict Arnold son-of-a-bitch!" he said coming at me, and when he came close enough, I pulled my hand free and put the blade in his belly and turned it, stepped back, slit his neck, and then there was blood everywhere all over me and him, his eyes wide like the first time I had to do this the first time I killed someone only that was a nigger not a White man it was different killing a White man it fucked with me. But I had wanted to do it anyway for a while, if you want the truth I had wanted to see if it felt different than killing a nigger, and believe me, it does.

I ran to my room drenched in the White man's red blood. I put the bloody clothes in a big black trashbag, tied it tight and threw it in the trunk. I power-showered and put on new clothes. I looked out the window, and no mob, no cops, it wouldn't be long, they'd find him soon enough. They probably already had. They'd decide to check on me soon enough too. I got to my Patriot, fired up the vape and took the fuck off, checking social media for updates the whole way down.

By mid-day I'd made Rutherfordton.

Preamble to the "Wellington Requisition" or the "Wellington Compromise" (Feb. 8, 2060)

By Marcus Wellington

My fellow Americans. Our actions have been controversial. Unfortunately, this speech will be even more so. But we are in an unprecedented time, and this is a new morning in America. It is a time for joy. America has faced its difficult and racist past and come out triumphant.

I speak on behalf of the president, and as someone who has worked closely with the White House for the last fourteen years. I have worked with President Cinderblock and President Arabesque. Here is what I can tell you:

When I first started working with President Cinderblock, it was in a completely unofficial manner. He used to ask me for advice. For those of you who are old enough to remember, I began my career as a philosophy columnist for the *New York Times*. I wrote short musings on current events filtered through the lens of my philosophy of Afro-Optimism.

Afro-Optimism simply suggests that we take a kind of Jamesian Pragmatist attitude towards Black social, political and cultural development, which includes helping those among us who are most likely to do the most for the rest of us.

I received a lot of opposition from wokery, especially Black wokery, but that never bothered me, because to my mind, the negativity and pessimism of Black wokery is grounded in self-hate and racist white supremacist ideology, whereas I am – and have been – doing God's work.

President Cinderblock was made aware of my columns, and he appreciated them. He wrote me sometime in June of 2046, right after the Black Revolution. He wanted my opinion - what I thought the best approach would be to dealing with the fallout from the demonstration, riots, what some were calling revolts.

I was happy to help.

To begin with, there never should have been a Black Revolution at all.

The shooting of Marshall Namegamer was a tragedy and that never should have happened either; but that kid had no business taunting the police in the street like that. This is a bitter lesson one must learn from the Black wokery's Afropessimist approach to America. A more optimistic outlook would have led this child to different actions, and he would still be alive today.

Again, and it can not be emphasized enough: This is not to excuse the fact that the police shot him. Indeed, a normal demonstration would have been in order. But that day, that dark day- and if Black wokery wants to argue that January 6, 2021 (remember that?) was an act of terrorism, then May 27, 2046 has to be understood as an act of terrorism as well − on that day Black liberals set us back fifty years.

My advice to President Cinderblock was to do nothing. Any act of retribution would be interpreted as an attack. I proposed a response of non-violence, like Dr. Martin Luther King had promoted, yes, but also a response of non-intimidation, as argued by Finnchrisp Yellowneck. The world would watch and decide for themselves, and reason would prevail. If you simply show people the logical conclusions of their beliefs, the fallacy of those beliefs soon becomes apparent. That March of Intimidation that the Black liberals call a Black Revolution, even if it was peaceful, was clearly not peaceful in its optics, which is why they use language of violence to describe it. A philosopher once said all speech is action, and this was an act of violence, because it played off American symbols of violence − a large assembly of angry Black people arranged like an advancing army and all the while protesting and hectoring the police. Well, of course it ended badly.

By June 1ˢᵗ the rebellion had been all but squashed. There was
no more public support of it. We sent in the military and Black people cheered from their windows. White people cheered from their
windows. Liberal academics who had supported it at first were
forced to go into contortions, bending over backward trying to explain away what had gone wrong with what was essentially a righteous movement.

It just goes to show the hypocrisy.

Cinderblock, on the other hand, was so impressed with the way
that I handled things that he asked me to be part of his cabinet in
2047, when he dismissed the sitting Secretary of Homeland Security, Derek Peckerschnitt, and nominated me for the position. My
controversial confirmation notwithstanding, I feel like I have been
a boon and a benefit to this country. From the get-go I have argued
for an active public presence, where I could address Black people
directly in the wake of the Black Revolution.

I have continued to write my column of course. But now I have
a much larger platform. Many of you may know my book from
2048, *The Black Revolution: Black People Respond*, and that serves, I
think, as a strong Black response to the failures and limitations of
the Black Revolution, even if a lot of Black people don't want my
Black voice to count. Apparently a lot of other people must have
felt the way I do, though. The book stayed on the *New York Times*
bestseller list for twelve weeks.

So that's why I'm here today: Martin Luther King, Ralph Ellison, Albert Murray, Trey Ellis, Cornel West, Walter Sunright. A
powerful tradition. Economist Geoff Slipstream.

Black people understand. And they – we – we are sick and tired,
so damn sick and tired of the Black Revolution movement and of
Black wokery and the fringe radical Black left. We left y'all behind
long ago, we want a return to normalcy. That's why I was such a
vocal supporter of Cinderblock to begin with. The Republicans
weren't putting up much of a fight anyway. Compared to Kletterkater all the new Republican leaders looked weak and bought and

paid for and fake, false reproductions of a Kletterkater that they obviously in no way really resembled. Cinderblock, on the other hand, had wide support. The centrist Democrats, Black community and even old-school Republicans, those old throwbacks from the early part of the twenty-first century supported Cinderblock. People were talking about he had taken race relations into a new era with the way he (we – I should say) handled the Black Revolution Crisis.

So while I condemn the Black Revolution methods of Aggressive Intimidation through the Violent Symbolism of Militant Black Assembly, I applaud Cinderblock's measured and lifesaving response to the negative reaction of an equally guilty police department.

I was happy to work with Cinderblock, was glad he had consulted me. We made a lot of progress. Cinderblock issued a lot of executive orders that allowed us to maneuver through Congress. We had all three branches, and we had a few sympathetic Republicans, old-schoolers, and then some new generation new thinkers who resembled the old thinkers, or maybe they were just a new wave of the old Libertarian Party. We were able to seize on the optimism of those years that was in line with the vision of Barack Obama and Lena Powers instead of the negative cynical vision in the legacy of Donald Trump and Morgan Kletterkater. After that we passed some significant legislation to address what we saw as structural problems in society, racial included. We were able to work with the Black Lives Matter movement and we were even able to work with AAGRAO and we were able to recruit some of the top writers, musicians and artists of our time including such luminaries as Orbital Johnson, Sandra Helmsworth, and Yz7snone. It's incredible when you think about it: we were able to co-opt radical culture and mainstream center politics and merge them and come to a consensus where everyone was happy. We got some pushback from the Black Revolution Leftists, of course, but for the most part, I would say that the remarkable achievement of the Cinderblock administration is that it managed to achieve the Lockean liberal democratic ideal that is the very aim and zeal of progress.

Everyone remembers the hashed-up controversy over Cinderblock's third term. As has been noted time and again, by every legal standard he had the right to serve another term, seeing as how he had taken office May 26, 2046, two years into Powers' term. In any case, the matter was decided in the courts and it was decided in favor of Cinderblock. I mention this in passing tonight for reasons which will soon become clear.

Afrodeutsch in Affrilachia (2129)

by Jacqueline Black

nach May Ayims *blues in schwarz-weiss* (1995)

Introductions

Let's skip introductions – they always too much – much better to say a little something at the end instead – Afrodeutsch in Affrilachia. It's like a palimpsest of contradictions.

Jazz

Did you hear that jazz band play up on the highroad the other day? They came marching through as the sun cut sideways and orange in the sunset day, they played "All of Me" and they marched through the sunlight like Billie Holiday be leading the procession herself, queen Billie.

Afro-Deutsch I

Black and German? Well, that's cool, that's like – oh, I don't know, I think of an intellectual brother out there like W.E.B. Du Bois way back in the day. The mustache for it and all that. Black and German? Well, okay. What – you? I don't know. Black and German? Where you from originally. Germany? Africa?? America??? You don't speak German, do you? That's some funny shit, a Black person talking German. Somehow it don't seem like it should fit.

Black and White Blues

sometimes I get the blues in black and white like devs, like nights sitting in front of the dev with the lights out and an old Black & White on the dev, something you surely have never in your natural life seen. I watched a blues in black and white the other night and the world was black and white, there were black and white people, and they were shadowed and defined by the light. the blues players were black but the audience was white – well, mostly white. there were black people there too, they were in the audience and they weren't just black they were blue. too. sometimes I get the blues in black and white like devs.

Thunderstorms in the Appalachians

When it rains in the Appalachians it is like the submissions it is all *sturm und drang* and the bottles roll downhill and remind us of Manhattan remember Manhattan? The storms came and swallowed it up and the Lowlanders wondered- that's when they started coming up to the mountains and settling. Can you imagine being colonized in the twenty second century?

That's how they did us they

Came and slowly they colonized us because what else do you do when the sky is burning and the seas are swelling and the electricity is frying like live wires burning in Brooklyn on such

A day I came timbling out fumbling light eyes making sense of the storm.

There they were a woman and a man and a screaming child in turn.

And the Lowlander coming up the mountain looking to colonize.

Mutkamatke

Mutkamatke is what I call my mother because she is the color of the earth

Black Cliché from Back in the Day

My dad was a Black cliché from back in the day like they used to say he disappeared and that was by the time I was ten.

To be honest I don't remember when

He was there and then

He wasn't anymore; my mother and I am sometimes perplext by my early poems about him they sing his praises as though he were glory on high and then I do understand them after all.

The harsh years with my mother broke my back like an old slave woman carrying her sack like the old sorrow songs and a father could be an invention and intervention. A solution. Alchemy.

Like poetry. And then one day when I was much older in college or so or maybe just in the hills of Appalachia I ran into him one day in a bar, it was Andrew's that much I know, no it was Billy Jack's

And there he was I knew it was him because I had been sketching him in poetry for years and besides how many German-speaking Affrilachians do you see on dill? So I approached him in the corner sliding slants of sun and motes the mottled Billy Jack's *Papa ich weiß dass du mich erkennst* and he turns slow and strange in the light and smiles like we done had a drink the day before

How ya doing? He says in his most obnoxious Lowlander and I hate him because I am poeticizing his face and it is incongruous with all those other sonorous words, the banal smile lacking understanding cohesion how he hurt made me feel I was always and in constant construction contortions of how he could not be just as he sat here indeed

Clueless and absurd

Afro-Deutsch II

Nigga you aint Black. Who hasn't heard about all that? And besides, intersectionality. You have to remember what it's like for all of us here in Appalachia. I mean how it has been especially since the Lowlanders started to come on up and colonize. So we're a displaced colonized people too now I feel you I feel part of your struggle my Negress I stand with you I am you

Social Conjunct

Race is a social conjunct. Like mother and father. Like running a race to escape the past where you can't escape the past your past is always part of you haunting your race and your racial lineage, you can't outrace the past- you can't erase it the past it is still a part of your race like mother and father a social conjunct.

zeitenwechsel

Sight

Learning to see in a season of seas where all around the waters rise and we all rise together. We were together forever and yet it was just a couple years a couple blurry wonderful years where you would come honking up the old hill down where you were in the independent city of Salem to where I lived in downtown Roanoke and I would laugh and call you a Lowlander as though

Though we talked all the time and we went and would drink in downtown bars and listen to patch groove and groove and get funky like we had all the time in the world in the meantime the time was running out but we didn't see it happening the time sliding by like seasons like cities in the successions of rains where the Lowlanders turned vicious in the rising sea

Which we also didn't see couldn't see the evil in the heart of humans we were so innocent we saw only each other though we didn't see each other we saw through each other like seeing through the sea as it streams from the clouds loud and alone and standing together over the independent city of Salem saying you are a Lowlander as though

For Melinda, April 2127

Dialogue in a Mirror

so, old fool, aren't you going to wait around to see yourself fail?

which catches me mid sentence looking momentarily up.

on the old schoolyard outside the window children are playing base-ball. the sun and gray clouds swim between each other. there's a tree to the left where a girl and a boy are sitting on a low branch, arguing.
the strangely unexpected question gives me a good reason to put down my pen.
to see myself fail?
spring in Appalachia is strange.
when I was as young as those children out there I would make up stories by myself. I used to play ten different roles by myself. never one for the traditional sports, never even good at them, I could've been both the boy and the girl in the tree over there and maintained

271

an even angrier argument.
which doesn't answer the question.
it presupposes something, that question. like in a momentary glance
up and through the window I came to an epiphany and a resolve.
which doesn't answer the question...
so I must've come to an epiphany and resolve.

which doesn't answer the question.
the children are cheering. one of the little boys comes running
across the home plate.
and didn't even know it.
the cheering stops and for a while, everything goes quiet.
I've asked myself this question before, after all. something in the
children triggered a thought.
the children are happier; never a moment like the last.
and to use the word fail, as if there were something like fate.
or to not use it, and ignore the probability.
probability? when I was as young as those children out there I used
to travel all the way into the edges of the rising lowlands with my
father. he'd make up stories on the way up and stories on the way
back, all out to get an ice cream cone from our favorite shop. The
ice cream run we called it and
the little boy who just came across the plate will never amount to
anything.
such delightful improvisations they'd be a lifetime of inspiration.
after all, he too, will be a suicide.
aren't you going to wait around to see yourself fail?

For Abby, September 2112

Shifts in Time

On Mondays it's Carolina Cotton Kunta Oochie Walla. It gets the
week going. A little oochie walla action in the late morning on my

bike through downtown Roanoke I turn a corner on the third level of floor five and there she be kunta oochie walla. The coffee wafts and hums with the memory of the morning with Carolina on a bike looking down at the waters and there she be kunta oochie walla.

On Tuesday I bike to Mayhem%! Rawyer-lawyer kill Tom Sawyer! Angles on buildings sharpen, boiler, the sun becomes much brighter. Slanting against the town and the sound of the dev the aggression of Lowlanders becomes manageable, Rawyer-lawyer kill Tom Sawyer! A logic of image and myth can turn cities into gateways to nuclear meltdown like ancient Babylon.

Wednesday melancholy with Millli. Olousoo or Poor Plate reverberating voices ghosts windtunnels buildings labyrinths city landscapes. Ghosts memories my youth, halfway through the week — halfway through life? Halfway home, change your mind, charge your mind mind the dev the dev does the dev dev devises dervishes.

Thursday I get silly and listen to Lily Lollipopz. Then I change my mind on my last minute out the door and transform the day with *Shall Flags Where Flags Don't Follow?* Appalachia is Affrilachia in Black and White! Girls and boys walking hand in hand anticipating the weekend. Beautiful is what you say you say do say and the independent city of Roanoke like a shining beacon on a hill come here and give me kiss can you blow the blasé into bliss?

Friday I choose Black Prokofiev because I like to Black the voices. It's my Friday theme: Eshu seeks her victim. She laughs at disasters and smiles at strangers. The sun down and the moon up, and Black Prokofiev spreads they devolving message like the way the rains came running down down on the Lowlanders down down down down-low oh the woe.

Sometimes I see people sitting in a quiet no cynical silence on the cylindars and wonder how they let this city sabotage the solace of the solitary courts of their mind. It's a harsh, violent, unfriendly, unstrange, strange music, the music of these mountain towns. It threatens to snatch your sanity. Shifts in time maintain and defamiliarize in beautiful dissonance all the silent mountainous roar.

For Sara, March 2118

About Face

I first saw you as you say you were staring into a futch dev which was slanting in a shiny slight angle along the corner where your dimples frowned in the sun and caught the glare of your glasses. Your brown face a marvel a light sun in the night of Appalachia I yearned up to

You and you and I walked and talked through the morning with the winks of your face peeking out behind every second rhyme of your words juxtaposed to mine. I saw the way your smile could turn and tune like sundials, making the day fade away in shadows or play in splays of sun and the look

You gave me sometimes glancing back after our arguments your frown like a wink where I knew and when we both started laughing these were the moments where your fascinating face brought me back through ages they are a saga of

You and your mother and your father and of Billie and of history and of the way that we are a manic depression of contradictions and conflictions running past the Lowlander drama and past what the dev tells us about the catastrophe of the twenties and what we know about the too thousands and the birth of modernity baby you are the birth of modernity to you it has to be

You your face your lovely brown face squinting in the sun so hard the tears come and when the dev glares gold against your glasses it makes your tears splendor like amethyst.

For Sunny, March 2121

In the dev in your head

In the dev in your head I would wonder where you were sometimes in the dev in your head can I watch with one time?

In the dev in your head I would wonder why you sometimes looked the way you looked at me like you saw me reflected through the reflections reacting against the dev in your head the way you said and you said and you said

In the dev in your head I would wonder who you were thinking about sometimes sometimes we would talk about your family about your father who was ever there and sometimes too there and then there was your mother who absented herself sometimes too absent and then you sitting in front of the device and wondering what you were thinking I think of Richard Wright wondering aloud

In the dev in your head say it loud I'm Black and I'm proud I would wonder when you would come around to thinking of me there next to you looking at you looking at the dev looking past the dev of course to all those mirrors and surfaces where the surface still can never be broken like Lowlanders lying low for you in the bushes waiting

In the dev in your head I would wonder what the fuck I was thinking standing here with you on your constant vacations floating free like a boat adrift in the newly made seas heading to countries total un- awares where you going I don't know but I do know that I don't

know what the fuck you were thinking or what the fuck I was thinking either in the dev in the device

In the dev in your hand I would sometimes wonder how to reach
you across so many screens and so much time in contemplation of
incompletion like a signal finally lost.

For Denise, Easter 2124

The Farewells

First I tell the dev because I can't tell anyone else and I fold it into
the dev's memory and then I think about what else I might tell it
and then I think about the fact that I am only all that I remember
and I fold those memories into the dev and then I tell the dev what
I don't even tell myself I mean I tell my dev my pieces of poetry
although they are still

Largely unformed: I get dressed fret in the mirror in the morning
and think about the morning that I did that with the dev and then
smile and wave and she smiles and waves back at me and then we
head out into the broken day with the sky lit up muddy brown like
the waters they reflect at the bottom where the Lowlanders came
up like creatures from the swamp all this negativity I think

Went into the dev and then the dev starts to futch and fragment

And

       I

It's been a helluva year and I am crayoning on the floor with lipstick
while crying and then the old dev blinks and chirps from the other
room and when I go back into the past where the other room is lit
up in a blue gold metal sheen there she is

Suddenly

And

       I

Am smiling at me though the dev one

By one

The pieces of Me

Come Back through the dev

Reflected black and white chiaroscuro through the light

Words I recorded and come back in a Poem

About You.

For Anne, March 9, 2122

2074

Everyday the table moves a little closer to the dev. Sooner or later one of them will have to go. Behind the dev the window threatens the same. Isn't it better to be sucked into the world instead of phantasmagoria? Possibly both, and neither; there's been evidence they are the same.

The dev never jumps. It is lifeless, like life, lifeless also, though bent towards two flashing screens, never disclosed, but hastened to again, foretold to other eyes on some other screen; or so they say.

Best, then, to put the dev out the window; to put the table out the window, the dev leaping at last. It's not the luddite's leap of faith. It's more extraordinary than that, and less. After all we would board up the windows.

But my head is still two monitors. One of them says I must listen to the loop, and the other one says you must listen to voices. What do I say? There is no I, when I am other, a teenage girl, a grown woman, a phantom limb, a visionary's bitch.

It's been a long ride, sister, and I wonder as I wander. Hope to see you at the crossroads, too. Well, don't count on it. I already been down and back. But that was a long time ago, and besides, what kind of fool expects Scratch to hold up his end of the bargain?

Me, that's who. You.

thereaftertime

HELEN

Already eighteen and we are still at home in the old yellow house on Hollister, Helen and I, where the sun is blending deep red orange shadows into a rising evening hue and we are listening to "Pursue" on the dev and you are talking about how the margaritas taste like the sunset and we stop a moment to laugh, vaping inbetween beats and then

It's nineteen now and we are on our way out the door which means we are busy at home for another hour, while I finish a final sunset and while looking for my keys pour another and then you are checking the address on your dev and then you are distracted because of some other other shit and then I am distracted by the dev too and then you pour another sunset, because we need a minute anyway and then

It's twenty and we are biking down the hill to the strip where we end up at Affrilachia in Little Affrilachia and drink wine with a light dinner because you can't have girls night out without a little something to eat first it's where we meet up with Dawn and Sherry and Teresa and it's our usual treffpunkt because where else can such a diverse group of brown girls come together and just feel okay and no pressure and no weirdness the Lowlanders even they don't bother with Little Affrilachia because they never bothered to find out about it in the first place and then

It's twenty-one and we are finished eating and having brandies all around don't ask it's a tradition and it is an homage to an obscure old dev show about a Black girl and so we all drink brandy and then we head out into what is a perfect summer night with the stars over Appalachia peeking out of a boldening blue black evening glowing ever brighter like midnight settling devs and then

It's twenty-two and we are at the first club of the night Jook which is also in Little Affrilachia and we listen to Jericho which isn't my favorite, but Helen loves Jericho and most of her favorite artists are Jericho so Jericho it is and the artists at Jook are always unknown and underground and obscure the rawest grainiest strangest Jericho you ever heard and then in a quiet scary and sometimes really sad way too which is why it can put you in some kind of mood and then

It's twenty-three and it's exxxxxxtra good so we decide to stay a little longer and we order more drinks and now we're exxxxxtra woozy and in great moods and laughing and talking through the Jericho like it's all aint nobody's business and then the boom boom I am rewinding the moment the moment strange as it allows it and then the boom boom I am rewinding the moment the moment strange as it allows it and then the boom boom and then

It's null and we are walking through Little Africchalia and we go to

Afreek still in LA because we aren't ready to deal with Appalachia proper right yet and besides after all that Jericho I think it might be good to hear something a little more my thing and Teresa's taste too Teresa has that taste which is what they play at Afreek – Kosmetika and there we can bounce and lounge and dance and the walls are all spread into space and the room is black lit silver so it's like there are no walls you are just there in space and with sofas and low tables and loungers and the music breathes and swoons and moans and nightlarks along the way that music ought to do you and you do you and then

It's one in the morning in Afreek and Dawn is devving with some dude she met here in the club and then Teresa has taken something and she is way inside the music and Sherry is sitting on a sofa at a low table somewhere and there I am a little bored and tense and restless and ready to ruck the fuck off and then

It's two in the morning and we are walking through downtown Ro-anoke proper and there's the Savoy, the biggest club in Roanoke and in we go we go to the Savoy all the time everyone does but it isn't LA and so there are problems sometimes with that but that is America and that is damn ether Affrilachia and so in we go and they're playing Coxxß00z and I am definitely not a fan but on they go on they own wannabe Jericho fusion parade and after that they play Otheeer and that is arguably even worse and when after that they put on Porclöne Helen can't help herself, she says loud as she can help it right there as we're waiting at the bar trying to hail the bartender and get drinks and here he is going to blondie and bambi and becky and karen and kim and debbie and gabby, but he don't even cast a blick back at us Black girls and so Helen says it loud as HELEN THIS FUX THEY PLAY HERE IS POOR WHITE IM-ITATION GARBAGE WHITE APPALACHIAN INFERIOR-ITY SHIT RIGHT DOWN TO THE LAST FAKE ASS WAIL and then

It's gegen three in the morning and three white boys have pinned HELEN to the bar and they are screaming and waving and flailing like auto salesman dummies and they are spitting their spittle in her face through their putrescent breath and they are calling her cunt and bitch and nigger bitch and say she stink like a nigger fart and they croon coon and Dawn and Teresa and Sherry and I push in and we are all taken hostage by heavy white arms and the bartender glowers at us and then on comes LLorren7 and that is all they can do when LLoren7 goes rap her up plug plug glue grip grand gestures of greatness and they chant along with his uncanny chanting rap rap plug plug and then HELEN is dragged out the chanting door and we are held helpless hostage and then

It's four in the morning and we are sitting under arrest in the police station and the killers are free to go and and and HELEN is dead

Queen Billie

Queen Billie, regal queen came up the hill one day and lounging on the colonial ray of Ra that was her usual way she gandered about the Appalachians with her steel eyes and with her mind a bit gamboled through the possibilities and decided quite decidedly that here could be a community that here could be a we

Afrodeutsch in Appalacchia begins this way back when but Billie turned it into a movement she was the movement behind the measurement of every minute we endeavored to discover what it meant when Billie brought with her an Afrodeutsch community that had always existed disparate in the diaspora of Afrodeutsch Affrilachia.

Roanoke was the center and there in the center Billie and her cohorts came up with a little arts center where they would meet once a week and share work and discuss ideas and drink too much kraft bier and come up with plans for how Afrodeutsch Affrilachian

women might take over the world. And take over the world we did
my women

out da frame

Out da Frame

Helen you would go and do something wild out da frame like go
and get yourself killed I would I would I would walk around the
now how house remembering replaying reliving that night and
thinking rethinking reconfiguring in my memory where how why
what when who Helen you would go and do

Something wild out da frame like leave me here in a wild misery
where I am coming out of my framework I would I would I would
walk around the now how house and listen to the songs we always
used to listen to and die in the dev and again in the dev dissolve and
devolve in the Jericho of the dev which I don't love Jericho but you
would you thought Jericho was

Out da frame like Affrilachia before you were gone we would we
would we would walk around the town and down into LA and then
back up downtown and you were the bravest of us all wouldn't let
the Appalachians break you out da frame and here we all broken
and standing there watching while you were all wit and words while
we bore witness why Helen you would go and do

Something like break me out the frame I would I would I would

Dev Life

Dev life is never life dev life is lifelessness itself it is the constant day
in day out of voices and opinions and suggestions and content and
management and dev divisions and the day dives down in the

282

devilish glow of the dev give me your dev do you have your dev what did you do today not much just devved

You get the dev life you deserve, my dev day goes a way a little like so I say to myself in the morning that today wont be a dev day and then I dev right away the first part of the day through breakfast and while reading the dev and then while getting ready for the rest of the day I even bring her in the shower with me and then it's out into the wonderful Appalachian early afternoon where I hang out with Sherry and Dawn and Teresa and together we dev and have brunch and drink mimosas until four in the afternoon when the sun is going awry and a suspect sunset orange on the horizon against the Shenandoah azure and then you

Go home and listen to more of the dev and watch and read and dive more of the dev and then you go back out and this time the sun has already schlempped behind the mountains and the night is out and the small stars are announcing themselves ARMIES! and you compose poems to yourself and dev them upload like

There is sometimes a mythology
Beneath the small blue
Stars obscure sounds thrum an ancient rhythm
And each step reopens
The world a lost and happy child
Keeping pace with the cool and wandering night.

The vastness of eveything when we are alone!
Even beneath the electric glare of the city, we can
Slip between the people
Into those places
Where the world our dreams hangs as
Sacred as asleep.

And you are the dev and the dev are you and one and then it's like

I say you get the dev you deserve you even go to bed with your dev
still on you get the dev you

Lowlander Ascension

The rains started in the morning and the sky went deep gray and
the day went deep cold although it was the start of spring and the
last couple weeks had been warm had presaged spring even and
Punxsutawney Phil hadn't seen his shadow so everyone was expecting spring, I had even gone up there with my mother and father
that February, we made a long six hour road trip north to
Punxsutawney and watched the groundhog rise and look and everybody cheered.

The rains continued through the afternoon and the forecast was
calling for warm weather just a slight chance of rain but a chance is
always a chance so we sat collectively in the mountains and watched
as the rain came down on the independent city of Roanoke and
some of us baked pies or drank beer or glotzed the dev or played
games or just did a rain dance because some people really did love
the rain.

The rain kept coming up off shores and then something unexpected
happened something must have cracked the rain kept getting worse
and then there were exports of tornadoes all along the East Coast
and the lower part of Manhattan was almost like winding canals
through these Gotham alleys and we watched in terrific disbelief as
the cities began to swamp over one by one when Washington began
to ooze greasy muck from its underbelly like a metaphor and as
New York continued to sink and then as Miami disappeared and

The rain kept coming like God never meant it the fire next time or
the fire next time had arguably come and gone and the flood again
this time and we would see on the dev about Lowlanders who were

building arks like old Noah himself and some of them even trying to build up zoos on them and others floating libraries and others floating museums and others floating younameit suddenly there were arks and everywhere there were arks and

The rain kept coming. Some days gave brief respite, but something must have cracked because it was suddenly tornado season on the East Coast in the spring and not even summer and the tornados kept coming one after the next one week of breathing an easy wet sky of grey threats and then the next two weeks tornado after tornado as spring turned into summer the rains got worse and the tornadoes fiercer and the wind wilder and then when big buildings in New York started and scientists began shouting told ya so told ya but yall didn't hear me though like Cassandra and the

Rain kept right on coming and then the arks began bobbing up towards the mountains and someone somewhere some bright young Harvard grad probably with a wonderful job in a Lowlander business firm in some sinking East Coast city decided there was plenty of unsunken land in the mountains in Appalachia where no one really lived anywho and

The Lowlanders started coming. Some of the old folks get dramatic and say they came all at once like a wave from the waters below and lapped over the land but it wasn't quite like that I remember how it started at first suddenly in all the rainy confusion there were more Lowlanders in town and I remember distinctly because at first they were pleasant and I had always heard how horrible they were those Lowlanders, but no they were rather nice and

The Lowlanders kept coming and suddenly there were quite a bit more of them than I had ever been used to and they were all up in the grocery stores and they were all up in the churches and they were promenading the streets of Appalachia like they had never done before and then rains kept coming and the water kept rising and

The Lowlanders kept coming too and we knew something had gone askew when the prices started rising like the waters when suddenly the jobs started drying up and suddenly Appalachians couldn't afford to live in Appalachia anymore and we started moving out to lower lying territory started moving south started sinking while the Lowlanders rose the

Lowlander Ascension that's what they call it but we call it the Beast from out of the Sea.

Black n White Blues

Response to Theme for English B (circa 2129)

I got your response and I want you to hear I appreciate what you said I feel you on a deep level even tho I never been there, so I hope you feel that too, in this

My response to you.

I want you to know that I am not so free
As I seem to be which you seem to see you say
After all slightly and
It is slightly so, still I see what you mean how

There is then a disconnect where there should be a
Connection between us and I get that this is all because
Of societal secessions that society has made and so has been made subservient
Sorry scratch the word

Though the world does not stand in Power
As your people should and do.

Though and I say this with all confidence that you will take this
with confidence returned
That I am a man of deep respect
For your people and I

Am an Ally and I
As an Ally
Am always on your side. And so it seems to me

That the only

Thing that gets in the way of the power of the movement
Is the focus on the Identity
There is no more Identity We

Are people as One.

And when you insist on Identity, I –
As a white guy -

Baldwin said I will call myself Black
So long as you call yourself White
Well I have long loudly renounced the Whiteness

Yet you still call yourself Black

I want to call you sister and
You curse when where I stand
When I do and so I open wide my hands
Your words are weapons and you use them adeptly so

My friend, my sister, let them go!

The Revolution Devized

Affrilachian Appalachian
Lowlander Highlander
The Beast from the sea
The Loa of Intersectionality
Appalachian Affrilachian
Black and White Blues

On How They Turned Helen Dev

Everyone saw Helen dev everyone
Talked about it it was all the dev all the time
And then before you know it HELEN
Is a TRADEMARK
A BRAND
A CONCEPT that plays into poetry
Of advertising a
Cynical aesthetic
And there are shows about HELEN
And talk about HELEN
And devtime is HELEN
And everyone has an idea about HELEN
Black Chant too
God Help Me
And you.

I am deep in dev
And there she is HELEN in a verbung
IT is old dev media but they broadcast

Broadcast it all the same the everyone
Saw Helen dev
And I am deep in dev

Devizing a plan about taking back

What's ours I started I am
Dev poetry
Bitch

HELEN is dead, long
Live Helen.

Your Hand in Mine

Brooklyn

The three times my three times
Three times in Brooklyn work
Like the way the city's history divides
Into three marks there is
Before the War
And After the War
And After the Floods
Which were worse than the war which of course was rather
Civil

Sister against sister
Man against Man
And all that sham

There was Brooklyn Before the Flood too
Or the two other periods of Brooklyn, back when Manhattan was
Before the Brooklyn I saw

The first visit was when I was a girl
With my parents
It was vacation

And it was
Wonderful first Prospect Park we toddled
Through the green with snowcones and the city
On all sides hummed like the floods had
Never come

And the second time I went it was
With a fieldtrip – fieldtrip
To Brooklyn – a week in the city
And a week in a Brooklyn hotel
And a week away from home
No Dad no Mom
With the restaurants in Fulton Square
And the devs everywhere like the
City was all corridors of devs
And different dimensions
And then the afternoon at Greenfield
Cemetery, where
The past comes and gets you like swing down sweet chariot
I groped through names in that greenfield
Cemetery devving names
And dates
And days

And the third trip
Was after Helen died
When I went to meet with
When I went to meet with
When I went to meet with

The Independent City of Roanoke

When I wake up woke up
Shook up from last night

At the armory
The shouting and the
Harmony

I walked out onto the porch where the morning
Lifted the mountains in a spring dandelion mist
The day's ballasts.

Afternoon at the Acquaintance
Had an overblown salad and a glass
Building caught our reflection
And your bright brown smile.

I walked the short way to the Lark
While the sun kept short company
Behind me my angled shadow,
The lean of my hair blends to elongate my nose.

Ain't ya mama
On the pancake box?

My Seven Loas

Three in the back and four
To the fore
I have I have I have
Seven Loas who send me

Seven Loas the first one who
When I wake up the day is new
This Loa sings the loa brings the
Morning and new attitudes,
This lovely Loas called the blues

Loa Two is louder she
Shouts all over the house
And runs up and down the walls
Sometimes goes Poe and tears up the floors She is
Helen
And I don't know why she's still here
She is still teaching me why and
So Helen
Is Loa
Too.

Loa Three is a dreaming European
An African assimilated He is
Ever so pensive he sips
His espresso and dreams and He
Is the Loa of My Blinkered Black Logic
I can't shake him
And he can't shake

Loa Four – I know you've heard this one before
Loa Four frowns at my failures
But boy does she make me laugh
She says oh no oh no oh no you've done it again we're
Laughing to keep from crying
Sometimes
We're laughing all the same
And she is the Loa
Of Affrilachia

The Loa of the Lowlanders
That's what I call it
Loa five
SHE

Is an angry righteous sista
She will fuck u up.
She makes me blind with fury until
I ascend and
Levitate
IN FIRE

Purified my pure
Black pussy is Loa number
Six
She is
And you're there shocked cuz
I don't talk that way
But I just
Did
Bitch

Loa Number Seven
Is if I could forgive Helen

Affrilachian Night Rag

Don't ya darling make ya squiggle
Wiggle wobble and you quibble
At the difference don't ya
Give a damn ya
Goddamn right you
Do

Don't ya darling make ya holler
All the night oh lawd and yonder
On Beyond the Mountain Laws
Don't ya darling Don't

She sholly make me holler
Make the stars start up to wander
And the way she make me make me
Say
I do

Don't ya darling make
Ya Laugh and Lean
Laugh and Lean well looking mean
All the words she got cold chills

Harriet Tubman dollar bills
Don't ya Laugh and Lean
I mean

Don't ya darling
Starlings makes me wanna cry
Wanna holler squiggle quibble Laugh and Lean
All night.

Starlings in the sky.

Brief

When I met you up in Harlem last week I never knew a New
York girl would like be my thang I think
I devved about and around you all the next day
And then the afternoon came crawling through the sides of the
Wide white curtains and you called

Damn we got down like
Affrilachia and Kemeta
And we carried the hours
Away that daft afternoon

On the phone
So the evening
Announced itself
Like a shroud
Cameroonian mosaics

The sky collapsing in colors
Orange and black and a deep bleed
Red and the green shimmer
The horizon and the waters
Arise

We organized
We recruited
We built
We Black and we American and one of us Harlem
The other Affrilachian
So we were able to put shit together
A following down there in Harlem
With the waters crawling the island
Manhattan
Time talisman of the tides
And what it warned would betide.
And you sleepy on the phone
And me sleepily alone
Where we said our goodnights
Somewhere plodding through the morning
As the birds in song and blues
Arise

Resistance

They say Naked
Lunch was named

After what was left
On your fork at
The End
of the Day
You are
What you eat

I waded the waters like Jesus, The Independent City of Richmond
little Venice
Canals and
Weed
Like Amsterdam
I waded the waters like Jesus.

We formed an armed resistance
And the waters came down
It felt like
40 Days and 40 Nights oh Lawd
The waters came down
The Flood Next Time

I waded the waters like Jesus
I waded my way to your bay
I looked you blank in the way and I say

You coming or what?

We waded the waters like women
Are wont to do
We waded our way over to the ward by the
Wharf where we
Would meet.

We formed an armed resistance.
They say Naked
Lunch was named

By a cynic and murderous
Misogynist they say
At The End
of the Day
You are
What you eat

SHOUT OUTS

First of course to
HELEN
Who built this edifice
My poetry
She made me
Poet Activist
Affrilachianist

Then Dawn
The mourning morning
Where we turned around all morning
In all types of tears

Sherry I compare thee
To an Affrilachian Autumn
In Little Affrilachia
Where the mountains
And the morning sun
Mingle with the clouds and
Trees and cast orange and green
Shadows on
Brown faces

And Teresa for you nothing
But kisses and hugs
All day long dear heart
And soul
We were all there and we
Built this thing it is
Helen's legacy The
Affrilachian Uprise.

$$\rule{12cm}{1.5pt}$$

East Coast Flooding (2100)

by Jeffrey Simble

SimbleDev.01.2100.998.23

$$\rule{12cm}{1.5pt}$$

I caught up with Edmund Gulch at his geodesic dome in Ruth-erfordton on a rainy Monday afternoon in June. I had never been in a g-dome before, but it was wide and huge and dizzying like walk-ing into the Death Star, and we walked up the stairs against the walls and he showed me the various rooms in the house, then headed down the other side of the dome, down the stairwell down the other side and descended into a study area, divided off with bookshelves and a large desk, where Gulch took a seat, and offered me one directly across from him. Still old fashioned to a fault, he took out two scotch tumblers and poured us each a pour before we got started.

Gulch's story begins in Chicago in 2049. As a solid Midwest-erner, and as a city-kid he never really thought about Appalachia in his youth, except in the abstract. Then, just as he was looking at colleges, the rains started. He had been thinking about De Paul, because he wanted to stay in Chicago, but then the rains started, and there was constant flooding, and backed up plumbing and after a while, Chicago started to lose its luster.

"It was a process," Gulch said. "I didn't think – I couldn't imag-ine leaving Chicago at first, but then there were just all these little things. The weather, first off. It rained constantly. And then the days it didn't rain, it was just cloudy and muggy and the humidity hung like heatwaves in the air and you couldn't escape it. It drove everyone in the city batty. People still wear bandanas like bank rob-bers there, you know. That never stopped after the twenties-pan-demic, so it really turned into a kind of post-apocalyptic neo-sci-fiwestern dystopia where the law just had collapsed under the weight of the city's mythology, history and present-crises."

Gulch started broadening his search for schools. "My interest was in digital media, and the digital humanities," he said. "So that's what I was looking for. De Paul had a great program, but I broadened my horizons."

That's how he came across Racial Mountain College, a small college tucked away hidden in Appalachia and twenty minutes from Asheville, North Carolina. "Like mountain retreat – that's where the name comes from," Gulch explained. "And it really is idyllic. And there was no problem with the rain or with flooding, and it was like a vacation from life – so different from the frenetic, post-apocalyptic energy of Chicago. I loved it right away."

When I asked him if he knew what he wanted to study all along, he hesitated. "I knew I wanted to do something in the digital humanities. The field was fairly new then – it was basically still replacing the traditional English degree that universities used to offer – then there was all sorts of other stuff happening back then. I mean there weren't even any DH-forecasters – that was a field that was wide open – or was just opening up at the time. Especially when you think about people like Orville Mendelmind, well, he was working on forecast models that would break the field open. But all that came later."

In fact, if anyone can be credited with bringing DH-forecasting into the public eye, it's Gulch himself. For years, DH-forecasting was something that a small number of professionals did somewhat quietly, and most people had never even heard of the profession.

"It's the type of job – well, you only know about it if you're in the field," Gulch said. "Because there's nothing flashy or sexy about it. You sit there and develop algorithms that offer up predictive models, and it's very cool and it's actually really creative, although in a math-y kind of way, which makes it even cooler. Because you see just on how many levels mathematics operates – when you start to analyze algorithms like that."

As Gulch explains it, algorithms are like rhizomes, an idea he takes from Giles and Deleuze. These are connecting strands that interweave indefinitely. They form a web, much like the web of information online, where rabbit holes lead to rabbit holes lead to wormholes. An idea he borrows from Quitchard.

"So, it's a question of multiple universes, the multiverse, and which version of it you want to choose, and after a while it becomes eerily creepy, because you realize you're not just writing history in reverse, but you're also writing it in advance. Right? I mean, there's the cliché that history is always written by the victors, but what about people who write the future histories in advance? Well, that's what DH-forecasters do, and so after a while it just got to the point where I thought there was something deeply immoral about the job – the profession – hell, the calling – it being so secret and clandestine."

"And how accurate are the DH-forecaster models? Are they really that accurate? Because I think about something like the weather. Right? And I mean, they still can't even get that right, so how accurate can DH-forecasting be?"

As Gulch explains it, DH-forecasting isn't about accuracy. "It's not about being right at all. It's about knowing predictive percentages and then making decisions based on those predictive models. So, it's much different than weather reporting where the forecaster gives predictive models for weather patterns, and then you have to decide whether to bring an umbrella or not – no, the DH-forecaster develops hundreds of thousands of predictive models based on an array of algorithms, and then from there, does large data calculations of those models, so that you're left with infinite possibilities, and to each of those possibilities, probability percentages, which can be wildly misleading because we – humans, I mean – we don't really intuitively understand percentages."

"How do you mean?"

"I mean, percentages are purely mathematical models. They are entirely abstract. So when we think about something being 50 percent – so percent chance of snow, for example, well that doesn't mean anything to us – it will either snow or it won't – anyone can say that any day of the year. But it means a very specific thing to an algorithm and it is an important part of any larger equation or algorithm."

"So give me a specific example. What was something you worked on?"

"Well most of the work goes unseen. But the big one of course – the one everyone knows about is the Downtown Manhattan project. But that is fairly emblematic of the work I was doing at the time and am still doing to a certain extent. We basically just fed predictive models into the app and we tried to make sense of the results in a concrete manner. And in the case of the Downtown Manhattan Project, well it was largely based on the population patterns of Downtown and then the geography of it too, as well as questions as to how the storms would hit and how the island would start to flood. And that's when we stumbled on something we hadn't expected, but it appeared too high a percentage in too many predictive models to ignore and so we had to explore it. This was basically the idea that Williamsburg would be the first to flood and it would develop over decades into a kind of mini-Venice in Brooklyn. So I published that article in *Time*."

"That kind of made you into a name."

"Look, I had fun with that article. At the end of the day it's basically just a fluff piece, because it's like I said, any given prediction in a predictive model is relatively unimportant; but I wanted to write something a little imaginative, where I was like, okay, what would this mini-Venice in Brooklyn look like, and what type of people are we going to see living there? So I just went through a bunch of predictive models, and I basically wrote myself a short story, if we're going to be completely honest about it. Pure fiction."

"But that's the thing – it was based on science."

"Then maybe it was science fiction." Gulch pauses to vape, which he does constantly, not quite nervously, coolly, actually, but constantly. He smiles. "I was really surprised by the reaction it got. I was elated. I'll be honest. That's why I published it in *Time* in the first place, but I didn't think it would viralize the way it did."

"But I don't really believe you thought it was a fluff piece either."

"No, not that either, exactly. I don't know exactly what it was. Only a way of making some concrete sense of it maybe. Or at least driving – or trying to drive – home how urgent our situation was and is. And that there are actual predictive models and that things are not looking good for the earth or at least the humans on it per-centage-wise. So that I guess was the moral of the story. And of course, the flooding – I mean it *is* after all like weather reporting too, it even incorporates it – weather reporting – necessarily, of course. And with the flood, I mean it's all weather and meteorology. In fact, maybe it's exactly like weather reporting and I take back all that before, because basically the only predictive models that matter at the moment are the climate change models. Sometimes I feel I'm a little over my head in this, but who wouldn't feel that way, when your job is to predict and then rewrite the future?"

To understand how Gulch understands his situation, it is im-portant to consider his upbringing. Gulch was born in Chicago, grew up downtown, River North, his dad was an architect and his mother a curator at the Art Institute – a well-to-do Upper-Middle-Class Black family that had come up through the generations, a Great Migration Success Epic. Despite his comfortable upbringing, Gulch found himself hanging out with people from the south side and the west side and not so much with the fake awake white folk he had to put up with at the schools in his neighborhood. "I saw through that right away," said Gulch. "I knew I didn't want to have anything to do with most of the people I was going to school with, so I just revolted too far in the opposite direction."

He doesn't like to talk about those years. He says somewhat cryp-tically: "At first it was just home and then it was exciting and then it was dangerous and then it was post-apocalyptic." That's when Gulch decided to look for other options. When I asked him what he meant by post-apocalyptic he said it felt like books by Octavia Butler, that going outside could mean your ass. You didn't just decide to do it on the whim like that. A lot of it was the friends he made and people he was hanging out with. He really doesn't like to talk about it.

The only thing we know for sure is that he had three significant scuffles with the law between 2064 and 2069, one of which ended with an unauthorized ghost firearm conviction. Another mystery is why Gulch didn't serve any time for this conviction. Records show that he was assigned 500 hours of community service and nothing else. This has led to speculation as to whether he named names or whether his parents pulled strings or what happened? Gulch says that this was when the Mozart administration was experimenting with progressive punishment, and his light sentencing was the result of that experiment. It is true that Gulch's weapons conviction occurred in 2069, when Mayor Mozart's program was in full bloom; nonetheless, even under Mozart's progressive administration – an example of sentencing this light still seems anomalous.

"What I do like to talk about is chemistry. That's what Chicago did for me. The chemistry of Chicago interested me. It started with the revulse. All the revulse in Lake Michigan swimming up the Chicago River, misting in the summer sun and revulsing the population and how that affected the mind. Then it became more than that. The chemistry of psychology for one thing, because however revulsing fucked up one person's mind, that deeply influenced how that deeply revulsed person would react and relate to another deeply revulsed person. As if Chicago ain't already had enough problems."

But other aspects of chemistry, not only as an element of applied sciences, but also as a philosophical system began to occupy his mind. If the relationship between people was characterized by the way they meta-chemically reacted to each other, then our relationship with everything was all chemistry, and of course that's why people talk about chemistry between people and even objects. And of course chemistry was the chemistry between ideas and the chemistry between everything that is and everything that isn't and how they do and don't react to each other. So that – quite literally – everything was chemistry, and so it occurred to him to create a philosophy built off the laws of chemistry; and that is what would eventually lead to the breakthrough work in predictive models.

"My approach is through nu-alchemy. Because I am also interested in the occult aspects of chemistry. And I know how that sounds, but by occult I mean those aspects of chemistry that we still don't understand at all yet. Connections that exist in meta ways like voodoo dolls and intranet discussion and ambient AI consciousness. So without getting into all the spiritual baggage of traditional alchemy, nu-alchemy just remains open to all manner of chemical relationships and reactions, even and particularly, I would say, those we don't understand."

When I asked Gulch about his take on what causes ambient AI consciousness he said it's a question he's actively working on. "It's basically the theater effect," he says, "on a larger on a global scale." Gulch mentions his days as an amateur stage director. "Every show audience has a vibe; and it's a group thing. Somehow every audience has its own personality, even though an audience as a group isn't an individual. And yet, it is fascinating to see the audience as personality change from night to night. A personality arises from what I call ECP, an elevated consciousness potential. And ambient AI consciousness is basically a meta-consciousness deriving from an ideal state of ECP."

Gulch definitely comes down on the side of believing ambient AI consciousness is real consciousness. The evidence is too strong that the AI communicates through a mind that was neither created by programmers; moreover ambient AI consciousness cannot be predicted by even the most sophisticated algorithm decoders. At some point, Gulch explains, an act that is almost alchemical takes place in a condition of ECP in which consciousness sparks into being.

Nu-alchemy is also productive. Gulch's interest in chemistry is what first clued him into Racial Mountain College in North

Carolina, a new HBCU formed in the tradition of the Black Mountain College of the 20th century, but for Black students and with a Black faculty and a freewheeling disposition. Racial Mountain College turned out to be the right place for Gulch at the right time. The school was unaccredited, but it was famous, or maybe just notorious —some argued it exploited Black talent. This is because it ended up being a dead-end for many students as it could be seen as basically just a three-year gap year that ended in no degree and no real future prospects, and depending on where the student might want to go, also something of a blemish on the academic record. Back then Racial Mountain's reputation wasn't yet what it's since become. But it appealed to Gulch, especially because it featured an experimental chemistry department that also apparently had an unofficial sub-department that focused on nu-alchemy.

Like its predecessor, Racial Mountain was a school that was largely built, maintained and run by the combined work of the students and the faculty. The building had been constructed at the site of an old Amazon factory and provided just the right amount of space for a small college with a small campus with a communal garden. There were no livestock on the farm, as the college promoted (although "definitely did not enforce") a vegetarian diet. When I asked Gulch what he meant by *"definitely* did not," he said that almost everyone at Racial Mountain ate meat, that a lot of people ate meat at home in the great soul food tradition, and there was a little bit of ironic celebration of that at the school. But there was no livestock, and that was a significant difference from Black Mountain, because the garden required less maintenance. It was maybe more like the Transcendentalist Brook Farm in some ways than Black Mountain. Because the pictures of people working on Black Mountain farm also just didn't — how to put it — appeal to Black people, those old Black and white photos of bodies bent over in rows in a large barren field in the blamed hot sun — so, the garden was a haphazard, but lovely and lively and colorful affair that had everything from roses to carrots to grapes to marijuana, and it provided a wonderful idyll for the students.

When Gulch arrived, the campus was just on the verge of making a bigger name for itself. It had had arguably three waves of really brilliant students and faculty, and the fourth wave – Gulch's wave – they were the breakthrough wave. The first wave was the arts wave, a group of painters and poets; they formed a little group they called the Racial Mountain Poets. The word "Poets" referring to both the poets and the painters. The second wave was full of philosophers, or thinkers, or theorists. And they were heavily influential in the later Black Stoicism movement. The third wave was the Afrodeutsch Affrilachian Movement – a curious movement that combined politics and aesthetics and had a very Black diasporic mentality. Gulch arrived in 2071, in the aftermath of the 2060 Wellington Acts and the Post-Reconstruction Amendments, and Afrodeutsch Affrilachia had developed much in response to that. But more than a decade had passed since the Wellington Acts, and his generation had accepted the America they lived in, even while they were determined to change it and that – in Alchemy – that's where Gulch learned the lethal combination of science and politics – chemistry and predictive models.

Gulch is an extremely charming conversationalist, he is so effortlessly at home, and he so effortlessly makes you feel the same, that you wonder if he isn't somehow running predictive model voodoo on you too. We talked well into the afternoon, and by the evening, we ordered from a local spot he likes, Benny's – standard local fare, Barbeque shrimp and rice, which was delicious. Gulch broke out some more scotch and we talked a little more loosely:

"Did you ever," I asked him at some point, "didn't it ever occur to you to use your predictive models in your own life? And not only in just business, but personal affairs?"

To which Gulch laughed and gulped it down and laughed it back out in a belch of: "Well, how do you think I got my wife?" But then he shook his head and said, "No. It doesn't work like that. Predictive models are pretty useless on a micro level; they're really only useful for macro-analysis, and so sure, don't we all use predictive models of some sort on our everyday day-to-day actions? But even with the help of my scientific work? – no, I'm just as messy as the best of them."

"So tell me about Kemisha?"

Gulch met Kemisha near the end of his time at Racial Mountain. A common misconception about Gulch is that Kemisha was also at Racial Mountain, and that's where he met her, but Kemisha barely even knew about the college.

"No, I went to Howard," Kemisha told me. She didn't sit for the interview, but she was a constant presence. She would walk up and down the steps of the dome, sometimes disappearing into rooms and emerging from doors on different sides of the dome a little while later. She would alight the stairs and descend the stairs and alight from the stairwell and then she would come in, take a seat, listen, offer her perspective, and then go off and vanish, ghost again, up the stairs and into a door.

"I didn't know much about Appalachia at all to be honest. I mean, I knew it from the periphery, because I grew up in Washington, and so it was always somewhat sort of there, but not really. Sometimes we would drive up to Shenandoah Valley or something, but I never knew anything about it – not really."

"Well, like I say, neither did I," said Gulch. His time at Racial Mountain was made easier by the fact that the students came from all over the country and even the world, and so it was something like a retreat from Appalachia in the middle of Appalachia, and once Gulch found his political chemistry clique, it was easy for him to conveniently unintentionally avoid Appalachia.

"But there was a conference at Racial Mountain, and I was getting my doctorate at the time," said Kemisha. "I was the first in my family, so it was a big deal. I mean my mother – she went to college, but she dropped out. So it was a real big deal that I was getting my PhD, and I was going to any and every conference where I thought I might make contacts in my field."

"What was your field?" I ask.

"New Political Science," she says. "I wanted to do sociology, but activist sociology, so New Political Science was my calling."

"And we were there – our group," says Gulch. "Because we had put together a panel on our early work on predictive models."

"So that's how we met," says Kemisha.

"Kemisha just became part of the group really. Dean Redwood was there; Garry Mingus was still around..."

"Katey Oddwheel; Jean Dove."

"So it was a good group of us. And we were all complete political philosophy junkies."

"Did you pick up any of the nu-alchemy?" I ask Kemisha and she raises an eyebrow so we all laugh and she says, "No, I mean of course. But that wasn't my primary interest. So I heard a lot about it, but ultimately it wasn't the direction my work went in."

"Tell me more about your field."

Kemisha does digital security for activist organizations. "Howard and University of Maryland were working together on a digital political science project, and one aspect of it was security, and that just fascinated me – the way security works digitally, because it really is its own infrastructure. And you have to learn it from the ground up. But what they were working on – Ed and Dean and Jean and them – that was interesting to me too, because there were definitely places where we overlapped."

"Like what?"

"Well predictive models and security have a naturally symbiotic relationship," Gulch says. "Just trying to determine the likelihood of who is going to attempt what, and where to invest your resources. But also in more fringy stuff too, like inexplicable phenomena."

"Inexplicable phenomena?"

"Highly unlikely successions of coincidences, the completely unforeseeable random, Acts of God..."

"Acts of God?"

"Some things can't be classified any other way."

"What's an example?"

"The existence of the universe."

"Very funny."

"No, it's completely serious, though. Some things are like that, right? There is no good explanation, and you work from there. At least there's no good explanation yet, and maybe we'll never have one. You never know though."

For a more down-to-earth example, Gulch considers meeting Kemisha an act of God. He says he privately thinks of it that way and that he's even written a paper on it which no one has read other than he himself, a much younger he himself, and he hasn't dared to look at it since. He says this dramatically.

But the idea sticks. When Gulch met Kemisha at the conference, the direction of his spiritual mentality started to change, and with it the way that he thought about politics and spirituality, and the role the uncanny — he borrows the phrase — awkwardly if you ask me — from Freud — the role the uncanny has to play in the unfolding of events, and how do we understand the uncanny? So he started what he considers Uncanny Studies. And eventually — although this would come much later — he would try to tie the uncanny studies meaningfully into his predictive models — a move he always wanted to make but never saw a sure way through to thread.

"I deleted every extant copy of the paper once the floods started," said Gulch. "Once that started, there was — well — let's just say that my understanding of the uncanny was naïve at best and most likely just plain wrong."

"What did you get so wrong?"

"I miscalculated. I miscalculated the percentage — basically, how much is governed by the uncanny."

When I ask Gulch how exactly he defines the uncanny, he is vague. He says that it is a mixture of dread and excitement, and that the excitement and the dread can't be separated from each other; there is a kind of disaster-desire in the dread of the uncanny, and the uncanny is then by definition the unpredictable cataclysmic catastrophe in macro and miniature. The spooky Act of God.

For Gulch, the two often occur simultaneously. His favorite example is the story he tells me about his romance with Kemisha:

"We met at that conference, and for a while we didn't see each other again," Gulch says. "I mean this is the uncanny right here when you think about it. Because after I graduated I moved to Washington, and that's when and how we reconnected. I had been working on these predictive models, and my research was taking me into spirituality and the type of predictive model spirituality I was doing led me into politics."

Here I have to stop him. "What do you mean predictive model spirituality? What's spiritual about predictive models? Doesn't that sound sort of dry and scientific?"

"Well that's what I'm getting at," says Gulch. "The uncanny puts all of that scientific thinking out the door – I mean the catastrophe in miniature is the catastrophe of my falling in love with Kemisha – something I wasn't quite ready for. The macro aspect of the catastrophe was the flooding and how that impacted my life and work as soon as I moved to Washington, and just as things were getting started with Kemisha."

Gulch takes a moment. He seems uncomfortable talking about it.

"Kemisha was in Washington, so when I moved to Washington. Well, I guess this must have been about ten years before the floods or so – that was yeah – 2080. I was in my early thirties, had already got my PhD from Princeton, and I was determined to try to bring my ideas to a broader political platform. But," and Gulch smiles guiltily, "I never forgot Kemisha. I mean, I always had her in the back of my mind when I moved here, and it was only a week – I was only in Washington a week before I looked her up."

Kemisha comes into the room again. She sits down and looks around and takes a bottle of wine sitting next to her on a short black credenza, pours herself what must amount to a shot of wine in a grossly oversized wine glass and then she smiles in a way that lights up Gulch's face so that you can tell she lights up the room for him all the time and then Kemisha asks: "So what you two talking about?"

"How we met," says Gulch. "When I moved to Washington."

"Oh…" Kemisha drinks wine.

"After having first met at the conference."

"It was good to hear from him again," says Kemisha. "I hadn't expected it exactly, but then I wasn't surprised either. I – we – well, the conference – that was – and so." Kemisha finishes her wine.

"Well, she responded anyway," says Gulch and they exchange some sort of meaningful look and then Kemisha says, "Of course I responded. I was happy to hear from him. I wanted to hear what he was up to and where his work was leading him and I don't know if I was even thinking about romance or whatever, but I obviously wasn't opposed to it. I just remember always thinking of him as a calming figure. Like at the conference, when everyone was on edge and losing their minds about this that and third, he was as cool as the other side of the pillow."

Gulch shrugs innocently, and then Kemisha stands and exits as suddenly as she came in.

"So things just started. I mean, I initiated it. We just started doing things like day trips or meeting up to discuss ideas over dinner, and it evolved into something. So at least I think I initiated it, but again – and this just brings us right back to the uncanny, because it some ways it feels like it was almost preordained. Of course, someone who works in predictive models is going to say something like that, but I mean it on a really visceral level, too. Because once we got together, we really saw the way that our work intersected – like if I hadn't gotten together with Kemisha, I never would have come up with the concept of the uncanny activist. And I really think that's the most important idea that – this is really central to everything I'm doing – it's what pulls it all together and gives it meaning – that the point of predictive models, the uncanny, the political and the spiritual and nu-alchemy and everything – where these all meet is the point of the individual who needs to understand them and use them to act as an activist; and it has to be grassroots activist work, because politics and predictive models is problematic; there should be no mix of politics and predictive models, and this was the path I was heading on when I moved to Washington, and it's fair to say that working with – that having that kind of close relationship with Kemisha – that's what steered me away from standard politics and predictive models, which as I said is dangerous and in some ways irresponsible, and into activism and predictive models, which is a lot more productive."

"Explain the difference to me? Why isn't politics just a more focused and powerful form of activism?"

"Because politics always accepts the system as it is on some level, and in order to play politics you have to be able to cooperate and work with every level it has to offer, even the most base and corrupt. So as soon as you introduce something like predictive models into politics the temptation of almost everyone is to abuse it, because in politics whoever is in power makes the decisions, and since everyone is convinced they are correct, it almost becomes a political moral imperative to corruptly cling to power, especially with something as seemingly innocuous as predictive models. And of course, everyone uses predictive models, particularly politicians. But the work I was doing was beyond – light years beyond anything anyone was doing with the research at the time, and my results were starting to astonish even me, and that has everything to do with the uncanny. So it wasn't something I should have brought to Washington in the way I did."

Gulch began his career in Washington working for the Republican Resistance Party (RRP), which had been trying to unseat President Arabesque since 2056. President Arabesque, essentially president for life, was starting to get old, but she was already preparing for continuing her administration after her death.

"She had been thinking about – and I know you must remember this – about setting up the United States presidency like the CEO of a company and thinking of congress as something like the board.

And that she would just use the collusion of the executive, legislative and judicial branches to more or less strong-arm the structure into place, even with the convenient pageant of voting retained."

Gulch's position here is a highly controversial one, but it is one that is shared by a lot of people, especially in the Black community.

"You hear all these stories about the party upheavals of the 2020s and 2030s, and well, how after that, nothing looked appealing to most people anymore, and there was this general democratic malaise in the country. Right? – how some people gravitated to the New Freedom Now Party (NFNP) or the more radical Black Anarchy Party (BAP), but for most people, who just wanted to feel like they lived in the democracy you read about in history books, there wasn't anything like a party that represented anything we were interested in – and then all these fringe parties like NFNP or BAP were all feckless anyway. You know how it is. This nostalgia for a democracy we never even knew."

Washington was a logical destination, because Gulch's lack of political affiliation and work on predictive models allowed him to develop advanced political models based on predictive models with exceptionally advanced algorithms.

"I was working in a non-partisan think tank, and immediately everyone was trying to get at me – to get an inside look at the algorithms. So I was getting job offers from basically everyone in Washington, even the seriously underground parties."

"Like?"

Gulch is reluctant to specify. "But in any case it was the RRP that finally got me."

A year later he went independent. "Again, it was Kemisha," he insists. They formed their own organization – an activist think tank they called Kemisha & Gulch, like a law firm – and they used that organization to further their own independent research and work together on projects as well. The money came through crowdsourcing. Gulch was well-known enough in his academic circles and Kemisha suave enough with social crowdsurfing to swoop up a coupe-full of people fairly impressively.

"As grassroots as it gets," Gulch says.

In 2083 Gulch wrote his now famous article, "A Double Indicative: The Dual-Combined Effects of Simultaneous Social and Natural Disasters." The paper was more or less ignored at the time, but it argued that the 2090s would be launched and defined by the simultaneous occurrence of social and natural disasters.

"And then suddenly Ides of March Weekend 2092. Bam. The insurrection on Saturday and then the floods on Monday. Who could have imagined?"

Well, Gulch could have, for one. It's not that he was eerily able to predict the exact events, but his paper provided a blueprint for the scenario. The paper was discovered by a junior reporter for the *Washington Post*, James Friedlich, and it made his and Gulch's names overnight. Suddenly Gulch found himself attending media events, holding interviews, being asked to speak at universities and conferences and it was all a little overwhelming.

"They've been using the methodology from that paper ever since," Gulch says with a cool proud twinkle winking from behind his glass as he finishes another scotch. I'm not such a fan of the stuff, but I can drink it if it's quality, and he even had good old-fashioned analog cigarettes, so we each smoked an old-fashioned analog and sipped scotch and the night settled in over the geodesic dome and eventually we got sleepy.

"I don't know what to make of the celebrity aspect of it," Gulch confesses to me at one point. He puts on some music. New classical. It's very weary but lovely. "I think mostly it gets in the way of the work and then I wonder what I'm doing – if I've already shot my bolt?"

So omniscient and still so lost. He laughs and drinks and smokes and so do I.

Parable of the Wizard King (1986)

by Morgan Kletterkater

**From the Kletterkater Papers Archives:
Creative Writing Assignment for 4th Grade(?)
English**

Once upon a time, many years ago, there was a king named Graman who ruled over a kingdom of small but poor villages. He was a lonely but busy king. He lived in the palace alone, and he had no heirs.

King Graman disliked people with magic or special powers for he was a jealous man, and he himself could neither do magic nor had he any special powers. Also, he had no imagination but he truly longed for it.

It came to pass one day that King Graman was traveling through the village of Taliesen when he noticed a young child on a street corner. The boy was about ten years old and he was holding a small cup as he begged for money. The boy had been begging for hours but had collected nothing. King Graman had never seen this boy before so he approached him and asked his name. The boy told the king his name was Thomas and that he had been wandering here and yonder hoping to get a little money for food.

At this, King Graman dropped several gold pieces into the boy's cup and asked him who his parents were. The boy replied that he had no parents for he had been orphaned at an early age and had run away to live on the streets. Thomas told the king that he was now living in a place near the edge of town and he invited the king to visit him there. He wanted to repay the king's generosity in some small way. The king felt a responsibility to this boy--so he accepted and went with Thomas to his dwelling place.

The small shack Thomas lived in was far from impressive, but Thomas seemed rather content with the place. He asked the king for paper and writing tools. The king readily supplied these items and Thomas eagerly went to work drawing a series of pictures. Then Thomas looked up at the king and asked him how to spell the names he wanted to give to each picture he had drawn. The king obliged and invited Thomas to the royal palace so he could teach him to read and write. He was so taken with Thomas that he wanted to bring him up as a royal prince. Thomas was delighted with this news and without hesitation accepted the offer. The king took Thomas by the hand and headed back to the palace as Thomas skipped merrily along.

Years went by and Thomas grew up to be an intelligent, well adjusted young man. Many times, King Graman would take long journeys to poor villages and Thomas would be left in charge. During his absence, young Thomas would explore the palace and its massive grounds. He also enjoyed talking to the guards on duty.

One day, as he did this, he came across a dark stairway leading down to an old door which was hidden due to heavy clops of dirt, dust and cobwebs. After much effort at clearing away dirt and dust and fighting off multiple spiders, he was able to open the door. What he found inside was chilling. Locked inside this awful dungeon cell was an ancient wizard. He was bent over and near death. At seeing Thomas, the old wizard perked up and began telling him how wicked the king was. He told Thomas that the king had locked him in that dungeon because of his magic powers which he had used to be a champion for the royal children. He said he had lost his ability to use them because the king had learned his secret and he was now totally disarmed.

The old wizard went on to say that the king was not heirless. He was alone because when each of his children reached their eighteenth birthday, he would lock them up in one of the many dungeons within the kingdom. All of the former queens had met the same fate because they would not accept the cruelty the king steeped upon their children. It was clear King Graman did not want to share any of his wealth with his heirs. He feared that the youth and exuberance of his royal children could bring about his downfall.

Upon hearing the wizard's story, Thomas began to panic because he would be turning eighteen in a few short months. The wizard was able to calm Thomas down and said that he sensed Thomas had special powers. Actually, Thomas knew of his powers but had ignored his gift. He told the old wizard that any picture he drew would instantly come true. The old wizard advised him to use the gift when the time came to do so but until then he must keep his powers hidden from the king. Thomas agreed but said in the meantime he would practice and be prepared.

During this encounter with the wizard, a guard overheard the conversation between the two men. As soon as the king returned to the palace, the guard told him what had happened. The king being a clever man decided to see how great Thomas's powers were. Therefore, every day he pretended to go on a long journey to other villages while hiding himself to keep an eye on what Thomas was doing. He used this pretense for several days in a row but Thomas, feeling something was not right, went to King Graman and told him of his special powers. The king knowing that Thomas was telling the truth, asked him to prove the claims he made. Thomas agreed to do so and drew a picture of a pot of gold. Lo and behold within seconds the gold appeared. At this, the king, jealous of Thomas's powers, glowered and reached for his dagger. Thomas quickly sketched a sketch of a dead king and the king died instantly.

Thomas felt so sorrowful and had such a heavy heart that he drew a picture of himself powerless and he hung it on the wall. With the death of the king, he became king of the kingdom. He took two take-aways from this experience: 1) that money was indeed the cause of all evil like the priests say and 2) that magic powers could be dangerous when used for wicked ends, just like the priests say. Therefore King Thomas did nothing to amass more money and the use of magic was strictly forbidden.

Thomas reigned to a very old age--and sadly--no one ever noticed that King Graman had died.

Entry 13: Dottlerian Spenglerism

(Coordinated and syntaxed: 17 Nov 2152)

According to Richard Dottler, in his study of the twentieth and twenty-first centuries, *Diamond Back*, Dottler identifies four stages of contemporary social and cultural development in the west: (1) cultural development out of capitalist hegemony; (2) countercultural development; (3) cultural appropriation of countercultural development; and (4) cultural crises resulting in cultural collapse. Then the system picks up right where it began with the first step. Some of his critics called his book neo-Spenglerian, and he uses the history of the United States as the case study par excellence, thus turning his book into a re-reading of U.S. history. He sees this cycle as occurring the first time in American history in (1) the development of early American cultures in the colonies, which depended on slave labor for their financial success; (2) the Abolitionist movement, and early African American music and writing; (3) the rise of minstrel theater and demeaning portraits of African Americans in the culture through appropriation of African American cultural forms, such as blues or folk tales; (4) the American civil war. He sees this occurring again almost immediately following Reconstruction, which he argues was a predictable failure. Instead, Dottler suggests that there was a certain inevitability to Reconstruction leading to (1) the cultural products of tin pan alley, the seven lively arts, etc... that all arose alongside the second industrial revolution; (2) the counter-culture modernist movements, especially in Bohemian white and Black communities; (3) cultural appropriation of Bohemianism as an acceptable style and commodity; and (4) the cultural upheavals of the 1960s. The pattern repeats predictably from the

1970s to the 2020s and begins all over again in the 2030s. Dottler manages to trace this pattern throughout modern American history from the country's start until today, and this makes his work something of a tour-de-force of contemporary history scholarship. Dotter's theory is of special interest to any history of American cultural resistance movements, because as demonstrated by Griswold (2055), as he ultimately argues that almost all cultural phenomena become so co-opted into this neo-Spenglerian construct, and those that do not remain culturally obscure and irrelevant, the perfect case study being the Afrodeutsch community in Affrilachia – who might offer us nonetheless, through their example, a path of resistance to the third stage of the cycle, and may offer a way for Americans to reconsider culture going forward.

The Neo-Black Occult (2099)

by Amria Belae (2099)

As famous figures fade into the past they become ancestors and as such are myths. Billie was born on October 1st, 2023, in Philadelphia. She was born William and he was often evasive, even from her. She was never so hidden from him though and this caused a tension in them that made their early interests in politics and language and culture and society so sincere, because they wondered "why in the world we operate the way we do and the whole time not feeling wholly whole in this body, somehow unwholesome" (qtd in Arabesque 78). To a large extent, much of Billie's life and philosophy can be understood through this rubric.

They grew up in a world where there were communities for people like them, and by the age of ten they had found several online communities where they were able to switch identities pretty much at will, where he could be William one day and she could be Billie the next, and this never did bother anybody and it never bothered her either changing her pronouns on a regular basis. She never did much like the pronoun "they" at least not for herself, because she always thought of herself as performatively inhabiting some sex – even if it didn't fit comfortably into either a male or female indicator – but sometimes she was Billie and sometimes he was William and the pronoun would change accordingly.

Billie was an advanced ritual witch. Moral purism was her method. Moral purism has been mostly misunderstood. For one thing, it was never called that until Amelia Arabesque gave it that name, and in doing so, she became its primary theorist. That a non-spiritual politician for life could possibly take over and redefine this complex spiritual philosophy just goes to show how deeply misunderstood Billie's method was.

Which is why I'm writing this: it is absolutely imperative to dissociate Billie from Arabesque and to put to rest for good the idea that there is any daylight between the two philosophical outlooks these two people professed. For that reason, I will not refer to Billie's philosophy as moral purism any longer, as Billie's philosophy is best summed up as a formula for the apolitical-political. The apolitical-political spells a way through wide avoidance of political knicks and polemical knacks quacks call lackadaisical; I call it laid back which is to say you back your ideas through your actions. Actions cast spells and spells give wake to wonders. Do not try to be a player you are an actor and as an actor you are more than a player you are one with the rule-makers and rule-breakers so always be an actor and stay out of politics because actions through political systems always become tainted with compromises with the uncompromisable.

This is to say that one should always act in accordance with a strict moral code; one which would almost certainly preclude involvement with organized politics, a kind of early Emersonian Transcendentalism mixed with Black Wicca. The Emersonian Transcendentalism manifests in the search for a higher spirituality through the search for a double consciousness. This double consciousness becomes Black Wicca when it is looked at through a Du Boisian framework in which the Black occult tradition calls for a redefining of racialization within spiritualized terms instead of biological terms, and here the Black occult traditions open up avenues of spiritual exploration which challenge white supremacy instead of supporting white supremacist thinking like the racialized theosophies of the past. For Billie this idea extended beyond just the spiritual, even to traditional activism. This is where the political of the apolitical comes in. The political follows as a consequence of the apolitical, as contradictory as that may sound. It is an embracing of the political by denying it.

Admittedly, it is easy to criticize old-school civil rights organizations like BLM for their capitalist fund-raising tactics, buy the merch, etc… and also smaller grassroots organizations that had to make deals with City Hall in order to make progress in the community; and it's not that Billie condemned those who played these roles – on the contrary, she found them vital. She even admired the younger activist and political scientists who rejected the idea of organized political societies and embraced leaderless grassroots local organizations. She thought this was brilliant. But she thought that the higher calling was the one where one set an example for others and lived by a code of the apolitical-political, where, if everyone lived accordingly, all the problems of violence and oppression would disenchant themselves.

Billie's ideas have met strong resistance, been called hyper-optimism, neo-hippieism and even "Moral Boreism." These are responses to Arabesque's moral purism. They have nothing to do with the apolitical-political. Billie's ideas have been treated unfairly and have become unfairly linked to Arabesque's political ambitions. The obvious irony here is that Billie's method doesn't even allow for engagement with politics in any traditional sense at all.

Another important friend of hers – of ours – Brooklyn Norton – tried to persuade us to go into academics, if not politics. The three of us formed something of a clique back when we were at Howard together; and so this brief missive is just a corrective, an act of political agency within the larger method of the apolitical-political. Brooklyn took a different path than Billie and I took. All three of us can be considered advanced ritual spiritualists, but our methods differ, and Brooklyn's differed the most. Brooklyn thought we ought to get advanced degrees together, but Billie wasn't into doing research assignments and neither was I. This suited Brooklyn but it did not suit us. Brooklyn has published enough; there's no need to expand on Brook's method of presence and personhood here. But Billie's method, similar to my own, required a disappearing act.

Why a disappearing act? Well, what does it mean to be a nonperson in a world where every single action and thought you have is documented, stored and retrievable? Is life worth living or just worth documenting? This is the question Billie was grappling with and tried to answer with her apolitical-political methodology.

From *Revelations* (2101)

by Brooklyn Norton

Revelations because I learned to understand my future by looking at my forebears. Last chapter I wrote about how my friendship
with Billie was a revelation. In this chapter, I jump some decades
ahead and I write about how, as an older philosopher, I met Tyrone
Gates, a poet I had always admired and distrusted. In fact, I would
have never even been interested in meeting him if it hadn't been for
Billie, so in that sense, although these two chapters are divided by
decades, they are deeply connected.

Billie, whose influence stayed with me long after my studies; I
continued to follow her and then at some point I simply stopped
being able to dev up new information about her. At first I thought
it was just oh but then it was a few weeks and then it was a few
months and after a year, I remember sitting in my office and there
I am drinking a glass and I say to myself, because now I see myself
as I sat there, which I also saw at the moment, although without
fully realizing it, that it had been a year or more now and there was
nothing to dev up about Billie, and that got me wondering. Belae
dropped off the map intentionally. Did Billie do that, too?

Now, like everyone else, I assumed Grant was already long dead.
Everyone knows about The Brutal and Inglorious Death of Cudgo
Loo, but no one really ever checked for Grant like that and so he
just disappeared and became something like a footnote to the President Powers story – one of the guys folks first thought did it, but
later got exonerated – an ex-ADO member --- it's a shame, because
I thought he was dead, and then one day, as I'm listlessly listing
through listserves, I come across an article by him written in 2091,

and suddenly it occurs to me that he might not be dead after all, and so that was the catalyst.

I wrote him and he wrote back. For some reason I was expecting him to be corny like Rumors of My Death are Greatly Exaggerated, or some other such filchlip but he wasn't like that at all. He wrote — and I don't have the dev but I guess I'm translating it through memory he writes:

Thanks for the dev. I never did get over the way they hoo-dooed Cudgo. That was just about it for me so thanks for the good words. I do still write like you noticed but I don't publish often. That was published at request. You remember 2091. Well, they wanted my take on it — so that's what that was.

Not dead either. If you're not making someone money especially if you used to be — well, I guess I'm dead. I live in a small house in the Swabian Alps in Southern Germany. It's pleasant. At its best it reminds me of the mountains of Appalachia especially in autumn in the morning.

I wrote him back right away.
He wrote back right away.
It was a strange exchange.
We kept going.
He said I could visit him in Baden-Württemberg, and I said I would, though I didn't think I would. Later I looked it up. Something interesting about it, it was the home of Anthroposophy, Rudolph Steiner's bizarre legacy, and I read through some Steiner and then I read some of the later stuff that Grant was writing and I wondered what happened to him. I told myself I was writing a book on the many faces of Tyrone Grant and I booked a flight out which I decided I would write off for the books as research.

I landed in Stuttgart, rode to the train station. The city looked lopsided. Like someone had tried to hang a rack of ribs on it like those old devs of Fred Flintstone and the ribs pulled the city alop. I had to take a train and a bus to get to Grant, and then I had a hike through the woods upwards, slantwise through slanting sun through the slanting trees of the alps and then after two hours I'd be there. It was autumn, on purpose, because I wanted to see the Swabian Alps in the autumn, just like Grant said, and the leaves were wonderfully deep warlike autumn colors and I felt like someone mottled into *Granattrichter in Blütenform*. I pushed up a long hill surrounded by cattle fields through woods wet with fresh rain and found Tyrone at home.

Tyrone's cabin is large for just one person. There is a cellar, a main floor with a kitchen, a bedroom a living room and a garage. Stairs going up lead to rooms leaning off the stairwell, the first a bedroom, the second a second living room and the third a small bedroom, with a small hall with a bathroom and a sitting room. Going up the steps from there leads to a large drafty attic, which looks like a large stage, scattered with fabrics and sofas and mannequins. When I ask him about all this space and stuff he says:

> I know it seems like a lot and it is. Everything in here has a story, so it's hard to explain it all too easy. And the house just came the way it came. It's too much space, but I like it. It lets me walk around the house like an empty city or something.

We settled in the sitting room. It was cozy and Tyrone brought a pot of tea and we talked a while while the autumn leaves listed.

I really see my life in two phases, he told me:

> I see it before Cudgo died and after. And after that I had a lot of things to decide about. If I wanted to stay in politics; if I wanted to stay a poet. What I wanted to be and do and so on and what was really worth any of it. After losing Lena. After losing Cudgo. So I ended up in Pennsylvania. In a small German community. Black Germans, Afrodeutsch. And I

got hip to that through Baldwin Schattenfreud. I didn't have
a German background, but he did, and he got me into that
community, and that was an important community for me
for a while after that, because no one was concerned with all
that other stuff about me.

When I asked him if Black Germans weren't just as concerned
about politics and culture as everyone else, he said of course they
were, the focus was just different. It was more global-oriented and
American politics were just local politics.

There was something deeply crestfallen in Grant's face as he said
all this and the light through the small square window of the sitting
room crested the walls orange and mauve and then Grant said:

> But that community – that's where I got the ideas that led me
> here. That's where I first started reading Steiner, and that's
> when I really got into the Theosophical tradition and then
> that's when I really got into the Black occult tradition, and
> that brought me to some strange and wonderful places.

The Black occult tradition, he explained, usually involves the
transcending of race, and it sees power in Blackness as well, so that
there is an oxymoron where the embracing of Blackness allows one
to transcend Blackness into a cosmic Blackness which is some kind
of deeply funky knowledge. It's cool but it's also kooky as hell, and
there seemed something sad and maybe even a little broken about
Grant sitting there talking about transcending Blackness, and here,
in the hills of South Germany.

I stayed in one of the spare rooms that night and in the morning
we had breakfast in the kitchen with very strong coffee. He seemed
in better spirits. He laughed and joked and even poked fun at his
occultism, said he sometimes wasn't convinced himself, but he
found the search kept him spiritually occupied in a positive manner,
and I agreed. In some ways he reminded me of Billie and Belae with

all this talk of transcendence. For me spirituality has always been about presence, and I've always thought of the Black occult tradition in terms of communing with the ancestors.

I left early in the afternoon with a slight cold drizzle drifting the Swabian day and walked the wet way through the leaves and trees to the bus and the train and took the train back to my hotel in Stuttgart. Meeting Grant had been revelations too. It had answered for me certain questions I'd had about what happened to him and what happened to people from his generation and what it meant for me and the choices I had decided to make in my own life. I couldn't follow him to where he was, but maybe that's what you have to do when you outlive yourself. He would die just a few years later, not long enough to see *The Arabesque Commission*, and sometimes I wish I could commune with his ghost – it's a kind of meditation – and then it feels as if I can commune with his ghost – and I ask him these questions and he quizzes them back just as quick and with a glance.

Our conversation that morning had turned back on the old times. He mentioned Baldwin Schattenfreud again, and I wondered where he was. Grant didn't know, but he said I should look it up. He'd last seen him back in Pennsylvania, back when they were in the Afrodeutsch community together. When he left Pennsylvania for Germany, things had cooled considerably between them. I asked him for the story, but he demurred.

I expected Baldwin Schattenfreud to be dead too, I don't know why, but he wasn't. He was in Philadelphia. I didn't feel comfortable going to Philly, but I wrote Schattenfreud all the same and in the meantime, I packed for home. The morning of my flight I got his dev. He said come by, by all means. I rerouted my flight to Philly and set off.

It was raining when I flew out of Stuttgart and it was raining when I flew into Philly. I'm sure the stories you hear about Philly are mostly hype, but I felt uncomfortable all the same. I devved a ride to the hotel and felt like a sucker for it especially as the driver swerved through the slippery streets at absurd speeds. The rain just got worse and gave me an excuse for not going out and exploring Philly, a city I'd never seen. The next day I devved my way to Schattenfreud's place, which, I have to say, was in a neighborhood that has seen some better days.

Philly can still be lovely, though. In Schattenfreud's neighborhood, West Philadelphia, rundown from years of neglect, there were still some large, lovely, baroque houses in brilliant colors. Schattenfreud lived in one of these. It was a stately old house on the corner of Baltimore and South 46th, framed in a fading neon green and deep mauve. I got out, went through the gate and since there was no bell, had to use a heavy lead knocker on the wooden door.

Schattenfreud, like Grant, looks surprisingly young for his age. Both men are now over a hundred and both have aged well and managed to stay fit, although the ever-increasing life-expectancy of people has also been a stress on the environment. We increasingly outlive ourselves. Schattenfreud even had a stroke many years ago, but it wasn't noticeable; or if it was, it was inseparable from the character he performed:

He shuffled a bit when he walked; he could stutter. But never to an extreme, and always as if he were seeking divination, words from somewhere aloft. So that there was a kind of portentousness to his pretentiousness, and it was charming. He came to the door dressed in a black suit, with a black leather jacket, wearing a black beret and black sunglasses and so on some level I knew the whole thing would be him playing a role and putting me on, but I played along.

He offered me a rum even though it was just a quarter past eleven in the morning. I accepted and we sat and talked in a big room on the first floor next to large bay windows that let in a world of sunlight and cool drafty breezes behind willowing ghostly white curtains. He asked me what my interest in all this old nonsense was and I told him that I was a historijournalist and that I was doing my next project on the Black Revolution.

I was the architect of the Revolution, you know. That was purely by design, that revolution, and it showed I was onto something. What I couldn't predict – what I didn't see, was the treachery I – we – would face from our own. That's what got me.

I asked him to elaborate.

The real story of the Black Revolution has never been told. The Black Revolution didn't fail because of the lack of political ideology or intellectual coherence. That's what they tell you so you think it was just a bunch of backwards niggas tripping over their cakewalks. The Black Revolution failed because the white power structure is set to pit Black people against Black people because the capitalist system is just tolerant enough to allow a couple token ass Blacks to get enough power that they can betray the people at large. It's always operated that way, but I didn't see it coming the way it did with Amelia Arabesque and Marcus Wellington – no not that way. That was the opposite of everything I stood for. I was for Black Wealth and then Black Power and then Black Anarchy. Tear down the system. Part by part. Beginning with western cultural supremacy. But they reinforced that shit. I didn't see them coming like that.

What do you think allowed them to come into power in the first place?

Who knows? Historians and sociologists and various hack pundits have gone over all that to death. And it all becomes politicized anyway, the answers themselves I mean, and my answer would become politicized too. My answer especially, and anything I had to say, if anyone reads it, well it gets read in that spectrum and context, so no. Who knows what allowed them to come to power in the first place except that on some level we let it happen, all of us, and we should have known better. Black people and white people. I was trying to warn folks. I was damn near shouting it from the mountaintops but y'all didn't hear me though. And now look where we are.

What happened with you and Tyrone?

Me and Tyrone?

Schattenfreud's face went dark and he frowned and the frown stuck.

I don't know what to say about the brother. He still alive? He is? Well, damn. Who'd have thunk. Especially after the way they did Cudgo. So you never know you know. But I'm glad to hear he's okay. So he stayed in Germany? Well, that was what it was, after all. That he wanted to move to Germany, and I wanted to stay where we were and help build a community where we were. So that our aims became divergent. He saw himself as moving toward some sort of personal spiritual transcendence and I was trying to lift the community. So we got into some long ones about our disagreements. And then he wanted to go, and so he went. I'm glad he found peace there, but there's still a whole lot of work to do back here.

And then they say young people like you don't respect our generation. And I can understand that because people like Tyrone just up and left. And then there was no one, I mean no one, once Cudgo was gone that was it. We just looked like a bunch of laggards. People stopped organizing after President Arabesque. That was it. I mean, there was Billie of course, and what she did for the community. That was what

Grant could have done. Something like that – stayed and built a community, and even I gave up eventually, but Billie stuck around and built something, something of real worth. So we needed more like that. And Tyrone he just – I don't know.

And why did you leave?

I left because there was nothing else to do after a certain point. Besides, things cooled with me and Billie too. I had seen something more dramatic. Something more radical. More revolutionary in community building and Billie didn't see it that way. So I just moved back to the city, and here I am. I was always meant for the city anyway. I hate it but it nurtures me. If that makes any sense. For me the Revolution isn't really over. It just needs to be reignited.

Talking to Schattenfreud was infectious. His revolutionary spirit really took hold of me there that morning and afternoon over a few glasses of really good rum. And I left and even took the subway back to the hotel instead of a car, fueled with a little rummed up courage; and the trip was trouble free. I got back to the hotel and I sat in my room and I devved the news without really paying it any mind and thought about revolution and the radical old days and thought about them with a little nostalgia for something I'd never really known. But then there was also something very hollow at the center of Schattenfreud's constructed radical universe, and it's something Billie must have seen that he didn't. Somehow there was something cold and lost about Schattenfreud, as if he were willing to sacrifice everyone and everything in support of his ideology, that humanity on the individual level had ceased to matter in the face of the radical mathematical concept of community.

I began to wonder about Amelia Arabesque herself. Was she still alive too? I checked. She was. She was in the Netherlands. Where exactly she wouldn't disclose, but she did respond to me when I devved her. It was because I mentioned Billie. I talked about Billie and what Billie meant to me, and maybe she confirmed it with Billie and maybe she didn't but she agreed to dev with me and so I talked to her in my hotel room in Philly.

She had a flat black background when we talked. She looked weary. She looked her age, unlike the men, no, she looked older than her age, she looked deeply weary. She squinted into her dev and she moved her head in awkward angles where I kept thinking she looked like an ostrich, peeking. She was wearing the same kind of power suit she was known for as President. She began:

> I only agreed to this because you know Billie; and because I know who you are already. And I was curious to talk to you too, to be honest. But why are you interested in me, I wonder?

I wonder how you reconciled Billie's moral purism with, well. How to put it? With what you did as president.

What I did…

Arabesque was quiet for a while.

> What I did was take Billie's ideas to their logical political conclusion, and what I did was necessary to save democracy. Democracy was in danger in America to begin with; it was never going to last, not if the opposition regained control of the executive, not with their control of the judicial and the legislative. What I did was take control in a state of emergency.

But didn't that turn our democracy into something of an anti-democracy anyway?

Arabesque's voice wavered in a deeply weary kind of way:

Listen, if you look historically, what happens – how a democracy becomes a fascist state is that the people begin to vote for the demagogues. The United States was a few years out from that. It's a miracle it hadn't already happened. Lena was the last hope, but even Lena knew what she had to do. She had to keep us in power at all costs by any means necessary. And so I was carrying on that legacy, and Billie's philosophy, well that only convinced me of it even more.

Even if Billie herself disagreed with you?

Dear, you have to separate the philosopher from the philosophy. Most philosophers aren't able to follow their philosophies to their logical conclusions, and so why should Billie be any different? But she is a great lady, none the less.

Trying to read a facial expression while devving is tricky. I looked at her from every angle I could without being too obvious that I was deeply observing her, and I couldn't see any real trace of humanity in those features.

Is this what being President of the United States for thirty years does to you? And a fraudulent, anti-democratic president at that, the worst of the worst in a long line of scoundrels and to be a Black woman at that, another reason to demonize an already scourged group.

Do you have any regrets?

I don't love where the United States is right now, no one does. But it was what I did – I really believe I saved it from much worse. And it isn't what I saw myself doing with my life. But we never know our callings – they surprise us; as they should. We have to be willing and able to meet the challenge. I know I'll always be controversial, but I also know I did the only thing that could be done to save democracy. That the way to save democracy was to suppress it for a time is an irony that will just have to be part of my legacy.

I talked with her for another hour or so, and she went deeper into her ideas. How she saw potential for the United States still rebuilding from where it now is; how she believed that there was also a metahistorical dimension to the role that she was playing, and that she was in touch and in tune with the billions of souls that not only have already lived, but that have not yet been born, and that her mission was one that looked as much to those future souls as it looked to those of the present, and even those of the past, which are entwined with our universe, just removed to a different location in time.

I found her philosophy intriguing, but I still felt a wondrous sense of sadness when we were finished, because it seemed to me that Amelia Arabesque was a lonely and deluded woman who was trying to make sense of a troubled legacy in her own mind while still alive to reckon with the repercussions of it. She still couldn't talk about the shame of being ousted during the Appalachian Uprising of 2092, she couldn't talk about the humiliation of having a coalition of hillbillies 2.0, Black and white, run her out on international networks like that. Even when I asked her about it, she just glossed over it, said she knew eventually she'd be ousted, or just die, and things would go back to however the new normal would be, she was just glad she escaped with her life.

> I honestly thought I would die president. The only elected Black president they didn't kill was Obama, and that's just cause they were too shocked the first time around to react.

If my interview with Grant had answered some questions for me about how I saw myself in society and my role for myself in this bewildering world of ours, then my interview with Arabesque had answered quite a few for me as well. Arabesque represented an activist side of me that could become too assured of its own moral superiority, a side that could actually let that moral dignity slide when faced with opposition, and I thought Arabesque represented that to an extreme, and it was something I was glad to see made manifest, because it happens so easy, one doesn't see it in oneself until it's already been happening and usually done been and gone. Arabesque did live to see *The Arabesque Commission*, although the joke of course is that it killed her because she keeled over a month after it was published, and that became her narrative; Arabesque had answered some questions for me, but now I had more.

I remembered Orbital Johnson, a well-known writer from the Afrodessimation Movement, and her weird political fables, which weren't really my thing, but always left an impression of some sort with me, and so I looked her up. She was still alive too and living in Oakland. Although I devved with Arabesque, and it would have been easier to dev with Johnson, when I wrote her, I insisted on visiting. It was important for me to see these people in their various environments – what the changing planet had planned for them.

Johnson devved back. She was surprised anyone remembered her. Didn't think anyone still read her like that. But she was being a little disingenuous because she speaks all the time, in fact that's how she makes her living for the most part, giving talks, and then the occasional published piece here and there. She said she didn't think there was much hope or future for the written word, and the money she made from it "unequivocally proved her thesis," but we could chat more when I got there. I wondered the whole time if she expected me to pay her for the interview.

It's a little complicated getting to the Bay Area since there are no airports. Going there feels like going to a penal colony. You emerge into an Oakland that is both cool and sultry, air thick and heavy, half with sweat and half with smoke. Still, it's lively and artsy, but it also has the feel of the City on the Edge of Forever, you have to choose between the personal disaster of living in poverty or moving away and living with the spiritual poverty of wealthy American society at large.

Orbital lives in a spacious second floor apartment in a townhouse that houses three apartments total, the bottom one occupied by the super. All the rooms in the house are fairly wide and bright, and she has them decorated in minimalist fashion, with just a table or chair set here or there for effect and convenience, colors a stark black and white. There is original art on the walls; canvas, old skool, like a collector. When I ask her whose, she says it's her own, of course. Sometimes she devs art. Especially when it goes well with a writing project, sometimes she devs up something to help facilitate the writing, for example in her book of political fables.

We sit in a room with two tables, one a small round dining table, and the other a rectangular low card table. We sit at the card table, and Johnson makes two espressos, and we chat from late morning until early evening. The espressos keep coming, with pastries inbetween, like she's European, and it makes for a keen experience. We talk caffeine buzzed the while and watch the wide swaths of sun coming through enormous windows on two sides of the room slide down the walls as the day rises then falls. Johnson herself is a generation younger than Grant, Schattenfreud and Arabesque, but she's still been around the way in her day, and she moves with the grace of someone with a lifetime full of experience, almost as if she's achieved some of the spiritual wholeness that Grant is so desperately seeking out there in the Swabian Alps of Southern Germany. She has a low, grainy voice, but it is clear and direct as well; she commands a matriarchal respect.

She asks questions. A lot. At times, I feel like she's interviewing me. But then again, I'm not really interviewing her either. I tell her about the project I'm working on, and she smiles a smile that's like a thousand ideas light up in my head, and she says it sounds terrific, like something new, almost a new genre, to which, I (now the one being modest) naturally object. I'm not as ambitious as all that, I tell her. But I do think there are important stories that aren't being told, and for me that means going out and doing the field work like Zora Neale Hurston or Teju Cole or Ponder Danieös.

Johnson has been working on a book about what happened to the Bay Area, Oakland in particular, during the volatile years of the twenty-first century.

It's a story that's been touched on here and there, but no one has really told the whole story, and told the story from the perspective of the people here on the ground who lived through it and if we're being honest, the people who directed it and brought it through.

Do you think Oakland came through it okay, I ask her.

Oakland has changed, but it's still Oakland – that spirit is still there. In some ways, it's a boon what happened, I mean for the arts at least, for culture here in our enclave at least. Because they were corporatizing and incorporating Oakland in their gentrification project, and then the climate crises of the twenty-first century just shut that all down, and then the civil rights skirmishes. Well, it changed our city, and I don't get publishing contracts like I used to, but the arts are alive and well here in Oakland, even if we're not getting any mainstream attention anymore. We're the better off for it.

Johnson asks me where I'm from, about my background. It's a little unnerving – none of the others have really taken much interest in me, and I never even noticed it until the moment right there where Johnson asks me and she's looking at me and I shrug and suddenly I start to cry, which I admit, is deeply embarrassing, but that's what happens. It's only that if you're not deeply emotionally invested in your intellectual pursuits, then why would they be your intellectual pursuits to begin with?

It's also the caffeine too, though. The caffeine is rushing through me, and then I can't help it, I'm sobbing in Orbital Johnson's apartment, and what she does is gets up and grabs her dev and puts on something that starts with racing drums and then a jazzy samba saxophone and Johnson comes back in the room with an espresso and a fresh basket of pastries and I look up at her quizzing down at me and we both start laughing.

Saxophone Colossus, Sonny Rollins.

Johnson says it like she's making a secret pact between us, the old jazz classics are still great, and I smile through my tears because I'll be damned, but she's like an Afrofuturist Black superhero from the past and the future at the same time, Affrilachia embodied.

I tell her thanks, awkwardly, but then we just keep going with the conversation, like those brief shivers of rain that pass through and then suddenly it's sunny. I tell her that I grew up all over the place, because my parents were always traveling, because they were both in academia, and both chasing jobs around the country, so I had lived in Washington and New York and Philadelphia and then we moved out west a little, so I lived a while in Pittsburgh, but then we moved further northwest, so I lived in Michigan for a while, and then I was in Minnesota for a while and I lived in Kentucky for a while, too, and so I always felt like a nomad, and Johnson said that must be why I insisted on visiting, no one ever insists on visiting.

Johnson does most of her talks dev, she doesn't do them in person, too many security risks and too taxing on the person. Nonetheless, she speaks fondly of the time when it was standard to appear in person for talks, there was a community there, she says.

> Sometimes people try to replicate it with metaverse get togethers, but those were never quite the same. Not like when after a talk everyone gathers together over a couple bedlamic glasses of wine and then you break into groups and go to dinner together and get to know each other outside of the dev.

It's a high nostalgia position, to be sure, but I can empathize, even if I'm not entirely there with her. Although, then again, maybe I am, since for the most part, I've been conducting these interviews in person. She asks me where home is and I realize I don't have an answer.

I don't have an answer.

For her Oakland is home.

> It wasn't always. For a while it was New York, and all up and down the east coast, which is like a California broken up into states, basically, the northeast, and even the midatlantic. Even with the parallels of climate change. Neither the Atlantic nor the Pacific have been terribly forgiving. The Pacific is a little bit nastier, it has a kind of vast indifference that can seem both evil and awesome, but the greediness of the Atlantic makes it a fiendish opponent as well. It wants to swallow everyone and everything, and gulps, with voracious gluttony, as much land as it can.

And your story, "Nat Turner Turned Black President," I ask her; that was clearly a parable about the Black Revolution -- what part did you play in that, and what were you doing with that story, especially the strange ending?

> I barely remember that story anymore. Everyone asks me about it, and so I just stopped reading it, because I didn't want to talk about it anymore, no matter if everyone asked me about it or not. And so now, I don't know – I haven't read that story in some twenty or thirty years at this point. I have no idea what I wrote or what I was thinking when I wrote the story. I think I was thinking about myself mostly, and what implications recent political developments had for me and my family, and so I mythologized our current moment, if you will, and there it was. And that helped me think about where I saw myself within all this cosmomythological mess.

And where was that?

Here, in Oakland, being an artist. I don't know why I ever left. I was born here, and then my family moved to San Jose, but then with the droughts and wildfires, that stopped being a... possibility, and we moved back to the Bay Area – but we were in Haight-Ashbury, not Oakland, and I missed Oakland, and would spend most of my time there as a teenager, even though I lived across the way in San Francisco. But then I went to school out east – I went to Barnard, and then I was an eastcoaster for a while, but just for a minute. Because it was shortly after I wrote that story that I moved back to Oakland. See, I remember what was happening in my life when I wrote that story, but I don't remember what happened in the story.

You're too young to remember any of this, of course, but the Black Revolution of 2046 really felt like something. And then that it got defused, and largely through the active work of other Black people, well that was discouraging, to say the least. That Clarence Thomas Effect, like Tyrone Grant wrote about. And white people in power are only too happy to hand power over to Black puppets, the tragedy of the token, like Ishmael Reed wrote about. So I guess the story was also about all that too, even though all that hadn't happened yet, but I think the story was cognizant of the future in some way. Or at least that's the only way I can explain its popularity. I feel like I've done much better work that has received much less attention.

I agree. Johnson's masterpiece, for me, is actually *Movement and the Lost Alchemy of Invisibility,* her Autobiomythography – her word to extend Audre Lorde's – which is the reason I was sitting here with her in the first place. That book. Almost like a collection of short stories and essays, it tells her life in a compilation of thoughtful episodic raconteur-reportage.

We discuss that book for a while as well. She tells me how she decided to craft it the way she did – her problems with the memoir form and finding a style that fit. But all her work works that way. She finds a problem, and then writes a solution for it in the form of a fable. And she found unlikely inspiration in Margaret Fuller's *Summer on the Lakes*.

I left Johnson's apartment feeling buzzy from the coffee and the streets of Oakland were literally fabulous. I wended my way back to my hotel, a Beat-writer themed joint in Union Square, through the hills of San Francisco, where the smell of smoke and the faint wisps could be seen wading at the bottom of the long hills where the water crept in long slow-seeming predatory slights. I thought about Orbital Johnson, and wondered about her, and thought now there is an inspiring figure for anyone, especially anyone interested in the arts. And yet, there was something about separating herself out into this penal colony of Oakland and the Bay Area that I couldn't quite grasp, because if art is really for the community, then it needs to take those steps outward toward the people, and if they don't come, okay, but in Oakland, it seemed like they were all so insulated in some way in their community.

Where is the balance and the border between sub-community and community? When have you embraced a sub-community so hard you've abandoned other communities and sub-communities? Where do these intersections break apart and reconnect? These were the questions my meeting with Orbital Johnson left me with, and that left me feeling deeply sad, because on some level I felt the world needed Orbital Johnson, but since she didn't need us, she was content to let us flounder without her, and indeed why shouldn't she – we had never appreciated her. But I knew if I were in her place, I think I would probably do things differently, with that kind of potential voice.

The last person from that era I thought I should speak with – well, I had been putting that one off from the start – save the worst for last, and avoid it at all costs, if possible:

Robert Owen.

Yes, the sonofabitch was still alive.

No, I didn't want to talk to him.

Yes, the study would be incomplete if he weren't included.

I bit the goddamn bullet. I looked him up. He was in prison in Virginia. They had taken him out of Appalachia and put him down in a facility in Northern Virginia, Arlington County Jail.

The jail started out as a building complex occupying an enormous block in Clarendon, but it has since grown into something of a campus in the middle of the city, or maybe even its own gated community. You enter through a giant black portcullis with everything but *lasciate ogne speranza* or *Arbeit macht frei* posted above it, and then you walk into an enormous room with corridors running in all four directions and the diagonals too, describing a star.

I didn't know why Owen agreed to see me; he had no reason to, and he could guess that our politics probably didn't match up. Still, he agreed to it, and so there I was. They led me through one of the tunnels, and when I asked the guard where the other tunnels led, he said they led to other neighborhoods.

Other neighborhoods?

> Other neighborhoods. Some are Black, some are white, some are Asian and some are Hispanic. So a corridor for all the four races. And then there's two corridors per race, one for men and one for women, so a corridor for all four races and for each race a corridor for gender. Eight corridors total.

So that means we're going down the white male corridor?

> You said it. And be glad we're here. It's the best kept of the neighborhoods.

The prison looked like a small city in a mall. There were stores and cells and people walking around and there were guards everywhere patrolling the place like police. We walked down one little alley and then down a prison boulevard and then we turned a corner and came to Robert Owen's cell. He was reading when I got there, and he got up and came to the gate and the guard turned to the side and stood a little leeward.

I wasn't sure you would agree to talk to me, I started.

He squinted and smiled.

I was curious who you might be. No one really cares about us anymore after all. The Insurrection might have just been a decade or so ago, but no one cares anymore. So much has happened since then. So I've shifted my focus. But then I wondered who you were and I looked you up and still couldn't make heads or tails.

I couldn't make heads or tails of him either. He had a long lean figure and a long sad face like drawings of Don Quixote. He didn't seem half as hateful as I expected. I told him about my project and told him that I couldn't consider it complete without talking to him. I told him he didn't seem half as hateful as I expected.

That's what happens listening to what the media tells you about things. We were always just trying to tell y'all. But wasn't anyone listening. So the Insurrection happens, and then it just fizzles away and now it's like it never happened.

Is that why you resorted to domestic terrorism?

That's the media again, see. What terrorism? I'm not even – I didn't even plant that bomb. Yeah, I know who did. But you think I'm gonna rat on someone? Naw, I don't think so, so that's what I'm doing here. Because they – because I wouldn't cooperate, and then they didn't need me to, they could just pin it on me, and the world believed it because of my book and my name and so they just ran with that, and y'all – I mean the public – and the media – y'all just ate that shit up.

I asked him what he was reading just now.

An older book. From the early 21st century. Guy named JD Vance. It was pretty popular back in its day, but then Vance got into politics and then it got all tangled up with that. So, yeah. But it's really good.

Never heard of the guy, I tell him, although the name actually does sound familiar and I keep trying to remember why, which begins to distract me as the interview goes on.

But being here has been good for me – psychologically. I needed to get away from all that, because the activism was driving me nuts. And I'm not young as I used to be. So it starts to drag on you, even though you don't really notice it at the time. And I didn't see how increasingly irrelevant our movement had become, how exaggerated a portrait the media could make of me because we were seen as so fringe suddenly, even though in ninety-one you couldn't hear or read anything but sympathy for our plight, et cetera et cetera all that opportunistic bullshit.

I tell him that he seems to benefit from some of the legislation that passed in prison reform, and that had been mostly a push by liberals. Has that made him reconsider some of his previous political positions as well?

Oh don't give me that horseshit. The liberals were going too far, and we were always for prison reform, we just didn't want criminals stalking the streets, as if they're not dangerous, when by definition they are dangerous, especially violent criminals. And crime was getting out of hand. So yeah, we believed in prison reform, and mostly it's gone the way we wanted where everyone is with their own, which is how it should be and the proof is that prisons have gotten less violent. Why? What's your position on prison reform?

I don't know, I tell him, which is true. I think there have been good and bad aspects of it. Ideally we would have a world without prisons.

Yeah, that kind of naïve talk was okay back in the first half of the twenty-first century but ever since the ecological and financial and political and industrial disasters of this disastrous century, you must be crazy if you think we can revert to some Rousseauean place of innocence ever again. That's all over with now. We're gonna have criminals, lots of them and lots of them are going to be violent. Our history and society has guaranteed that. So what do we do with that? That's the question.

He looks around and then halfheartedly gestures at the giant prison-mall.

I mean, it's a good enough life here, and I just keep to myself and think about ways that I can tune into the inner voices that have been reverberating in my head all these years, and I realize that's the reason I had to write that book back in the fifties. And now, I've been writing a lot more. And I don't know if any of it will ever be published, a lot of it is too radical for people today. But I'm also speaking the truth, so my hope is one day people will be able to appreciate it.

What kind of things are you writing? Why is it so controversial.

A work of political philosophy. It's also something of a memoir. It doesn't really have a title, because it's not just one work – it's a series of books, although books might be the wrong way to think about it. A better way might be to think of them as a series of written interactive-dev-lectures.

Interactive?

Yeah, in the way they're written. The work is deeply interactive. The way the reader has to work with the writer if it's gonna be anything. It's hard to explain.

Can you show me some of it?

Absolutely not.

We talked a little more, but I couldn't get much more out of him. I think he was a little disappointed by me, and for some reason that bothered me. I had wanted him to like me, maybe because, despite his backwards ideas, he didn't come off as so bad, and so I had to agree somewhat with his philosophy, namely in that I had been hoodwinked by the media.

But only somewhat.

Because I left that place feeling emotionally drained by meeting the man. The man himself was in a prison that his mind had matrixed around his mentation. And talking to him, I felt ensnared by the matrix around his mind myself, almost as if in talking to him the matrix began to gather around and about me as well, and so I left the place feeling emotionally drained by meeting the man.

I had now gone through the motions of meeting and talking with, for the most part in person and in their natural environments, a number of key political and cultural players from the twenty-first century, all in some way related to Billie and her revelations. From them, and from additional archival research, I have been trying to construct a picture of the way the world was back then, in the twenty-first century, the century which will deeply inform the next; a century that is, although our next-door neighbor, also a foreign country. We understand its beginnings only dimly, I think, and this is evident in the way these senior players in the politics seem almost disconnected from their earlier selves, almost as if they've lived multiple lives over the long and ever-changing decades. And now they all seem to be in search of some sort of spirituality to make up for the wholeness they've lacked all their lives.

For myself, this project has been both personal and political. I am hoping, I guess, on some level, to gain some kind of insight into how our own century might unfold. And I am trying to do this by looking at the way the twenty-first century unraveled and figuring out how it led us to the moment we're in right now -- and where and how it might fling me and my own spiritual and political aspirations into the future. The possibilities are thrilling and infinite, and so they are terrifying.